REACH FOR THE STARS

MAXINE MORREY

B
Boldwood

First published in Great Britain in 2024 by Boldwood Books Ltd.

Copyright © Maxine Morrey, 2024

Cover Design by Leah Jacobs-Gordon

Cover Images: Leah Jacobs-Gordon; Shutterstock

The moral right of Maxine Morrey to be identified as the author of this work has been asserted in accordance with the Copyright, Designs and Patents Act 1988.

All rights reserved. No part of this book may be reproduced in any form or by any electronic or mechanical means, including information storage and retrieval systems, without written permission from the author, except for the use of brief quotations in a book review. This book is a work of fiction and, except in the case of historical fact, any resemblance to actual persons, living or dead, is purely coincidental.

Every effort has been made to obtain the necessary permissions with reference to copyright material, both illustrative and quoted. We apologise for any omissions in this respect and will be pleased to make the appropriate acknowledgements in any future edition.

A CIP catalogue record for this book is available from the British Library.

Paperback ISBN 978-1-83751-139-6

Large Print ISBN 978-1-83751-138-9

Hardback ISBN 978-1-83751-137-2

Ebook ISBN 978-1-83751-140-2

Kindle ISBN 978-1-83751-141-9

Audio CD ISBN 978-1-83751-132-7

MP3 CD ISBN 978-1-83751-133-4

Digital audio download ISBN 978-1-83751-135-8

This book is printed on certified sustainable paper. Boldwood Books is dedicated to putting sustainability at the heart of our business. For more information please visit https://www.boldwoodbooks.com/about-us/sustainability/

Boldwood Books Ltd, 23 Bowerdean Street, London, SW6 3TN

www.boldwoodbooks.com

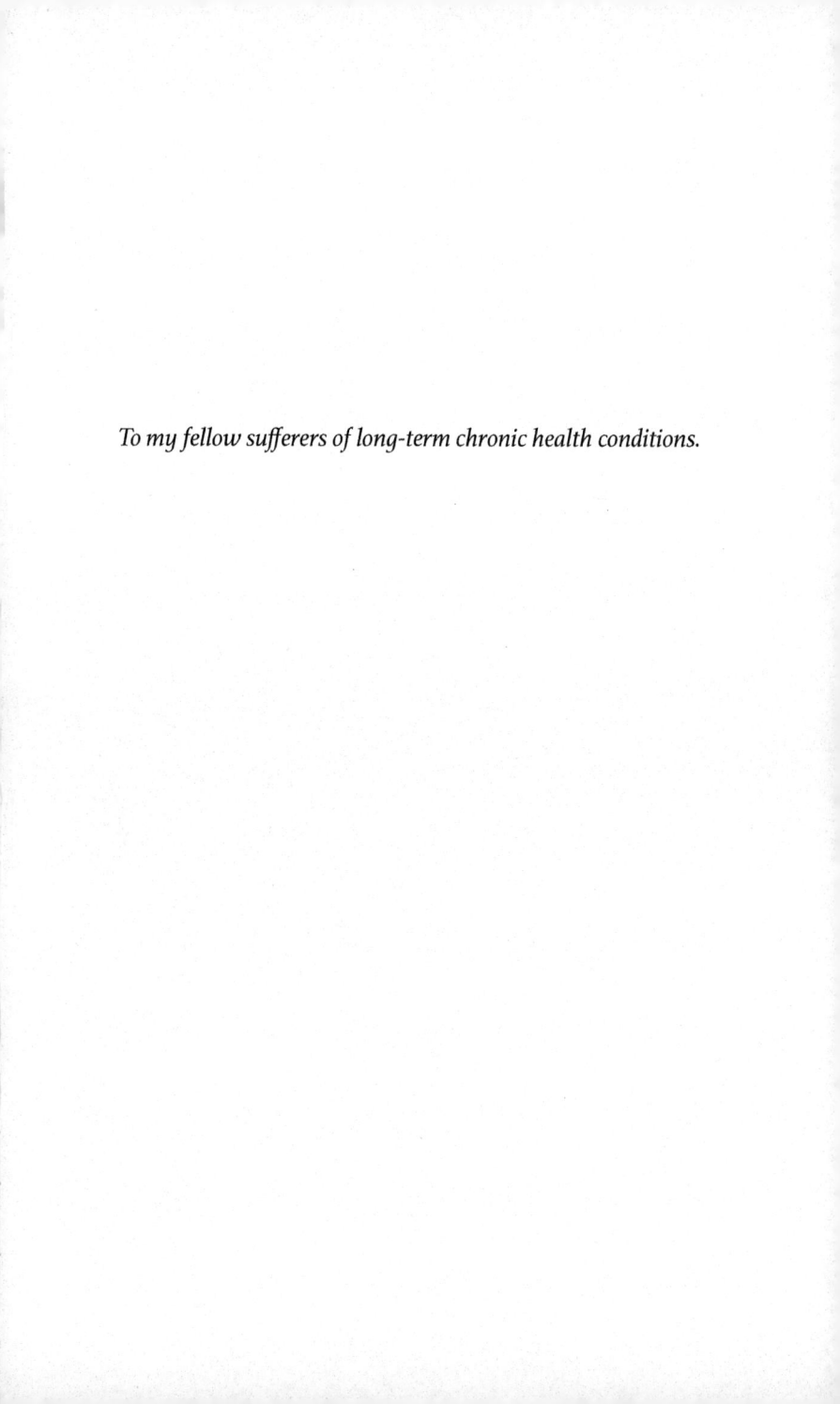

To my fellow sufferers of long-term chronic health conditions.

1

'Oh God!'

The man at my feet looked up at me with tornado-grey eyes set in features so chiselled, they made Michelangelo look like an amateur. I say looked. Glared would be a more accurate description and the sculpted jaw was so tight, I reckoned there was every chance it might crack at any moment. A thin trail of blood began trickling down from his brow.

'What the...' he paused momentarily, took in the audience of assorted ages now gawping at him on the floor and chose to swap out a word '...hell are you doing?'

I jolted out of my shock. 'Sorry! I didn't see you! I'm really, really sorry. Are you all right?' I put out a hand to help him up although, as I would be trying to haul up what appeared to be six feet five of solid muscle, it was more an apologetic gesture than to offer any real help.

He gave me another glare and got to his feet, unaided.

'You're, um... you're...' I touched my hand to my temple and then reached up, almost automatically, to do the same to his. He backed up and I snatched my hand down. I cleared my throat. 'You're bleeding.'

The man briefly put his fingers to where I'd been aiming for and brought them back, now covered with a little blood. He rolled his eyes. 'Great.'

'Do you want me to take you to the hospital?'

He'd begun to turn away from me but at this, he snapped his head back. 'Thanks, but that's a definite no. You can't even steer a two-by-four! Christ knows I'm not going to get in a vehicle with you.' With that, he turned away and began striding down the aisle of the DIY shop. A few muffled sniggers rippled through the onlookers as they began to disperse and within a few moments, I was left standing there on my own, still holding the plank of wood I'd knocked the most gorgeous man I'd ever seen flat on his arse with. This was *not* supposed to be my life!

Not that I had ever planned to knock anybody on their arse, but if the same scenario had happened in one of the romcom movies I loved to watch, the results would have been very different. It would have been the perfect meet-cute. For a start, I'd have been dressed in some sexy cut-off shorts showing off my toned legs and a fitted T-shirt, or maybe a checked shirt, knotted at the waist. There'd be some barely there, but just-enough, make-up on and I'd have salon-perfect hair tied back in a perky ponytail, sunglasses perched on top of my head. The guy would have sat up, made some funny remark, smiled at me and next thing you know, he'd be helping me do my house up, with several accidental touches, a steadying hand around my waist as a ladder wobbled until, finally, that first kiss would happen…

Except this wasn't a film. It was my life. And my life wasn't remotely like a romcom. In fact, if pushed to categorise it by genre, right now it would be closer to disaster movie. I was not dressed in a way that anyone would describe as cute. Having already ruined several ridiculously expensive outfits, I'd finally succumbed to adopting protective clothing. However, not having the first idea what I needed and, at the time, being far too tired to be in charge of a credit card, I'd ordered something more suited to entering a crime scene. The one thing the universe had got right was that the guy was gorgeous. But after that, it had all gone a bit off-piste.

'Shit,' I mumbled to myself as I grabbed another plank off the pile, checking three times that no one was around me as I did so, and made my way to the tills. Having paid, I lugged the wood out to my car. The sun of earlier had, at some point during the melee inside, decided to take a nap and hand the baton over to a large, ominously grey rain cloud. As I slid the planks into my car, the raindrops got heavier until it felt as if I were standing in a cold, exposed shower. The coveralls begin to stick to me, each plop of rain turning them more and more transparent.

'Come on!' I growled through gritted teeth. My car was not meant for jobs like this. When I'd bought said car, the thought of ever putting items from a DIY store into it had never, and would never have, crossed my mind. Even the thought of me entering a DIY store was laughable. But I had not had the last laugh. That honour appeared to about to be awarded to the man from earlier. I gave the wood one last shove, hoping it would stay in position, then slammed the boot lid closed. The wood did stay in position. The glass in my rear window did not. I stared as the glass shattered then neatly fell inside my car.

'Perfect.' I swallowed hard, squelching down the tears of frustration that threatened to spring with alacrity from my eyes to join the rain now pouring down my face.

It was then I noticed my paper hazmat suit disintegrating

around me, the greying bra and oversize pants I'd worn underneath beginning to show. I pulled my keys from my pocket – the material of which proceeded to stick to said keys, leaving a gaping hole by my hip. 'Bloody hell!'

That was when I saw him. Looking at me from the truck parked opposite me, windscreen wipers sloshing side to side. The threatening frown was long gone, replaced now with a bloody great smile. I turned away and grabbed the car door handle. As I did so, I caught sight of myself in the window. I looked like a papier-mâché school project that had gone terribly, *terribly,* wrong. Bits of paper were now stuck all over me and with each move another bit of my suit parted company with the rest of it. Yanking open the door, I slid inside, rammed the key into the ignition and burst into tears. This was *so* not supposed to be my life!

* * *

Isn't it funny how your best ever, absolutely bloody fantastic ideas come along when you're three sheets to the wind? Except usually you wake up the next morning with a raging hangover that feels as if the entire population of South America is doing the tango in your skull and decide, after a little more sober consideration, that the idea is not quite so stellar after all. Well, that is how it is supposed to happen but here I refer you back to the disaster movie that is my life. Unfortunately, I did not take that vital sober reconsideration time. Instead, I got exceedingly drunk, came up with a fantastic idea and, never one for hanging around, and having a reputation for getting the job done, I acted upon it.

Which was why I was here. Now. Crying in an old bra and the enormous pants I'd once bought in error. It was only when I'd got them back from the laundry service that I realised they weren't my usual thong style. Of course, by that point, I'd had them washed so I couldn't take them back. They'd got shoved to the back of the drawer and forgotten about. But today was huge pants day because a), I'd run out of clean thongs and b), I have to say, despite the fact they were now stuck to my wet body, they actually were far more comfortable than having dental floss between your bum cheeks. I mean, it wasn't as if I had needed to worry about VPL in this get-up. Until now. I glanced down at myself through my teary eyes. I hadn't banked on the rain or the disintegration of both my clothes and my dignity in front of a handsome stranger I'd just brained with a plank of wood. The truth was I hadn't banked on any of this. I was so out of my depth, I'd need a helicopter to winch me to safety. But I'd made the decision and now I was stuck with it.

* * *

It was the social media post that pushed me over the edge. There was my ex-fiancé with a woman a good ten to fifteen years my junior on a far-flung white-sand beach getting married. That would have been bad enough, considering it was less than three months since we'd split up after over ten years together, but the best bit – you'll love this – is that they were having *my* wedding. I paid for *that exact* wedding. I knew it was non-refundable when we booked it but I didn't pay much attention to that. After all, we'd been together ten years and I was finally getting the dream wedding I'd always wanted but had had to pretend not to want because that's not the done thing these days. Not if you're a successful career woman.

It's all very confusing. One minute, you're told you can have it all and then you can't. Then you're supposed to not want it all but by that point, you're doing it all anyway. Either way, I had dreamed of this wedding. My Sindy doll had had this wedding and I was supposed to have it too. But I didn't. Because, as it turned out, when my fiancé was away on business trips to secure a very important client for his law firm, he was also securing the owner's heiress daughter as a new fiancée. And I, the old model, was out. So last season.

To add insult to injury, he then took the wedding – the wedding I had saved for since I left university. The wedding I'd dreamed about. The wedding I'd paid every damn penny for because Adrian was going to put the same amount down as a deposit on a new house together. The wedding that was non-refundable but still named him as the groom so he'd just changed the bride's name and gone through with it. He looked so damn happy I actually punched him in the face. Or rather I punched the photo, which meant I then had to use my phone to order a new laptop and now have a scar on my knuckle where a piece of the glass got stuck and I had to pull it out with my eyebrow tweezers.

Luckily, I didn't notice the pain too much for that – or any of it really because, as luck would have it, the wine subscription box had arrived the same day and over the next four days, I proceeded to drink the entire contents. I rang work and told them I was sick, but illness is no excuse when you have important meetings, and my presence was 'requested', which was code for 'demanded', at a conference on the Monday morning. I was granted permission to attend online instead. And that was my downfall.

Used to messaging with a friend using the chat function in the app, I did so now. Thanks to getting pally with Bacchus, what I didn't realise was that it was set to 'All'. Therefore my comment turned out not to be the confidential exchange I'd thought it was.

> I can't believe we're all bowing and scraping over this dick.

In itself, typing this was a harder task than it usually was, then I looked up at the screen to watch my friend try and cover his giggles. But there was no such reaction. As I scanned each of the little squares on the screen, expressions ranged from shock, embarrassment, confusion and, in the case of my boss, outright, purple-faced rage. Kind of like the girl in the old Willy Wonka film. My brain scuttled off to find her name. It never did come back. I think it passed out on the way there.

Even through the pleasantly soft-edged wine haze, I realised something was amiss.

There was another, very short meeting after that with fewer people involved. I remember something about 'conduct unbecoming' and 'utterly unforgivable' coming up but the rest was pretty fuzzy. I got the gist though and that gist was that I was most definitely fired.

Now that would have been bad enough. But, oh, no, I wasn't done yet. I was on a roll! When all the bottles were empty a few days later, I came to with the mother of all hangovers and discovered that not only was I unemployed but that I had, during my mind's hiatus from sensible decision making, agreed to a sale on my apartment and bought a Victorian farmhouse in need of renovation and several acres of land with the proceeds. And a flock of sheep. Apparently, they were yet to arrive. I felt a fresh wave of nausea as my mind helpfully played out my life implosion in full technicolour for me. What the flock was I going to do with a flock of sheep?

Surely there should be a sensor built into all digital devices that assesses your blood alcohol level and bans you from doing anything monumentally stupid until it registers that you are sober. Unfortunately, there isn't. So I did. And here I was.

And now I had a new humiliation to add to the ever-growing pile. The image of Hot Plank Man looking at me and grinning as he drove off replayed in my head and I gripped the steering wheel tighter as I turned into the driveway that led to the farmhouse. What the hell had happened to my life?

2

As much as I would like to say that I had embraced this new life and was now a whizz with a power tool, I don't think there's any need for me to disavow you of that belief. I was not. I had never done an iota of DIY in my life. Not once. And now I had a ruddy farmhouse to renovate. My last few days had been spent trying to block up a gap in the fence where some random chickens kept wandering through into the garden and pecking at the French windows. Well, they would be if there were any French windows there. Currently they were pecking at the plastic that was covering the gap. God knew who they belonged to but the way it was going, one might end up in the oven! OK, that was a lie. There was no way on God's green earth (and to be fair, it was exceptionally green around here. Probably because it hadn't stopped raining) that I would ever cook anything I'd spoken to.

I dashed out of the car in my huge knickers and third-rate bra and fiddled with the lock, pushing myself into the hall, and grabbed a coat off the hook before running back out and wrangling the wood out of the car while trying to avoid the remaining bits of glass that used to be my rear window.

'Come on!' I yelled. Yelling at inanimate objects was another of my more recent hobbies. After I'd been so keen to get the wood into the car, the planks had now got wedged in. I gave them another good heave to release them, which did the trick perfectly. It also released me from my standing position and I ended up flat on my back in one of the many, *many* muddy puddles that surrounded this 'idyllically situated residence'.

'Oh, for *fuck's* sake!' I screamed out the words to the leaden sky and lay there, freezing my arse and every other exposed part of me off as tears of frustration flowed down the side of my face. A tap on my shoe made me lift my head the tiniest amount to see a chicken pecking at my now-pretty-much-ruined three-hundred-quid trainers.

'Go for it. Just carry on and eat me alive. I don't care any more. Bring your friends.' I plopped my head back down in the mud. The only sounds were the rain and this persistent sodding chicken clucking softly. In another situation, that might be quite soothing but right now, I'd give anything for the sounds I'd grown up with. The ones I was used to. The ones that suited me. Traffic, sirens and the general hubbub of London. Even the birds were quiet here, sheltering from this infernal rain.

'If you don't feed them, there's every chance of that happening.'

My eyes flew open and, with horror, I found the handsome face of the man I'd clobbered earlier looking down at me. The planks I'd bought were lying next to me.

'Need a hand?'

I pushed myself up, hands sliding madly in the mud as I did so. He reached down, hooked one hand under my armpit and hoisted me to my feet.

'Thanks,' I replied, immediately wrapping my Barbour around me in an attempt to cover as much as possible. Although I was aware he'd already had an eyeful earlier this afternoon. 'Don't take this the wrong way, but how did you get here and what do you want?'

'There's a bloody great gap in your fence line the other side of the paddock.' His voice was deep with that hint of gravel that normally made my insides do a little sexy dance. Unfortunately, my insides were currently frozen solid and dancing was the last thing on their mind. Raindrops dripped off the brim of his eminently sensible waxed hat as the grey eyes considered me with a blank expression before he dropped his gaze momentarily to look at the wood that was getting wetter by the moment. 'Is that what that lot's for?' He pointed at my purchases.

'No.'

'Good, because it's completely wrong.'

I swallowed the lump I felt forming in my throat. 'Thanks for that,' I snapped back. 'Did you actually have a reason for trespassing or are you just testing out illegal ways onto my property in order to critique my buying habits?'

He held out a packet of nails. 'You dropped these earlier while you were fighting to get the wood in your car.'

'Oh. Right.' I reached out to take them with one hand while making sure my coat was still tight around me. 'Thanks. Um... how did you know where I lived?' I was suddenly aware that I was in the middle of nowhere with a strange bloke twice my size. I shoved the packet of nails in my pocket and wrapped the coat even tighter.

'Don't worry. I didn't follow you. It's a small village. Everyone knows a buyer from London purchased this place recently and you're a strange face, so I just put two and two together.' He took a step back. 'Sorry. I didn't mean to frighten you.'

'You didn't.' The words fired out automatically. I'd been

fiercely independent for long enough now that this had become my natural response.

He nodded but it was obvious from his expression he didn't believe a word.

'Might be an idea to get some sort of security system fitted. The village isn't far but you are still out on your own here.'

'I'll add it to the list,' I replied and even I could hear the despondency in my voice.

The man did a tiny squint before holding out his hand. 'Jesse Woods.'

'Felicity DeVere.' I took the shovel-sized hand and shook it. I'd seen his brow twitch as I rolled out my name but he kept any comment to himself. I was sure it would be part of an 'amusing story' at the local pub later. Right now, I didn't care.

Squaaaaaaaaaaaaaauuuuuuuk!

Both of us looked down at the persistent chicken.

'You really do need to feed them. They should probably be in the coop in this weather anyway.'

'Then their owners need to take care of that. I've got more than enough on my plate!'

Jesse did that squint again. 'You are their owner.'

'What?' My head snapped up from looking down at the sodden and apparently hungry chicken.

'The chickens came with the property.'

'No.' I held up a hand. 'No. No, they didn't.' I felt the panic rising as my voice did the same. 'There was absolutely no mention of chickens. I know about the impending sheep, which I haven't figured out what the hell to do with, but I'm not getting fobbed off with a load of bloody chickens too!'

He gave a shrug. 'Definitely yours. And it was on the property details.'

'How come you're so well informed about all this?'

'Because my family were the previous owners. My cousin, to be accurate. I saw the details. The chickens were specifically mentioned.'

I stared at Jesse, looked down at the chicken, who looked back up at me, before I returned my gaze to Jesse.

'I take it you didn't read the details too well.'

I remained silent. What was I going to say? *No, I didn't actually because I was on a massive bender, busily throwing away everything I'd worked for so that I could end up in the arse end of nowhere, soaked, freezing cold in a dilapidated house wrapped in a Barbour and little else, being judged by a beady-eyed hen.*

'You should really get inside before you freeze to death.'

'It's not like it's any warmer in there,' I blurted with a shrug, dislodging a small pool of raindrops off my shoulders. I'd begun to forget what hot water actually felt like and, should I ever get the luxury of experiencing it once more, I would never again take it for granted.

Jesse frowned. 'The heating was working when I checked it over for my cousin. It was left on frost setting to stop the pipes freezing. Have you changed it from that?'

Changed it? I thought these things just all worked automatically...

He tilted his head, water running off the waxed hat in rivulets. 'Would you like me to pop in and go over it with you?'

I hesitated.

'Here.' He pulled a wallet out of the back pocket of his cargo trousers. 'Do you have a friend or someone you can send this to?' He held out his driving licence.

I nodded. 'My phone's in the car.' I backed up and opened the door, sitting down carefully, aware that if I'd bent in to grab it I'd have shown him my arse. Not that a man who looked like he did would have taken much notice, bearing in my mind the granny pants and the fact I'd already brained him earlier in the day. I hadn't missed the butterfly stitch now holding the cut above his eye together.

'Oh!' I said, standing up again and pushing the door closed behind me.

'Problem?'

'No,' I said, snapping a picture of his licence. How did he manage to even look good in that? Most people looked like a wanted poster in theirs. I bet his passport photo was good too. Git.

'I was just remembering... erm, earlier. Sorry again about whacking you with the wood.'

'No harm done.' He touched his head under the brim of his hat. 'Well, not too much anyway. There are those who'd argue I could do with some sense knocking into me.'

'Sorry. Again.'

There was the briefest flash of a smile. So quick that I wondered if the cold was making me hallucinate. It was such a great smile, I might well have done as by this time, I felt I was pretty susceptible to hallucinations. I tapped on my phone and, with lack of anyone else to contact, sent the photo to myself and shut it off.

'Done?'

'Yep.' I nodded.

'Good. Come on. You need to get dry and I'll get the heating on for you.'

'Are you sure you don't mind?'

'Yes. I assumed the agent would do all that, but I guess not.'

'I asked if there was anything I should know but the estate agent just handed me the key and said it was all pretty self-explanatory.'

The grey eyes momentarily turned stormy once more. 'OK. I'll show you some basics.'

* * *

An hour later, I was dry, dressed – including yet another pair of enormous pants – and my house was warm. Well, kind of. There was still plastic sheeting covering several of the window gaps, a material not exactly renowned for its heat-retaining capacity. Not to mention the fact that when you shut the front door, it was so warped that the wind still blew freely through the gaps. The back door wasn't much better.

I sat staring around me. What had I done?

'You OK?' The deep voice jolted me out of my daze.

'Oh! Yes. Fine. Thanks.'

'You look...' I met his eyes, the handsome face set in a thoughtful frown. 'Stunned,' he finished.

'Me?' I replied, too quickly. 'No. Not at all. Absolutely all going to plan. Just a couple of hiccups which,' I put my hand out, 'thanks to you, are now under control.'

Jesse looked back at me, clearly not buying it for a second, but I held his gaze, determinedly, attempting to block out the fact that he'd already seen me lying flat on my back in the mud, raging at the sky.

'Right. All under control, eh?'

'Absolutely.' I gave him my best winning smile, the one I'd used to close the many deals I'd made as I'd clawed my way up the ladder of success. The one that always worked. The smile that won clients over when they were wavering, just as Jesse was now. And then he returned it. Just as they always did.

'Good effort but I'm not buying it.'

I felt my jaw drop.

'What?'

'I can certainly imagine it fools a lot of people but I'm afraid I'm not one of them.'

I turned back to the strong black coffee I'd made when I'd returned from the shower.

'I don't know what you mean.'

Jesse shifted his weight. 'Pretty sure you do, but I'm not going to argue with you.' I glanced back at him. 'There's too many planks of wood around here to do that.'

'Ha ha.' I turned away, partly to hide my confusion. I'd honed that smile over the years and it always worked, closed the deal, swung a decision my way. Until now. 'It was an accident.'

'It was a joke.'

I threw him a glance and he gave a shrug. He held my gaze for a moment then blew out a sigh.

'Well, then, if you've got everything under control, I'll be on my way.'

'Right.' I got to my feet. 'Yes. OK. Thanks again for the help.'

'You're welcome.' He took a few steps towards the badly fitting front door and I followed him. Suddenly, he stopped and turned and I was unexpectedly a lot closer than I planned. He smelled of clean laundry. No aftershave. Hurriedly, I took a step back, putting a little more space between us, and swallowed.

'If you change your mind about having it all under control...' Jesse glanced down at the minimalist and ridiculously expensive console table I'd placed by the door. The receipt from the DIY shop was on it, amongst a pile of yet unopened letters. His eyes took in those too, but his expression gave nothing away – another new experience. I'd made a point of studying people, learning how to read them, and it had held me in good stead with my work. It had helped me tailor my pitch to clients. But this guy? He wasn't just a closed book; he was a closed book with a lock on it under a pile of other closed books. In a locked library.

Jesse leant over, picked up the Mont Blanc pen sitting alongside and scribbled something on the back of the receipt. 'That's my number.' I raised an eyebrow and the grey eyes danced with amusement. 'You think I'm hitting on you?'

'Are you?'

'No. Just to be clear, that,' he pointed at the paper, 'is me offering help in case you need it. That's all. Nothing else.'

'Good to know.' There was a hint of tease in my voice.

'You'll be relieved to know I don't go around trying to pick up women in DIY stores.'

'Big relief,' I replied.

Jesse gave me a glance. 'And,' he added, 'if it makes you feel better, you're not really my type.'

The smile on my face felt like a rictus. *How on earth could that make anyone 'feel better'?*

'I see.'

He turned to go, his hand on the latch.

'Just out of interest, what *type* exactly do you think I am?'

He looked over his shoulder, the eyes wary now. I saw his Adam's apple bob.

'That feels like a question I probably shouldn't answer.'

'No, please,' I said, moving around him and leaning against the draughty door. 'I'm interested.'

He looked down at me. My uniform for years had been sky-high heels and I was used to meeting strange men on a more even height. But right now, in two pairs of thick woollen socks and some cloud sliders, I was at a distinct disadvantage in that department. Not only was he taller but he was also built a whole lot sturdier than the wreck of a house I'd bought.

'I'd better be going.'

I moved to block the latch he'd momentarily let go of with my body.

He met my challenging stare with one of his own. I was more than aware that, if he'd wanted, he could quite easily have moved me aside with one hand and been on his way. He let out a sigh.

'I'm not really into city types. That's all I meant.'

'And you think I'm a city type?'

He glanced around at the minimalist furniture that looked entirely out of place, the high-end branded sweatshirt I wore that clearly wasn't a knock-off, and then studied my face, my well-honed 'natural look' having been applied following my shower.

'I know you are.'

'And clearly you feel there's something wrong with that.' I had no idea why I suddenly felt so defensive. Since when did I care what some random bloke thought of me, even if he was Greek-god handsome and had delivered heating and hot water into my disaster of a home?

'That's not what I said.'

'You may as well have.'

'Then I apologise. It wasn't what I meant. I just wanted to reassure you that I wasn't interested so you had nothing to be worried about.' He reached around me, gently but purposefully, before looking down and meeting my eyes once again. 'The offer of help is still there. If you want it. Enjoy your evening.' With that, he twisted the latch and waited for me to move. When I did, he strode with long-legged paces back to his pick-up. I closed the door but could still clearly hear the engine turn over and the tyres splash through the mud on the way out before I was once more surrounded by the overwhelming silence of the place. Being efficient, I entered Jesse's number into my phone, typed, *Thank you* into a message and sent it off before dropping the paper into the bin. His words, however, were still tumbling around in my head.

'Who cares what he thinks?' I snapped before grabbing my laptop from the coffee table and stomping up the creaking stairs to bed. There, tucked under three blankets and two duvets against the chill wind coming in through the rotten windows, I began looking for tradesmen to help me turn this old house into something liveable. If I did it right, I might even be able to make some money on it.

I had no intention of staying here. Obviously, I wouldn't be able to go back to my old job. That ship had most definitely sailed, hit an iceberg and sunk in the middle of the ocean, but I could certainly get my old life back. The *city* life that Jesse had so sniffily dismissed. I'd built that life from nothing once before and I'd do it again. This time, I had my savings and years' worth of wisdom behind me, unlike the teenager I'd been back then. I could do this. I would do this. And without Jesse... I pulled up the picture on my phone and studied his driving licence. Without Jesse Woods' help.

3

'Hi!' The woman gave a cheery wave as I walked into the snug little café in the village. I'd spent the last few days doing research for the restoration, making spreadsheets and costings, and now I just needed a change of scene from the same four walls and plastic sheeting I'd been staring at since I got here.

'Hi,' I said, my Manolos clicking on the floor as I walked to the counter.

'You must be the new owner of Paradise Farm.'

I let out an unintentional laugh. 'Yes. That's me.'

'Julie Woods. Nice to meet you.'

Woods?

'Felicity DeVere. Likewise.'

Her smile seemed genuine and at least she was making an effort, unlike the other customers, who I knew were looking at me while pretending not to. But I'd dealt with that before. I ignored them and focused on what I'd come here to do.

'How's it going?' Julie called over the surprisingly unobtrusive sound of the coffee machine as it ground the beans. She saw me glance at it. 'I know, quiet, isn't it?'

'It is.'

'The other one was driving me mad and I was moaning about it once when my brother was here and next thing I know, this had arrived.'

'Wow. Nice brother.'

'Yeah. He's all right,' she said with a grin. 'Take a seat anywhere you like and I'll be with you in a minute.'

I click-click-clicked over to a table for two by the window, took a seat and began to study the menu.

'So, how you getting on up there?' Julie asked as she got to my table, pad and pen in hand.

'In Paradise?' I asked, with a wry smile.

Julie laughed. 'Yeah. I gather it's not quite that just yet.' She pulled a sympathetic face. 'But the views are amazing.'

'The weather hasn't really been the best since I got here but I'm sure they are. Although I'd prefer to view them through glass rather than plastic sheeting.' Why I'd mentioned the plastic, I had no idea. Usually, the minimum amount of small talk was enough for me. But I was so grateful for this woman's warm, friendly smile and greeting after everything that had happened, I was surprisingly eager to extend the conversation.

'I can't believe he left it like that. That wasn't the deal.' She shook her head.

'The deal?' I asked as I chose the avocado on sourdough and Julie scribbled it down.

'My cousin. He made a right hoo-ha about wanting the place and how he had always dreamed about having it. Everyone knew my brother was the one who was supposed to get Paradise Farm once Gran died but he's such a softy, he let our cousin have it. He even lent him the money to do it up it as he'd made such a song and dance about caring for it. Instead, Joe ripped out all the original fittings that were worth anything and flogged them to a salvage dealer, sold the place and scarpered with the money.' She threw a dark look. 'Jesse's money.'

'Jesse?' I repeated.

'Yeah. He's my brother. Oh, that's him now,' she said as the tiny bell above the door tinkled and her brother's large frame filled the doorway. 'I'll introduce you.'

Before I could speak, she was beckoning him over from where he'd stopped to chat to a young couple with a newborn who were sitting near the door. He glanced over, gave her a wave, gave me a brief nod then turned back to his conversation.

'That's OK,' I said. 'Some other time.'

'OK. I'll bring your order over when it's ready. Cutlery's over there.' She pointed to a wooden dresser, its shelves displaying a stylish mix of teacups and saucers and teapots. Below those stood utensil pots and mini condiment sets along with a water dispenser, slices of lemon and lime bobbing inside it.

I clipped over to the dresser, aware of the sound of my shoes, which suddenly seemed deafening over the quiet chatter of the café. Back straight and chin up, I gathered what I needed, including a glass of water, then made my way back, sat down and pulled the laptop out of my Hermès shoulder bag and resumed my project management of the house.

A short time later, Julie appeared at the table bearing the most delicious-looking brunch.

'This looks amazing,' I said. 'Thanks.'

'Julie's food is the best around by miles,' a deep voice added, pride in his tone.

I looked up to see Jesse now standing by his sister.

'He's biased, obviously. And probably just wants free food.' She gave him a nudge with her shoulder.

'Well, if there's some going,' he replied, exchanging a grin with her.

'This is my brother I was telling you about,' Julie said. I didn't miss the brief shadow that passed across his face as she said the words.

'Jesse, this is Felicity DeVere. She's the new owner of Paradise Farm.'

'Felicity.' He nodded. 'Nice to see you again.'

Julie's head snapped round towards him. 'You've met? When? You didn't tell me.'

Jesse folded his arms across an expansive chest and tilted his head the smallest amount as he eyed his sister. 'I wasn't aware I had to report every new acquaintance I made.'

'No, obviously not.' She rolled her eyes at me. 'Eat, eat!' she said, chivvying me up, but it felt a little uncomfortable to start eating with the audience I now had. I was also more than aware a few more ears had perked up in the meantime. 'I'm just surprised you hadn't mentioned you'd met Felicity here, what with her being the owner of the farm now.'

'I left something behind at the DIY shop and your brother kindly brought it round for me,' I explained, sensing Jesse's discomfort.

'Oh.' Julie seemed disappointed. 'Right. So, are you eating?' she asked, looking up at her brother.

'That looks good,' he said, pointing at my plate.

'Coming up.' Julie laid a hand on my shoulder, then headed back behind the counter, leaving her brother standing by the table.

'Sorry about that.'

I looked up.

'About what?'

He inclined his head towards his sister, who was now busy laughing with another woman as the café began to fill with what seemed to be regular customers. 'She's always been pretty chatty.'

'I think she's lovely,' I replied genuinely and my words brought a smile.

'Thanks. I'll... I'll leave you to get on with your lunch.'

He turned to take the last table behind me just as an elderly couple swooped in. 'Sorry, Jesse, love. You don't mind, do you?' they asked, making themselves comfy.

'Oh... No, not at all.'

I caught his eye and pushed the empty chair at my table with my foot. He hesitated.

'I won't bite,' I whispered, widening my eyes at him as he rested his hand on the back of the chair. 'Besides,' I continued, 'you're not my type.'

The smile was slow and way too sexy, something he was apparently unaware of. 'Touché.' His gaze fell to the laptop screen taking in the builders' website I'd pulled up.

'Don't use them. You want someone who's a specialist in restoration ideally.'

'They've got a lot of good reviews.'

'That's as may be, but you've got a Victorian farmhouse. That's not the same as sticking an extension on a new build.'

'Thank you for that excellent example of mansplaining but I'll do my own research, if you don't mind.'

Jesse looked as if he very much did mind, judging by the tiny muscle in his jaw that was flickering away like a dodgy light bulb.

'I'm trying to help.'

'Which I appreciate but, as I said before, if I need it, I will ask.'

He sucked in a deep breath and let it out slowly. 'Right.'

'Here you go!' Julie appeared at the side of the table and put Jesse's lunch down in front of him.

'Looks great, Jules. Thanks.'

His sister squinted her eyes then stood back and put her hands on her hips. 'What's wrong with it?'

'Nothing!'

'Then what's with the face?'

'No face,' he replied, jaw still tense. 'Same old face.'

'I don't think so.'

He threw her a look that told her to leave it. I knew exactly what the problem was and, having witnessed their close relationship earlier, had no wish to cause any ripples in that particular pond by her thinking he was turning his nose up at her cooking.

'I just think your brother would rather eat elsewhere. We have differing viewpoints on the renovation of my house.'

'Oh,' Julie said, apparently relieved that the problem was not with her food. Then she cast a glance around. 'Well, sorry, big brother, we're full, so you'll both have to just agree to disagree for the moment. Enjoy!' she said and walked back to the counter.

I took another bite of my food, trying not to smile.

'Don't think I can't see you smiling over there.'

I widened my eyes as I swallowed my mouthful. 'I don't know what you mean.'

Jesse gave a grunt and concentrated on demolishing his lunch. I finished mine, put the plate aside and returned to my research, sipping on the refill of coffee Julie had just provided me with. I switched screens back to my vision boards for the house and scanned through the one for the bedroom. The scheme was soft and feminine, romantic and cosy – all of the things that my London apartment hadn't been. But then I'd been a fan of the minimalistic look. Working long hours had meant I wasn't always there an awful lot and if I was, I had my head buried in a laptop. So it had been quite a surprise to find that the mood board I was creating for the main bedroom began to come together in a style I'd never thought I'd consider. But it felt right.

'Is that for the main bedroom?' Jesse interrupted my thoughts, and I looked up to see him glancing over at the screen.

'Yes,' I replied. 'Although I suspect you're about to tell me that's all wrong too.'

He wiped his mouth with his napkin and placed it back on his lap. Interesting. For someone who seemed so rough around the edges, his grasp of table etiquette was on point.

'Nope. Not at all. From what I can see, it looks perfect.' The smile flashed on his face. 'Don't look so shocked. And...' he cleared his throat '...I apologise if earlier seemed like "mansplaining" to you. That wasn't my intention. I just wouldn't want you to waste your money on a bad job.'

'Thank you. I appreciate the apology. Well...' I drained the last of the coffee and then pushed my chair back. 'Things to do.'

'People to see?'

'Unlikely, as I don't know a soul, but yes, that kind of thing.'

'You should come round for dinner.' Julie popped up at my elbow.

'Oh! No, that's really kind of you but it was just a turn of phrase. I'm fine, really.'

Her hand was back on her hip.

'Do you know anyone around here?'

I opened my mouth, glanced at Jesse, who was now resting his chin on his steepled fingers, watching, the faintest hint of amusement on a mouth that some might call tempting.

'Well, no, but—'

'That's that, then. We always have a big roast on a Sunday and you have to come. It's got to be ever so lonely up there. Oh, go on, say you'll come. We never get any new and interesting people around here.' She had the same big, grey eyes as her brother and they were hard to say no to. Just as I imagined it would be hard to say no to him, given the right situation but that was certainly not something I needed to worry about.

'I wouldn't want to inconvenience anyone.'

'No inconvenience!' Julie replied, grinning now. 'Lunch is at one so Jesse can come and get you about half twelve. Sound OK?'

'Oh no, I don't need a lift, honestly.' Now that I'd had my rear windscreen repaired, at least one thing I owned had all its windows as they should be.

'Of course you do. You've got to have a glass of wine, or two.'

'What if I wanted a glass of wine or two?' her brother asked.

'Then you'll manage without,' she replied, not skipping a beat. 'Ah, that's great. I'm going to ring Mum and let her know.' She pulled her phone from her apron pocket. 'See you Sunday if not before,' Julie said, touching my arm as she left, her phone already to her ear.

I turned slowly back to face Jesse. 'What just happened?'

'She might look like a stiff breeze would blow her over but she's a steamroller when she wants to be.' He stood from the table, placing his napkin on top of it now that he was finished. 'Guess I'll see you Sunday, then. If not before.' He echoed his sister's words then held out a hand, indicating for me to go first as we made our way out of the café, its windows now steamy with the heat being generated inside. Outside, the sky was a leaden, flat grey with the promise of yet more rain. A gust of wind howled around the corner. I wrapped my ankle-length, fitted, wool coat around me and knotted the belt.

'I need to make some calls about getting some replacement windows fitted sooner rather than later I think,' I said, casting the sky a disapproving glare.

Jesse nodded, his gaze dropping to my stiletto heeled shoes. 'Kind of amazed you made it out in those.'

'I have some most unflattering wellies in the car that I found in the boot room for commutes between my car and house until I get some paving laid.'

'I see you're learning.'

'I wish I'd learned that huge spiders like to hibernate or whatever they do in said wellies before I put them on my feet.' I shuddered again at the feel of long, furry legs tickling my feet as I'd shoved them into the oversized boots earlier today. 'I'm amazed you didn't hear the screams, to be honest. I was sure half the county did.'

'Not a fan of spiders?'

'No, not terribly. Especially not on my person.'

He looked down at the scuffed toes of his work boots before suddenly returning his gaze to me. 'I'm really sorry about this, you know. I had no idea what a state the house had been left in.'

'It's hardly your fault,' I replied. 'Even though I know now that the place was supposed to go to you.'

'Ah.'

'Your sister told me. I can understand why you don't like me—'

'I never said that.'

I stopped mid flow. 'Well, no. But… I can see how irksome it must be to have me swoop in from out of town and buy the house of your dreams.'

'To be honest, that's not the house of my dreams.'

'Oh!'

'It looks a hell of a lot better in my dreams. For a start, it's got functioning windows.' He gave a flick of the dark brows.

'Hilarious.'

'What's that for?' He nodded towards my car. Two straw bales were stuffed into the back seat with another on the front.

'Bedding for the chickens, according to Google. I know it's not enough, before you say anything, but it's a start. The chap at the supply store said he'd drop the rest round for me.'

'Brendan?'

'Yes.'

'Blimey. Special privileges there. He must have taken a shine to you.'

I flicked him a look. 'Hardly.'

'Coming round to the idea of them now, then, the chickens? Didn't seem so keen on them when you first met.'

'Thank you for reminding me of that particular moment in time but, yes, I think I am. They're really rather sweet, if a little untrained when it comes to being herded back into their house.'

'Herded?'

'Yes.'

'Why don't you just pick them up?'

I looked up at him. The only chicken I'd ever picked up was pre roasted and in a wrapper from Waitrose.

'They might flap a bit at first but they'll settle as soon as you've got them and they're quite cosy to cuddle. Nice gentle breed you've got there.'

Never in my life had I imagined that I would ever be talking about how cuddly any chickens were, let alone my own!

Jesse sensed my hesitation. 'One step at a time though, maybe.'

'Yes, I think so. I'd better get back to this... whatever I'm supposed to do with it.'

'Need some help?'

'That's very kind but I'm sure between Google and YouTube, I'll work it out.'

He nodded.

'Thanks, though.'

'No problem. Glad they're growing on you. I'll see you half twelve Sunday.'

With that, Jesse gave a nod and then strode across the narrow main road of the village to where his pick-up was parked. As he went to get in, a lithe-looking woman stepped out from a nearby shop and called his name. He turned and I saw the woman's face light up with a huge smile as she walked towards him, reaching up to kiss him on the cheek. I guess she was more his type.

He was right about the chickens. They were growing on me. Having done some hasty research online, I was now feeling rather guilty about the grubby state of the coop I'd inherited. By the looks of things, I'd also need to investigate getting the run repaired too as the chickens still had a tendency to be found in various parts of the farm that they shouldn't be and the last thing I wanted was for a fox to get them.

I flashed the locks on my car and slid behind the wheel onto the soft leather just as large droplets of rain began to gather pace on the windscreen. Great. Did it ever do anything but bloody rain around here? As soon as I got home, I was ringing someone to sort out the windows. If I could at least weatherproof my house, that would be a start.

4

'Oh! That wasn't exactly what I thought you'd be putting in.' I looked at the windows now lined up against the wall. They were nothing like original Victorian-style sash windows and, although I was a total newbie at this, even I knew they were going to look hideous.

'You said you wanted it done quickly. These are the ones we've got in stock that fit the measurements. You didn't say anything about having fancy ones put in.' The man shoved his hands in his pockets and gave me a shrug. 'It's these or nothing.'

I looked out at the once more darkening sky. Every other supplier I'd rung couldn't do anything for weeks yet, so I'd ended up going with this company that I'd finally found buried several pages in while trawling the web. A voice in my head that sounded remarkably like my sexy neighbour's told me this might not have been such a great idea.

'What's the verdict, love?' He sounded tetchy now. 'If you don't want them, plenty of others will and hanging around here doesn't pay my bill, if you know what I mean.'

Definitely not such a great idea. But what could I do now? They were here. They had new windows and I had completely rotten ones. How bad could it be? At least when I went to bed tonight, I'd be warmer.

It turned out I wasn't warmer. I could hear the wind whooshing through gaps between the building and the window frame. Not to mention it looked hideous. The existing windows had been ropey but were beautiful period sash ones, perfect for my romantic vision. Now my bedroom had one basic, white uPVC one that, weirdly, only opened a couple of inches. The fitter had said that was normal until it bedded in. He'd seemed to know what he was doing so I'd taken his word for it. In the end, he'd had to leave the other one as, once again, the heavens had opened and trying to fit any more had been impossible. I'd suggested paying for them all together but the man had insisted he be paid for the work he'd done and that he'd arrange with me to come back when the weather was more conducive. He and his mate were both big blokes and, unlike Jesse, who never appeared to use his size as a threat, there was something about these two I hadn't felt comfortable with. In truth, I'd been regretting the whole thing. I'd paid them for the bedroom window in cash as requested, locked the door and waited until the van was out of sight to let out the breath I hadn't even realised I'd been holding.

And now, here I was, under a mountain of blankets, listening to the wind howling through one rotten window and one new but badly fitted one. I'd spent the last couple of hours on my laptop trying to find suitable house insurance, something that was proving difficult given the current insecure state of my house. But eventually I'd given in to the weather and snuggled down in the bed, trying to get warm. At least the old window had kept out the worst of the rain but I could hear the tap tap tap of raindrops on the floorboards under the newly fitted one. I'd put a bucket down earlier but now I could hear a new spot letting in the weather. Perfect! If Jesse knew, I was sure he'd be laughing his arse off and telling me he'd told me so. Which he had.

A loud crack outside made me squeak in shock. Another was emitted as the sound was followed immediately by a crash. Was that a tree? The wind was hammering into the farmhouse, thumping against it like a solid force. Branches from another tree scraped and tapped at the glass, reminding me of a ghostly Cathy from *Wuthering Heights*, begging to be let in. I pulled the blanket over my head. Was the place actually haunted? It was old enough to be. People used to die at home in the Victorian era when the house was built, didn't they? Oh God, was I trying to sleep in a room where someone, or more than one person, had taken their last, rattling breath?

I shoved the blanket back sharply. This was ridiculous. I didn't even believe in ghosts! It was just a bit of weather and I was working myself up into a frenzy about it because I was already running on Stress Level Defcon 1 – at least! I flipped the switch for the bedside lamp and pushed myself up the bed. Leaning over, I could see the puddle forming under the nearest edge of the window while the other side was still dripping steadily into the bucket. And then the thunder started.

'Great.' I sighed and swung my legs out of the bed. I was out of buckets, having only found one, but I could mop up the mess and then put another towel down to soak up the leak until I could get hold of the fitters again in the morning to redo the appalling job. The thought of them coming back didn't exactly warm the cockles of my heart. Maybe I could ask Julie if she'd be able to take a bit of time off from the café to be here too, just so that I wasn't alone. No, that was ridiculous. I'd done everything on my own for decades. I wasn't about to start relying on others now. Apparently my independence was something that had appealed to Adrian. Or so he'd said. I guess it had left him free to do his own thing. Like get cosy with heiresses.

'Right!' I slapped my thighs and stood up. As I took my second step, an enormous clap of thunder rolled around the building, shaking it, and me, to its core. The lights flashed then everything went dark as a cave. That was another thing, along with the assorted smells, none of the many property programmes mentioned about moving to the countryside. It was dark. I mean, properly dark by 4 p.m. Having always lived in the city and surrounded by streetlights, this was still taking some getting used to.

Outside, another deafening crack was followed by a second loud crash, at the same time as lightning lit up the room like a flare. The thunder followed immediately, competing with the wind as each tried to drown the other out. The wind slammed into the house once more and blew the new window from its poor fixings. the frame catching me on the temple as it fell to the ground, taking me and a glass side table with it. As it landed, glass sprayed everywhere, the shards lit up like a glass fountain by the next flash of lightning.

I lay where I was, stars tumbling in front of my eyes in the pitch black, my head already beginning to thump. Another sharp crack outside brought me back to the present. I made to push myself up and promptly put my hand on some glass.

'Shit!' Snatching it back, I stayed where I was, waiting for the next bolt of lightning to illuminate the area so that I could at least get to my phone and use that as a torch. As the next flash lit the room, I groggily stepped back and reached over the bed to grab my phone, almost overbalancing as I did so. Steadying myself on the bed, I switched the torch on, revealing a blood-red handprint on my ridiculously expensive cashmere blanket.

'Fantastic,' I said, focusing my anger on that in an attempt to keep the rising panic at bay. My house was falling apart around me and I was leaking blood from at least one part of my body. My head was pounding and my right foot was stinging too so I wasn't putting either of those in the clear either. I turned the torch onto the floor where the shattered table and broken window frame lay, then followed the spray of glass as the shards caught the light way across the room, twinkling back at me like tiny, vicious stars. I sat down heavily on the bed.

I looked down at my phone. Who did you call in this situation? A family member, a friend, the police? No, that was ridiculous. What the hell could the police do? *Hello? I'd like to report a rogue window.* More like rogue window fitters. As for the other two, I didn't have any family and the only friends I did have were miles away back in London. Not that anyone had called to see how I was. I'd always been too busy to nurture any real friendships, and perhaps a bit suspicious. Trust wasn't exactly something I excelled at and I'd been with my ex for a decade so his friends had become my friends. Or so I'd thought. I guess in the end, they were just his friends after all.

I took a deep inhale, tried to ignore the creak and groan of the tree just outside the window and turned to bum shuffle across the bed. The longer I stayed here, the colder I was getting. My teeth were already chattering as I grabbed the bloody throw from the bed and wrapped it around myself. It was already ruined so in for a penny, in for a pound and all that. I pushed myself up and tottered unsteadily towards the door, my hand stretched out to feel for the doorframe. As I grabbed it with relief, a loud crack reverberated around the room, the rain lashing in through the gaping hole where there had once been a window. I turned back just in time to see a huge branch tear through the roof and land sprawled on my bed, its end sticking out through the wall. My room, my house, was totalled but all I could do was stare at the huge log that now rested in the same place I had been just seconds ago.

* * *

Through the howls of the wind, I heard another noise. Still stunned as I stood staring at how much closer than planned I suddenly was to nature, I didn't react. The noise stopped. Almost immediately, it started again. Finally the familiar sound jolted me out of my stupor and I put the phone to my ear.

'Hello?' I answered without checking the screen.

'Felicity?'

'Yes.'

'It's Jesse. Are you all right up there?' His words were quick and sharp, tension resonating through them.

'Umm...'

'OK. That's not the positive reply I was hoping for.'

'There's a tree in my bedroom.' My words sounded oddly calm.

There was silence on the line and I went to drop my hand, assuming the storm, not content with crapping on my house, thought it would round out what I hoped was its finale by destroying my only contact with civilisation.

'Felicity?'

I lifted the phone back up. 'Sorry. I thought we'd got cut off.' My words were as casual as if I'd been on a train and gone through a tunnel.

'No. I was just... Did you say there's a tree in your bedroom?'

'Yes. I think I'm going to need a new roof. Actually, I think I'm going to need a new house. In fact...' reality was peeling back the layers of shock and waving enthusiastically '...I could really do with a new life. This one's rather turned to shit.' And then I hung up because I felt the tears, frustration and downright fury about to blow and I had no desire to embarrass myself in front of my handsome, disapproving neighbour any more than I already had.

I was about to do what he'd likely expected me to in the first place. Something I'd never done in my life before, no matter how hard things had been. But right now, as I sat on the landing of my partially destroyed house, I couldn't see any other way. I was going to give up. There was no way I was going to make my money back on this place, especially with its impromptu roof garden, but I'd take what I could and get the hell out of here.

For a while, I'd thought I could do it, thought I could make that shift from city living to the country. The quiet was definitely growing on me and I'd sort of made a friend in Julie, who didn't appear to want anything in return – which in itself had been novel. But I couldn't win against this. Where did I even bloody start when there was a sodding tree lying on my bed – or at least the remnants of the beautiful, period-style bed I'd bought with the insanely expensive mattress and seven-star hotel-quality sheets? The one bit of comfort in this disaster of a so-called house and it was smashed to pieces and sodden.

I screamed with frustration at the tree, the wind, the storm and life in general. Everything I'd done, everything I'd battled and won and worked for. Where the fuck did I go from here?

A hefty gust blew through. The painting on the wall next to me that I'd hung myself – thank you, YouTube – slammed against the wall then lifted and crashed to the floor, glass splintering everywhere, the paper inside already crumpling in the rain. I let out another lung-busting scream that encompassed all the feelings I couldn't even begin to put into words.

'Felicity?' The shout came from outside and I snapped my mouth closed. 'Felicity!'

I staggered upright, gripping the wall as heavy footsteps came racing up the stairs, torchlight dancing in front of them. Jesse. His arms reached for me and I let them. Suddenly, the muscles in my legs that I'd trained at the gym religiously four times a week felt like blancmange.

His gaze left mine momentarily to take in the surroundings. 'Jesus. Are you all right? Are you hurt?'

I shook my head.

'You screamed.'

I shook my head again. 'I'm all right. Honestly.' I looked down, suddenly embarrassed at the thought that he had heard my screams of frustration, despite the fact that they had oddly made me feel a little better.

His hand caught my face. There was a slight roughness to his skin, a man who used his hands. This was in contrast to the men I usually associated with, some of whom had a better hand and nail regimen than I did.

'You're sure?'

I nodded against his hand.

'OK. Can you—?' As he stepped back, glass powdered under his boot. 'What's that?'

'It blew off the wall.' I pointed to the sad, crumpled, soggy mess that had once been my favourite painting, surrounded by splinters of wood and glass. Jesse looked down at my feet.

'We need to get you out of here.'

I went to step forward but suddenly, one strong arm was under my knees and I was scooped up and resting comfortably against a very solid chest. 'Apologies but if that's smashed, there's glass everywhere.' He looked up as another flash illuminated the room. 'You also appear to be missing a window.'

'I think that's the least of my problems right now,' I replied, looking up at him. I couldn't see his expression but I felt his arms tighten a fraction.

'Buildings can be fixed. People are more important.'

'If you're going to be nice to me, you need to put me down right now because I'm in a very emotional state and I refuse to cry in front of you.'

'You've every right to be emotional,' he said, turning towards the stairs and making his way carefully down them, his arms solid and reassuring around me. 'But I'm not putting you down until I know your feet aren't going to be cut to ribbons. Besides, we need to get you out of this house.'

'I can't leave it!'

'You have to, Felicity!' Jesse said. His torch sought out a pair of my shoes, which he picked up and placed in front of me, and then he put me down so that I could step straight into them.

'No, I don't. I'm sure the storm will be over soon and I need to be here to assess what the damage is once it's light and then sort out getting it back on the market.'

'Wait, what? The market?'

'I'm done! If there was ever a sign that I am most definitely in the wrong place, then I'm pretty sure this is it!' I flung my arms wide. 'The sooner I get out of this, and back to civilisation, the better.'

'Right. Well, in the meantime, this house isn't safe for you to stay in. We don't know what structural damage that tree has done and the storm isn't over yet. The safest thing for you to do now is get out of here and come back in the morning when it's light.'

'Fine!' I grabbed my keys from the bowl and marched to the door. My foot and hand stung and I had a splitting headache but I was getting out of here.

'Felicity, wait. I'll drive you.'

I yanked a coat off the hook, shrugged violently into it and pulled open the door, mentally adding 'more substantial lock' to my shopping list bearing in mind how easily Jesse had got in.

'Thank you, but I'm quite capable of... You have got to be fucking joking!'

Jesse took the keys from my now limp hands as they hung at my sides, gently moved me outside and locked the door. I was still staring at my car. At least what was left of it. The universe, or whoever the hell was in charge, not content with letting me ruin my career and jettison everything I'd worked for in order to come to this disaster zone, had not only sent a tree through my roof, barely missing reducing me to a pile of goo, but had also aimed a whole tree at my car and dropped it right down the centre. I now, effectively, owned two cars. Or at least two halves of the same one.

I felt my body sagging. I'd thought I was done before but apparently not. Now, though, I was utterly, totally and completely done. I began to slide to the ground.

'Upsy daisy.' Jesse's arm was back round me, holding me up. My feet felt leaden.

'Just leave me here. Please.' My voice sounded small.

'Not going to happen.'

I wriggled out of his arm. 'Why?' I stepped back, suddenly finding my voice again. 'What are you even doing here? Why do you care if I stay here or not? You know what?' I yelled against the weather. 'I wish I'd never moved! I wish I'd stayed right in that bed when that bloody tree came in!'

Suddenly, I was back up in his arms, back against that chest. 'We're going home.'

'This is my bloody home.' I kicked my feet and one of my shoes flew off. Of course it did. 'Put me down!'

'I'm about to.' He pulled the handle on his truck door, kicked it open and deposited me inside, not especially gently, then slammed the door shut. He'd left the lights of his pick-up on when he'd come in and I saw him cross their beam, his eyes squinting against the driving rain, mouth set in a grim line. Then he pulled himself in behind the wheel, the engine bursting to life, and the truck cut through the quagmire that was officially my drive. In the light of the truck's interior, I could see the tension in his face. Well, good, because I was angry too.

'You know this is kidnapping.'

I caught the tiniest headshake.

'What?'

'Nothing.'

'There's clearly something. Where the hell are we going anyway? You do realise I have absolutely nothing with me?'

'I'll ask Jules to drop something round in the morning.'

'Drop something round where?'

'My place.'

'Erm. Thanks, but no, thanks. I'll stay at the hotel if I'm staying anywhere.'

'It's the middle of the night, Felicity, and we're not in London now. There's no twenty-four-seven service in the village hotel. The owners are asleep.'

'I'm sure they'd be happy to wake up at the prospect of trade.'

'No. They wouldn't. They've got a kid who's only just started sleeping through the night so sleep probably wins out. Not everyone is driven by money alone.'

'I suppose that's a dig at me?'

He let out a long breath through his teeth. 'Look. I've got a guest room with its own en suite. I'll send Jules a message explaining what's happened. You're about the same size from the looks so she'll drop something round for you in the morning. That way, we don't have to bother anyone else tonight. Then we can go back to your place in the morning and assess the damage.'

'We?'

He turned briefly to face me. 'Yes. We.' He cleared his throat. 'If you want.'

I looked out of the window but all I could see was rain streaming down the glass and my own tear-streaked face reflected in the low light of the cabin.

'I'm sorry... I'm... Thank you.'

'You're welcome.'

5

Jesse pulled into the drive of a Georgian-style house. The tall wooden gates were open and subtle uplighting highlighted the handsome building.

'This is your house?'

'It is.' He slowed to a stop and applied the handbrake. 'I'm assuming from your tone it's not what you expected. Probably best if I don't ask what you did expect but I'm guessing more of a hovel.'

'No!' My hand shot out and caught his arm before he reached for the door. He turned back to face me, the planes of his face catching the light from his house. 'Not at all. And... and I'm sorry if that's how it came across.'

'Felicity. You don't have to apologise. The guest room is yours whatever you think of me.'

'This isn't about the bloody guest room.' I snatched my hand back. 'This is me trying to apologise.' I swallowed and tilted my chin up, facing Jesse just as I'd spent the last few decades facing the world. Head high while inside, my mind and heart were racing with panic and fear. 'Sorry. It's been a bit of a crap night.'

He let out a huff of air through his nose. 'That's an understatement. Stay there, I'll come and get you. I've no idea where your other shoe went.'

'I can walk. You, unlike me, have a gorgeous block-paved driveway.'

'Which is cold and wet.'

A slightly hysterical laugh bubbled up and spilled over. 'Jesse. I don't think it's possible for me to get much colder or wetter. Remember my al fresco house?'

He stared me down.

'I promise I'll wipe my feet.'

He got out of the truck, walked round to my now open door and held out a hand. 'I don't think I've met a more impossible woman.'

I took his hand, holding on tighter than I planned as I descended from the truck's cab. Despite the heater that had been blasting, my body had begun to seize with the cold. 'Thank you.'

'You're limping.'

'I think I trod on a bit of a glass. It's probably out now. I promise not to bleed on your carpet.'

He turned to reply as I joined him under the shelter of the porch. 'Jesus!' His fingers caught my chin gently as he tilted my head. 'What happened? Why didn't you tell me you were bleeding? We need to get you to a hospital. Get back in the car.'

I wrapped my hand around his wrist. 'I didn't tell you because I didn't know. The window frame hit me on its way to the floor and we're not going to hospital. I'm fine.'

'You are not fine! You're bleeding!'

'Then could you take a look? You patched yourself up all right when I clobbered you. Honestly, I really just want to sit down right now somewhere warm and quiet.'

The grey eyes were laser focused on me. After a beat, he

wrapped an arm around me and unlocked the door. 'Like I said. Impossible.'

* * *

'Ned. Stay!' he said as we entered and a black lab gave a soft whine and tilted his head. 'Go back to your bed.' The dog dropped his head and turned around, plodding out of sight as Jesse turned back. 'Come into the kitchen and I'll take a look.' He moved to lift me again but I stood back.

'Thanks, but I can manage.' I wasn't used to people fussing about me and the words had come out sharper than I'd meant. Jesse took a step back. 'Sorry. I didn't mean—'

'It's fine. Take a seat.'

I did as he asked.

He ran the tap and put a glass of water down in front of me, then reached into a cupboard and brought out a neatly packed caddy of first-aid supplies, and put that beside the glass. The dog watched from his bed, nose resting on his paws.

'Your dog is very sweet.'

'Thank you. Right. Head first. Do you mind?' His hands hovered in mid-air for a moment.

'No. I'm just sorry to be such an inconvenience.'

'You're not. This might sting a bit.' His touch was gentle as he wiped the blood from my face. 'I'm going to put a Steri-Strip on it. Shame mine's come off. We'd be a matching pair.' He flashed a grin and I felt some of the tension in my shoulders seep out.

'Thanks for coming up tonight.'

'Not a problem,' he said, continuing with his work. 'Any headache? Blurred vision or nausea?' I shook my head. 'Let me know if any of that changes.' He then turned his attention to my hand. Reaching over, Jesse grabbed a pair of glasses from the counter top, sliding them on to his face. And just like that, a man I thought couldn't get any more sexy did so. 'Couple of shards in there. Hold still.' Deftly, he lifted them out with a pair of tweezers from the well-equipped box and cleaned my hand once again, popping on a large plaster. 'Now for the feet.'

'I think it's just the one. Only one hurts anyway and it's really not that bad.'

'Best to check anyway. Allay-oop!' He lifted my foot and rested it on his knees as he sat on the floor. A brief study resulted in the tweezers being employed again and another waterproof plaster applied.

'Right. I think that's it. You were lucky.' He stood up, taking off the glasses as he did so. 'From your expression, I can see you don't agree.'

'It's not that.' I stood, placing my weight unevenly onto my good foot. 'Well, yes, it is that. I'm not sure I feel all that lucky right now.'

'It could have been a lot worse. You saw your bed, right?'

'It's hard to forget. And yes, you're right, of course. I'm sure I sound incredibly ungrateful.'

Jesse gave a shrug of his wide shoulders. 'Probably a bit of shock still lingering there.'

'No. I'm all right now.'

He folded his arms. 'It's OK to admit you're not OK, you know? No one is going to think any less of you for it. A bloody great tree nearly landed on you. That's enough to put the wind up anyone.'

Before I could reply, and probably knowing I was about to disagree, Jesse continued. 'I'll show you to your room. You all right?' he asked as I put my hand out to steady myself on the counter top, his hand on my upper arm.

'Yes. Thanks. Just tired, I expect. All the excitement.' I returned a wan smile.

Jesse gave me a long look but remained silent as he led the way up the stairs to the second-floor guest room.

'There's a robe on the back of the bathroom door in the en suite,' he pointed to a door, 'and there should be everything you need. Feel free to have a bath or shower to warm yourself up. Might help you unwind a bit, but only if you feel stable enough.'

'Thanks, Jesse. This really is very kind.'

'You're welcome. My room's the next floor up so just phone if you need anything, in case I don't hear you. OK?'

'Yes. Thank you. I can't think there's anything else I would need though.' I pushed open the door to the bathroom. 'This is beautiful.'

'Thanks. Labour of love and all that.' His gaze dropped to his feet momentarily. 'I'll leave you to get on.'

'Thank you.'

He nodded briefly and closed the door behind him. The moment he was gone, I stripped off my wet clothes and slid into the soft, fluffy robe. Bliss! Some of the high-end spas I'd been to could take a tip from Jesse when it came to robes. I could happily live in this dressing gown forever. Leaning over the clawfoot bath, I turned on the taps, adding some of the lavender-scented bath essence from the choice on the vanity to the stream of hot water, and inhaling the calming scent as the surface of the water became a mass of bubbles.

As I turned the taps off, a knock at the door made me turn. Wrapping the robe tighter, I opened the door and peered around.

'I thought you might want this.' He held out an expensive cut-crystal glass, Waterford if I wasn't mistaken, containing a dark liquid. 'Brandy. Will warm you up and help settle your nerves.'

I stood a little straighter. 'Thank you but my nerves are fine.' I did my best to keep any edge out of my voice, but I'd been in the habit of rebuffing any suggestion of weakness for so long now, the words formed almost of their own accord.

Jesse's eyes stayed on me for the briefest moment before he began to turn.

'I'm sorry.' I opened the door a little more. 'That's very thoughtful of you and the brandy would be lovely. Thank you.'

Those intriguing grey eyes were looking back down at me now as he handed the glass over and I rested the bowl of it in my hand to warm the liquid inside and cupped the other around it.

'You're not someone who likes to accept, or admit you need, help, are you?'

It was refreshing, if a little startling, to meet someone who said it like it was. No games. No preamble. And he was right on the nose.

'No. I'm not and I apologise that I've come across as ungrateful. I'm enormously indebted to you. Thank you again for this. And for everything you've done tonight. And before that.'

'You're welcome and there's no debt. We help each other here. Look out for one another.'

'Yes. I can see that.'

'Plus it was my family that sold you a house that is in a far worse state than you were expecting.'

'That's not your fault. It's mine. I should have been more astute.' I sipped at the drink. Strong. Warm. Smooth. 'Don't they say when something looks too good to be true, it probably is?' I gave a one-shouldered shrug.

'That they do.' He paused. For a moment, I thought he was going to elaborate on the statement but he didn't. 'I'll let you get to your bath and bed. Is there anything else you need?'

'No. Thank you. You've done more than enough already.'

He shook his head. 'Nothing anyone else wouldn't have.'

'Oh, I don't know about that,' I said, almost without thinking, my breath expelling a humourless laugh.

Jesse looked at his feet, bare now and oddly sexy.

What?

I did not just have a moment thinking about this man's feet. Seriously? That whack on the head must have been harder than I thought! My eyes drifted to his forearms. Strong, corded and dark with hair – but not too much. Just the right amount...

'Are you OK?' he asked, taking half a step back towards me. 'You look a little...'

I tilted my head up to meet his eyes. The colour of stormy seas, concern now shining in them, drawing the dark brows closer.

'I'm fine!' I flung the words out. 'Absolutely. Sorry. The evening is probably catching up a bit with me.' I downed a mouthful of drink and felt it burn my throat as I desperately tried not to cough. 'Fine!' I squeaked out.

The brows rose this time and the concern of a moment ago was replaced with confusion and, judging by the merest tilt of his lips, amusement.

'I'll let you get on with your bath, then. Get a good rest and we'll go and take a look at the damage tomorrow.'

I landed with a thump back in the real world.

'Yes. Right. Damage.' I lifted the glass to my lips again as my brain raced around, holding up flash cards prompting me to remember all elements of the disaster my life had turned into during a few short weeks. A large, warm hand on mine stilled both my hand and my brain – my thoughts drawing up short in my mind like a cartoon character coming to an abrupt standstill. I was half expecting to let out a Scooby-Doo-sounding 'Huhhhhhhh'.

'Maybe a little slower this time.' I met the dark eyes. 'Sips.'

'Yes. Yes, of course. I'm not sure what came over me. I'm not normally this uncouth.' I gave what was supposed to be an easy laugh but it came out far more strangulated than I'd anticipated. What was it with this man? Even though I'd basically imploded my entire life, I still knew how to walk the walk and talk the talk. That was unless Jesse Woods was in the vicinity, when it seemed that all the skills I'd been brought up with, and, more importantly, those I'd had to learn once everything fell apart, deserted me. I gave myself a mental kick up the derrière.

'Thanks again. Goodnight,' I said, closing the door with what I hoped was an enigmatic smile, as cool as if I were visiting one of my many – apparently ex – friends in their country homes. Except I wasn't. This man who'd opened his home to me was almost a stranger and yet the kindness and concern he'd shown were beyond anything I'd received from anyone in what felt like a very long time.

I stepped into the soothing water, the bubbles tickling my skin as I sank down, feeling my tense muscles relax and react to the warmth. It had quickly become obvious that the days of being invited down to the country for house parties were clearly over. Not one of those so-called friends had called or even messaged since I blew up my own world. They'd all hastily distanced themselves from me as soon as the poop had hit the fan.

Would I have done that if the Louboutin had been on the other foot? I wasn't sure I wanted to examine that particular question too deeply. I'd like to think that I wouldn't have – that I'd be as kind and welcoming as Julie and Jesse had been to me – but, of course, that would have meant standing out from the crowd. Putting my head above the parapet of the general group consensus. And as tough and independent as I had worked at being, the truth was I'd also been desperate to fit in. To be part of the crowd I'd always been. Would I have risked being ostracised on someone else's behalf? My brain felt full, my head was throbbing with a dull ache and my whole body felt suddenly exhausted. I pushed the thoughts to the back of my mind, took another sip of the brandy and reached over to switch on one of the many true-crime podcasts I had stored on my phone, distracting myself from both my current situation and the truth of the answer to that question.

* * *

Total fatigue, both mental and physical, claimed me before I'd even thought about closing the curtains. The night was black as tar; no street lights shone into the guest room, the only noise the wind scouring the land and thumping into the solid walls of the house. It was only as the early tendrils of light tiptoed their way into the room through the glass in the morning that I noticed the curtains weren't drawn. I pushed myself up from one of the comfiest beds I'd ever slept in and pulled back the soft, thousand-thread sheet and down-filled duvet. I slid my feet into the guest-room slippers, padded my way over to the built-in window seat and looked out.

If I hadn't experienced it in such a visceral manner, it would have been hard to believe that such a storm had raged the previous night. Glancing around, I saw Jesse's house seemed to have survived the battering, thankfully. The hedges lining the edges of his garden and the field beyond were full of birdsong. I had no idea which birds but obviously tough ones if they'd avoided being blown away.

I heard a door close and the man himself stepped out onto the porcelain-paved patio and, after a quick wipe, took a seat at the marble-topped table and sipped his coffee. Ned trotted out to join him, his dark coat shining in the early-morning sun. He plopped down beside him and looked up expectantly. Jesse rubbed the dog's head and then held out a biscuit. Unlike Araminta's chihuahua, who'd go for a finger as soon as look at you, this dog took the biscuit so gently, it was almost as if it were moving in slow motion. I felt myself smile. But only for a moment. Suddenly, the present crashed back in and I pushed myself away from the window and set about making myself presentable.

Unfortunately, as I hadn't had a chance, or forethought, to grab any clothes last night while making my hasty exit, I had to make do with the robe as my morning ensemble. The dressing table set let me at least get my freshly washed hair in some sort of order and the locally produced, organic face wash and moisturiser gave my face the perk-up it needed. I looked back at my reflection. Not great but it would have to do.

'Good morning.' Jesse turned at the sound of the door and the dog stood to attention beside him, glancing at his owner then me, his tail a blur of motion. 'How are you with dogs?'

'I'm a fan,' I replied, smiling. It was hard not to as the dog kept looking from me to his owner and back again, clearly eager to say hello.

'Go on, then, Ned. Remember your manners.'

Ned didn't need to be asked twice and within a split second was sitting politely in front of me, his tail swishing in a speedy arc, his bum almost hovering above the ground in excitement.

I bent, ensuring the dressing gown was wrapped and tucked in well so that I wasn't accidentally exposing anything to either Jesse or his dog, and scratched his ears. Ned closed his eyes in bliss and made a contented groaning noise.

'You've got a job for life doing that.'

'I can think of worse jobs.'

'True. Did you sleep OK?'

'I did, thank you. To my surprise. In fact, it's the best night's sleep I've had in a very long time. I'd fully expected to be lying there all night stressing about what I was going to find today and what to do about it.'

'One step at a time. A good night's sleep always helps.'

'Yes. I suppose so. Thank you.' I straightened.

'Would you like some breakfast?'

'No, I'm OK, thanks.' Now I'd woken, I actually *was* worrying about all the things I'd anticipated worrying about last night. 'I'll get out of your hair just as soon as I can.' I looked down at the dressing gown. 'I'm just in rather a sartorial pickle at present.'

Jesse stood, pushing the chair back with his legs. 'Jules is popping over with a couple of bits for you to wear shortly.'

'Oh, I'm not sure…'

He was closer now, looking down at me. 'It's either that or go in the robe. Your choice. I'll make you a coffee. Come on, Ned.'

The dog followed him immediately, a solid, black shadow.

'Right,' I said to myself quietly and took Jesse's place at the table. The sky was a vivid blue, washed clean by last night's storm, the earliest budding trees hinting at the oncoming spring and the faintest hint of warmth in the air. Jesse's garden was large and exquisitely planned, with colour still in some of the borders and a good structural base with something of interest all year round, if its current appearance was anything to go by. I'd once dated a three-times Chelsea gold winner – it was hard not to pick up tips by osmosis. Of course, then he'd designed a garden in Tuscany for a lord and consequently met Lady whatever-her-name-was, heiress to an absolute fortune, and I'd suddenly been a weed in the beautiful garden of his life and consequently dispensed with.

'Out there or in here?' Jesse's head peering around the back door pulled me sharply back to the present.

'Oh! Sorry. I'll come in.'

Jesse remained at the door, opening it wider for me. As I passed, I caught a subtle whiff of something earthy and woody with just a hint of spice. It suited him.

'You really ought to eat something.' Jesse reiterated the advice once I was sitting in the sunny breakfast nook, sipping on rich, dark coffee that sent much-needed caffeine spiking into my system. 'I've got granola and can probably rustle up an avocado if you want that?'

'What are you having?'

'Bacon roll.'

'I'll have one of those, then, please, if it's not too much trouble?'

'Not at all.' He pulled open the fridge. 'You sure? I don't mind doing the avo toast. It's probably healthier.'

He had a point and it was what I normally chose each day. Even if I had started eating it because all my friends were, the fact remained that avocados were full of good fats and very good for you. But now that he'd planted the seed of a bacon roll, my mouth was watering. I shook my head.

He laid the rashers in the pan and the sizzle teased all my senses. I'd tried being vegan a couple of years ago but I couldn't get past the odd late-night bacon sandwich. Jesse placed the roll, stuffed with thick bacon and melting butter, in front of me. 'Get that down you. Breakfast of champions,' he said, pulling out the seat next to me and biting into his own roll.

'Not sure I qualify for that particular breakfast,' I thought, then froze with the bun halfway to my mouth. 'Shit. I said that out loud, didn't I?'

Jesse chewed a couple of times, swallowed, then nodded. 'Yep.'

'Could you please disregard that last statement?' And yes, I did go out with a barrister.

'Nope.' He took another bite.

'What do you mean, no?'

'I heard it. You can't just disregard something you've already heard.'

I always knew that was a scam by lawyers to get the information across to the jury!

'Well, if you could just try and forget it.'

'Why?'

I looked round and met his eyes, swallowing a mouthful of the heavenly breakfast. 'Why what?'

'Why do you want me to forget it?'

'Because...'

Because it makes me look weak and that is unacceptable.

He waited.

'Knock knock! Anyone home?' Julie's voice saved me from answering but the look Jesse gave me told me that he most definitely wasn't forgetting it.

'In here, Jules,' he called.

Her smiling face popped into view, a large paper carrier bag in her hand. 'Hi! Oh my God, are you OK?' she said, hurrying towards me and giving me a most unexpected hug. 'When Jesse told me about the tree, oh God, I feared the worst.'

'She always did like a bit of drama.' Jesse finished the last of his roll and wiped his hands. His sister stood back, hands on hips.

'A bloody tree fell on her house! I don't think I can be accused of exaggerating anything!'

'No, unfortunately not,' I agreed.

Jesse shrugged.

Julie turned to me. 'He makes out like he's all cool about stuff but if he wasn't worried, then why did he turn up at your house?' She arched her eyebrow at him. They were a great shape. I really needed to ask who she went to for them.

'I was being neighbourly,' her brother replied. 'We all know the house still needs work. I'd have done the same for anyone,' he said, shooting a meaningful look at his sister. 'Did you bring Felicity some clothes?'

She stared back at him for a moment, clearly unintimidated despite the differences in their size. I smiled at my petite, but fierce friend.

'I've brought some jeans and a couple of T-shirts and a sweatshirt. I've left a coat and trainers in the hallway. There's a couple of pairs of knickers in there too but I wasn't sure about the bra…'

A grin slid onto my face. Julie had been at the front of the line when boobs were being dolled out. I was later to the party and consequently got the leftovers, which wasn't much.

'Thank you. I'm pretty sure I can get away with going braless.'

Beside me, Jesse's coffee took a wrong turn and he gave a sudden cough. Julie whacked him on the back. 'You all right there?'

He nodded, cleared his throat and took another sip, which apparently knew the correct way down.

'Thanks for this, Julie. It's really kind.'

'No problem at all. I'm just glad you're all right. You must have been terrified! You should have rung me. Oh, of course, you don't have my number. Good job this one was on the ball.' She jerked her head towards her brother. 'What's your number, Felicity?'

I reeled it off and a moment later, my phone beeped.

'There, now you've got mine too,' Julie said.

'I'm hoping no more trees plan on launching themselves at my house!' I smiled, only half joking as I picked up my phone and sent a kiss face and the words, *Thank you* to Julie.

'I'm sure they won't. But now I can see if you want a coffee some time or something.' She looked at the message, grinned and leant over and gave me another hug. 'I'm so glad you're safe.'

A lump formed in my throat, constricting my reply, so I made a small nod instead. These two people, people I barely knew, had both put themselves out for me, come to my aid, with no expectation of anything in return. It was a rare and unusual experience for me and I was a little off-balanced by it.

'Thank you,' I forced out. 'Thank you, both of you, for everything you've done. I don't know how to repay you.'

Jesse's chair scraped as he stood. 'No repayment needed. Do you want to go and get changed and we'll go up to the house and see what's what?'

I pushed my own chair out, a sudden wash of nausea rolling over me as the thought of what we were going to find – and how much it was going to cost – hit me. I gripped the edge of the table as Jesse's shovel-sized hand came to rest gently on my shoulder. 'Hey.'

I started. 'Sorry. Yes, of course. I'll just go and change. Thanks again, Julie.'

'You're welcome,' she said, seeing herself out. 'I'll call you later.'

'OK,' I said, already looking forward to it. The door closed behind her. Jesse's hand remained in place and I looked up at him.

'It's going to be OK.' His voice was soft, assured and steady, and if I hadn't witnessed a sodding great tree land on my house last night, I might have felt better.

6

'Thank you. I really do appreciate the sentiment but I'm pretty sure everything's a disaster. What I don't know at the moment is exactly how much of a disaster it is.' I looked up at Jesse.

'We'll fix it.'

We?

'I'll help you get the house secured and weathertight for now and the insurers should send someone out to assess it. They'll find you somewhere to stay in the mean...' His words trailed off as I slowly looked up at him through my lashes. 'Felicity. Please tell me the house is insured.'

I chewed my lip.

'Felicity...'

The disappointment in his voice speared through me. 'I tried!' I said, standing back from him. 'Nobody would take on the risk because they said the house wasn't secure. I was in the process of looking into it more. I didn't expect a sodding great tree to plonk itself right through the roof the moment I moved in!' I took a step away towards the stairs. 'Look. Thanks very much for all you've done so far but I can take it from here.'

'Nope.'

I stopped. 'I beg your pardon.'

He folded his arms across his broad chest, the strong, muscled forearms bare.

Focus!

'I said, no.'

'I'm well aware of what you said. What I don't understand is why.'

'Well, for a start, you need a lift back to your house.'

In the short time I'd been here, I'd already realised that even thinking about calling an Uber or a Lyft around here was pointless.

'Fine. Then if you wouldn't mind dropping me back to my home, I would appreciate it, but as for—'

'Let's discuss this on the way, shall we?' He glanced at his watch.

I stopped talking but only out of surprise. Who the hell did he think he was, speaking to me like that? OK, yes, he did come to the rescue last night. But still. People didn't just cut me off like that and tell me what to do!

And yet there he stood, immoveable and as solid as my nemesis tree.

'Ugh!' I spun around and ran up the stairs to the guest room.

Having chosen a pair of jeans and a cute T-shirt from the selection Julie had brought over for me, I pulled a sweatshirt over my head and headed downstairs. I shoved my feet into the trainers she had dropped off. I was a little taller than Jesse's sister but a similar build and thankfully we had the same-sized feet.

I took a seat on the bottom step to do them up, then stood and grabbed the coat she'd also brought.

'Ready.'

Jesse didn't reply, merely called Ned to his side and together, we left the house. As we approached the pick-up, Jesse opened the passenger-side door for me but before I could get in, Ned zipped past, jumped up onto the seat and sat facing forward, ready to go.

'Ned! That wasn't opened for you.'

Ned looked round at his owner, his eyebrows rumpling in confusion.

'Is that where he usually sits?'

'Yes but—'

'Then let him stay there. I'll sit in the back.' I reached for the handle to the back seats of the pick-up's cab, but Jesse was there before me.

'No way. I'm not driving you around like a bloody chauffeur. Ned, back seat.'

His dog looked at him for a moment then turned and scooted through the gap between the front seats into the back. Jesse opened the back door, clipped the dog's harness to the seat belt and closed the door.

'Your chariot awaits.' He indicated the empty front seat.

I gave him a tight smile and got in, yanking at the seat belt as Jesse closed the door behind me before striding around the front of the vehicle and hoisting himself in behind the wheel.

'Look, I know it's not ideal with it being uninsured, but I really don't need any more grief about it. Believe me, I'm angry enough with myself for the both of us.'

'I'm not angry at you. There's just a lot to do.'

'I don't want to take up your time. If you could just drop me at the house, you can get on with your day.'

Jesse turned to look at me, his expression impassive and unreadable.

'What?'

'Nothing,' he replied as he switched on the ignition and then pulled out of the drive.

Thankfully, it was a short journey, otherwise I'd have bitten all of my fingernails down rather than just four. The acrylics I usually had were long gone and, right now, getting replacements was the last thing on my mind. I couldn't remember the last time they'd looked this much of a state. I added 'ask Julie about beauty salons' to my mental to-do list and tucked my hands under my thighs so I didn't chew them any more.

We turned down the drive and as we got closer, I had to call on all my stoicism not to cry. The base of a tree stood splintered and jagged to the left of the house, the body of it cutting square across the roof of my bedroom. Glass from the one remaining sash window in the bedroom was scattered around, glittering in the bright morning sunlight. Branches and other natural detritus were strewn around the place, and as Jesse pulled the truck to a halt the final indignation was before us. My once beautiful, sleek convertible was now two rather less beautiful cars thanks to the tree that had sliced it right down the middle.

'I'm guessing that, at least, is insured.'

I ignored Jesse and opened the door, turning first to Ned. 'Stay here, Ned. There's glass everywhere and I don't want you getting hurt.'

Ned looked back at me and, the moment I stepped out, hopped through into the front seat and stayed there. 'Good boy.' I smiled, ruffling his ears, then closed the door.

I walked up to the car. Thankfully, yes, it was insured, which was something but, right now, it didn't help much. I'd loved that car. Also, it was my only means of transport to and from this dead-end place. Now what was I going to do? I pulled my phone out of my pocket, took a few photos and then scrolled down the contacts and stopped as I came to the one labelled 'car insurance'. I was, if nothing else, organised. Pressing the dial button, I waited. And waited. And then I remembered. There was no signal here. Shit. I wondered if my router had survived the storm. At least the Wi-Fi calling had worked last night long enough to allow Jesse's call to connect. Turning, I saw Jesse leaning on the front of the pick-up. He studied me for a moment but thankfully didn't say anything.

'I suppose I'd better go in and see what I'm dealing with.'

'What *we're* dealing with,' he corrected me.

I stopped and turned to face him. 'This is my problem, Jesse. I appreciate the rescue last night but—'

'It wasn't a rescue. You'd have been fine. Somehow I get the feeling you're not the type of woman that ever needs, or would even accept, rescuing.'

'What's that supposed to mean?'

'Exactly what I said.'

'I suppose you still expect every woman to swoon and drop into your arms – or bed – then?'

He laughed at this, although I hadn't meant it to be funny. 'Definitely not. But there's a difference between being capable and refusing to accept help because you're too damn stubborn.'

I opened my mouth to reply but he was already on the move.

'Let's go and see what the damage is.'

'I think it's pretty obvious what the damage is,' I mumbled a few steps behind him. 'There's a bloody great tree in my house.'

Jesse turned, flung an amused smile at me and carried on walking.

Did he have to have quite such a great smile? And, as my eyes followed him, a pretty exceptional bum.

'Oh...' was the only word my brain was able to process as we both stood on the threshold, looking at the disaster zone that had once been my bedroom. The only room in the house that had been close to being finished, barring the dodgy windows. Now there was a skylight where the roof used to be. Or at least there was sky.

'You OK?' Jesse asked.

I made a noise that could have been taken for affirmation. However, I was definitely not OK. I was, in fact, very far from OK, but it seemed the appropriate reply for the moment. Plus the only other response available to me right now was 'complete meltdown' and I was saving that for later when I was on my own. Jesse had caught me off guard last night but I wasn't about to show any more weakness to him than I already had. I'd learned a long time ago that doing that generally came back to bite you.

'Do you want to go and check on the chickens?'

I looked at him blankly for a second. 'Oh my God!' I took off down the stairs and ran to the field towards the newly painted coop. It wasn't the best job but, considering it was the first time I'd picked up a paintbrush, I didn't think they'd mind. The dull-brown colour didn't do much for me either, but it was the only thing labelled as suitable for outdoor wood I'd been able to find in the outbuilding.

Thankfully, unlike mine, their house looked untouched by the storm. I entered the run, making sure the catch was in place, and opened the door to the coop. As I did so, the birds clucked and squawked their way out, hustling and bustling until they got to the bottom and began pecking around at the grass, apparently unbothered by the previous night's events. A couple toddled over and began pecking at my laces.

'Right, yes. I suppose you want food.' I walked over to the storage unit within the compound, scooped out some of the feed, and scattered the grain onto the ground. The birds descended with zeal and began happily pecking away. I moved around them and pulled open the egg door. There sat at least a dozen fresh eggs waiting for collection.

'Bugger,' I said, realising, in my haste to see whether my chickens were scattered far and wide, that I'd come out without the basket. Hurrying back, I rushed into the utility through the back door and walked slap bang into a solid chest.

'Oof!' I bounced backwards as Jesse grabbed me to stop me falling on my backside. He hadn't moved at all from the impact. It was like an ant bumping into a rhino.

'Sorry. I was coming out to find you. How are the hens?'

'Fine,' I said, reaching past him to grab the wicker basket I'd bought to collect the eggs in, which was not something I'd ever thought I'd be carrying, if I'm honest. I was more used to hooking a Hermès bag over my wrist, but then my life had taken a massive swerve and right now that was the least of my problems. And I had to admit, I'd never tasted an egg so flippin' delicious.

'Want some company?'

'Sure you're not just checking that I'm pretending I've managed to keep the chickens alive?'

He smiled as we walked. 'Not at all. The way you dashed out of there told me all I needed to know.' We approached the run. 'You painted it?'

'I know it's a bit of a mess, so please don't criticise it.'

'I wasn't going to. Looks good.'

It didn't but I appreciated the compliment.

'Did you buy the preserver from Brendan too?'

'No, that was already here. Actually,' I asked, having popped the last egg in my basket, 'you couldn't give me a hand putting the lid back on it, could you?'

'The paint? Of course.'

'Great, it's back in the utility. I don't suppose you'd like some eggs, would you?'

'Love some, if you're sure.'

'Perfectly. I still have yesterday's.' I ran a hand back over my hair, smoothing my ponytail, my go-to hairstyle for the last however many years. 'I can't believe I forgot about the hens. I'm not sure I'm cut out to be responsible for other living creatures.'

'Don't be so hard on yourself.' Jesse dismissed my comment immediately. 'It sounds like this is all quite a different lifestyle for you. You've barely been here five minutes. Give yourself a break.'

'It's different when something is relying on you for its well-being though. Thank God I'd remembered to put them away last night. That's one miracle.'

Jesse gave a brief smile. 'Where's the paint? Let's do that and then we can discuss the roof.'

I pulled a large tin out of the cupboard that I'd covered with foil – a tip from the Internet to keep the paint from drying up. It didn't seem a long-term solution, in case it got knocked over, so I'd kept the tin lid just in case. I lifted it and placed it on the counter.

'Was it the right stuff?' I asked, suddenly panicking I might have put something toxic on my birds' enclosure.

Jesse was removing the foil, a frown settling into place between his brows. 'Yep, it's the right stuff.' He peered at the tin, then the lid, then the tin again. 'Felicity?'

'Yes?'

'Did you remove this lid with a tin opener?'

'I... yes. It's a tin, isn't it? I must admit it seemed a little odd because I'm not sure how you're supposed to keep the rest. Or is it a one and done? That seems quite wasteful. Could I decant it into something? Why are you looking at me like that?'

He shook his head. 'Nothing.'

'No. Tell me. Obviously, there's something obvious I'm

missing here. I'd rather you told me than I be the butt of the village joke.'

'I would never laugh at you, Felicity.' His eyes were serious now.

'You laughed at me trying to get that wood in my car while my protective clothing disintegrated around me!'

The smile returned. 'Fair enough. But you had just knocked me on my arse in front of everyone so you've got to let me have that one.'

It had never occurred to me that Jesse had been embarrassed as well as cross.

'So come on, then. Tell me.'

Jesse laid the lid back in place. 'See that groove that runs around the outside of the lid?'

'Yes.'

'That's how you get in.'

'What? How?'

'Screwdriver, usually. You stick it in there, maybe a couple of other places until it prises up easily.'

'A screwdriver.'

'Yes.'

I looked at the tin. 'Right. So that's buggered, then?'

'Pretty much, yeah. Although I'm sure we can find something to decant it in, like you said. Good idea to try and save it in case you need to do some more treatment.'

I suddenly felt like a massive idiot. 'I'll do it later,' I said. 'So.' I raised my eyes to the ceiling. 'Is it as bad as we feared up there?'

'I'm afraid the tree through the roof wasn't a hallucination, as much as we'd both hoped it might be. There's damage to the furniture and other items in the main bedroom from the rain. Obviously, your bed's a goner. But, from what I can see, the other rooms look undamaged. Obviously, I can't really comment on the structural side. That's above my pay grade.' He shifted his weight. 'Sorry, I wasn't being nosy. I just needed to check to see what we're dealing with.'

There was that 'we' again.

'Of course. I didn't think for a moment you were snooping! Honestly, I know it probably doesn't feel like it, but I'm incredibly grateful for what you and Julie have already done for me. I don't know what I would have done without you both.'

He shrugged off the compliment. 'Like I said, we'd have done the same for anyone.' He began to turn away and I reached out and caught his arm. He stopped, looking down first at my hand then letting his gaze travel to my face.

'I'm certain that's true but, in this case, you helped – are helping – me and for that I'm very grateful even if I'm not always very good at showing it. For that failing, I apologise.'

Jesse was silent for a few moments, our eyes fixed on each other. I felt my chest heave under the scrutiny of his gaze.

'There's nothing to apologise for. Do you want to come up and take a proper look?' He stepped away and I felt the loss of his warmth and... something else... The only word I could form in my mind was 'security'. When he was close, I felt safe. As if nothing could touch me. But now I was alone again. Which was ridiculous, because it'd been a hell of a long time since I'd trusted, or even wanted, a man to provide any sort of security in my life.

It was why I'd always kept my bank account separate from Adrian's and kept my flat. And he hadn't seemed to mind. Perhaps that should have been a bigger clue, but I liked my independence so had just assumed the situation suited us both for the right reasons. Besides, Jesse Woods was nothing to me, apart from a helpful and, yes, admittedly pretty damn hot neighbour. And I was nothing to him. The feeling, the thought, was confusing and ridiculous. I shoved it into the dusty corner of my mind where I'd pushed all the things I didn't want to think about, mentally shut the door on it and dragged a bookcase in front of it for good measure.

'Coming?' he asked, one foot on the bottom stair.

'Yes.'

His features softened for a moment, as if he was mistaking my hesitation for nerves.

I dragged up a smile. 'Thanks.'

He turned and led the way up to the first floor.

'Holy shit.'

I went to an exclusive and very expensive private school to enable me to come out with such erudite statements. As you can see, my father got his money's worth. Then again, in all the scenarios and education we were given, never once had there been a situation even remotely like the one I was currently taking in.

'Yep. That pretty much sums it up,' Jesse agreed with my succinct appraisal. 'But it could have been worse.'

Remaining silent, I turned to face him.

'I know that seems hard to believe right now,' he replied, accurately interpreting the disbelief written all over my features.

I looked back up through the large, unplanned skylight I now had in my bedroom roof to the freshly washed blue skies beyond.

'On the plus side, it's brighter in here now.' If I didn't make light of it, I was going to cry and there was no way I was doing that in front of Jesse. Or anyone. I'd had girlfriends who switched on the waterworks any time they wanted their own way but that had never been my style and I wasn't about to change now. Also I had the horrible feeling that if I started crying, I might never stop. By rights, I should still be back in London, in a relationship that was working for both of us but with our own freedoms and that would continue in a similar manner even after the wedding. In the meantime, I'd be living in a beautifully styled apartment that overlooked the Thames and crucially had a fully functioning roof. I let out a sigh and felt my shoulders droop, forgetting momentarily that I wasn't alone.

'That was a heck of a sigh.'

I started out of my thoughts. 'Sorry.'

Jesse held up his hands. 'Nothing to apologise for.' He scratched the stubble on his chin, dark growth shadowing the sharp features I'd seen on previous meetings. 'You're handling it brilliantly, as far as I can see.'

Little did he know that inside my head there was a tiny me screaming hysterically and running round and round in circles.

'Thanks.' It seemed like the right thing to say.

'Did you feel that it was a little dark in here prior to this?' He pointed up.

'Obviously, I haven't had a lot of time to get used to it and my previous apartment had lots of large windows, so it did seem darker compared to that, of course. But yes,' I said. 'I think it could have been lighter.' I paused. 'This wasn't exactly what I had in mind though.'

He stood at the doorway, assessing the room. I stepped in and his hand wrapped around my upper arm. 'Hang on, I want to just check things first. The last thing we need is you taking an unexpected trip into the floor below or getting clonked on the head again by something.'

'This isn't enough?' I asked, flinging my arm out at the obvious damage and kicking myself when my voice broke on the last word.

'There's probably nothing else. I just want to make sure it's safe. OK?'

I stood straighter and nodded. 'Yes. Of course.' Then added, 'Thank you.'

'Perhaps we can look into enlarging some of the windows with the rebuild. Let a bit more light in?'

'Is that possible?'

'I don't see why not,' Jesse said, looking up at the ceiling again. 'We'll get the tree removed and will be able to see more then, but if you want more light, that's a good option. I can have a word with an architect I use to see what he thinks.'

'An architect you use?'

'Yeah.'

'I should have asked this before but what exactly is it that you do? Am I keeping you from it?'

'Not at all. I've got my fingers in a few pies, but my main career is property investment.'

'Renting?'

'Some, yes. It depends on the area. Something like this I'd have bought with a view to selling. There's not enough interest for renters in this area.'

'Is your house one you did up?'

'Yep. It was a bit of a state when I bought it but I'm pretty happy with it now.'

'You should be. It's stunning. So why didn't you buy this one off your cousin to do it up?'

'My cousin and I don't especially get on. He'd made noises about wanting to really settle in the area and this was the perfect opportunity when he was left the house by our grandmother. I offered to help him do it up, but he refused. Said he wanted to do it his way, which I respected.'

I didn't let on what Julie had told me about Jesse having lent him a pile of money to do it up and him then scarpering with it.

'As usual, that turned out to be a load of bullshit.' He turned to me immediately. 'Sorry.'

'No need to apologise.'

'I hadn't been up here since he got it. I only found out he was selling it once it was a done deal but had understood that the work was finished. He didn't use anyone local on the job so I had no idea what a state it was actually in when he sold.'

'That's a shame. By the looks of your house, if you'd been involved, I'd have at least got what I paid for.'

Jesse remained silent.

'It's my own fault. I should have come and looked at it. That's what you get for making important life choices in the midst of clearing a month's worth of wine subscription in less than a week.'

Jesse blew out a breath. 'That's a lot of wine.'

'It was a lot of wine.'

'I don't understand how the sale was completed so quickly though.'

'I have an ex who works in property. He'd told me if I ever wanted to sell my flat to contact him. So I did. He had a cash buyer ready who wanted it as soon as possible, I wanted to get out of London as soon as possible and this place was empty. Now I know why. But it's amazing what can be achieved when there's a lot of money involved. Within a few days, all the paperwork was signed so I couldn't have pulled out if I'd wanted to.' I paused. 'That particular ex always did like to get things done quickly.'

Jesse rubbed his jaw but I didn't miss the flash of amusement in his grey eyes.

'But I'm certainly the one paying for it now.'

The dark brow creased. 'Paying for it? We've all made hasty decisions, Felicity. Agreed, it's probably best not to make such important ones while three sheets to the wind, but it's not some sort of punishment. It's just bad luck. If it had been me, I'd have had that tree removed during the renovation anyway. It was too close for comfort. But apparently my cousin was looking to do the bare minimum and make a quick killing. There will be legal measures you could take, you know? You've been sold a lemon.'

I leant on what was left of a pricey table, only for it to creak and falter, having soaked up the night's rainfall. I stepped back. Clearly that was done for too. I looked at the matchsticks that had once been my sleigh bed. Maybe that wasn't a bad thing. A new bed that had no associations with my former, failed relationship was perhaps a wise investment. But before I spent any more money, I needed to find out whether any of this was fixable and, if so, how much it was going to cost.

'Can we make lemonade instead?'

'Lemonade?' Jesse asked, confused.

'You're right, this place is a massive lemon and, given the chance, I wouldn't do it again.' I looked up at him. 'I know what I said last night but the truth is I'm here now. I burned my bridges in London so I need to make the best of what I've done. For the time being at least. In your experience, would it be possible to make something out of this place? Make lemonade out of a real lemon?'

Jesse scanned the room, the ceiling, the sky, before landing back on me.

'I reckon so.' And then he smiled and I couldn't help smiling back.

7

We returned downstairs and I put the kettle on. I'm British, what can I say? If there was ever a moment for a cup of tea, this was it. A few minutes later, we were both sitting at the small breakfast table I'd put in the corner of the room near another draughty window so that I could read with my breakfast, two large bone-china mugs in front of us.

'I've called in some help. They'll be up shortly with some equipment to remove the tree and cover up the gap and make the house as weatherproof as possible.'

'Thank you so much. I do appreciate all your help. Please send the bill to me, won't you?'

Jesse shook his head. 'There won't be a bill. A few people owe me some favours.' He shrugged his broad shoulders then took a sip of tea.

'Yes, but they don't owe me the favours, which means they, and you, need paying for the time you're spending here.'

Jesse took another sip of tea, placed it carefully down on the table and turned towards me.

'Felicity.'

'Jesse.'

'The fact that you're in a house that wasn't up to standard is down to a member of my family—'

'But not you.'

'No. Not me. But in my eyes, that is just semantics.'

'But not in mine,' I replied, drawing myself up. 'Which means if you do work, I pay you.'

'And if you insist on paying me, I won't be here at all.'

'What?' My voice pitched up in panic, much to my annoyance. I cleared my throat.

'If you insist on trying to pay me for something I feel duty-bound to fix, I won't come at all.' He lifted the mug to his mouth, his eyes remaining fixed on mine.

'Fine! Then I'll just hire the people myself.' I crossed my arms, feeling pleased with myself.

'And I will tell them if they take up any offers of work from you, there won't be any more work from me.'

My eyes widened. 'You... you can't do that! You wouldn't!'

One dark brow quirked. 'Watch me.'

For a beat, we both stared at one another, neither blinking, neither wanting to back down.

'Ugh!' I allowed myself to slump for a moment. Nanny would have been horrified.

'Do we have a deal?'

'What sort of person doesn't want to be paid for work?'

'What sort of person lets a friend buy a house when they're clearly drunk?'

I swallowed and looked away.

'Seriously? Did this ex not question your decision at any point or was he just focused on the bottom line and the hefty commission he was obviously going to earn on a swanky flat in London?'

'How did you know I sold a swanky London apartment?'

Reach for the Stars

'The village is a small place. People talk and others listen. Word gets around.'

I squinted at him.

'There's something else. Tell me.'

'You're very demanding, anyone ever tell you that?'

'Once or twice.' That made him smile but he looked away to hide it.

'I can see you smirking and I wasn't referring to where your mind has clearly taken itself.'

OK, there were a few times there too but sometimes, you have to jiffy things along a bit, don't you?

'I don't know what you mean,' Jesse replied, in control of his features now.

'Liar. Anyway, tell me whatever it is you're hiding. Believe me, I can take it, and I'll find out anyway.' I folded my arms across my chest. 'As you said, it's a small place and people talk.'

He shook his head. 'I knew you were going to be trouble when you clocked me with that two-by-four the first day I met you.'

'I apologised for that,' I replied, glancing at his brow where the cut was now healed over but still obvious.

'You did, and I forgave you. But the point remains. You're trouble.'

I stayed silent and waited, fixing him with a laser-like stare. Jesse blew out a sigh, reached into his pocket for his phone and pulled it out. Laying it on the table, he pressed a couple of times on the screen then scrolled around a bit before bringing up an email and pushing the phone across to me. I looked up at him.

'You asked,' he said.

Jesse
 The sale on the cottage has gone through this morning. Some London broker had a woman paying cash. He'd just

done a sale on her flat and wanted it all pushed through quickly. Said she might sober up before it completed otherwise! Apparently it was some ex-girlfriend of his. Obviously no love lost there if he was willing to screw her over like that. Another idiotic Londoner wanting the idyllic country life with all the amenities of London! She's in for a shock in more ways than one. All cash and no surveys needed. Lucky me!

Anyway. Just thought I'd let you know I'm off abroad now everything's signed and completed. Not sure when I'll be back. Or if.

Joe

I returned his phone, my stomach tight.

'I'm guessing it wasn't a good break-up.'

I swallowed, which was harder than it should be, but then usually, I didn't have a massive lump in my throat.

'Actually, it was a perfectly civil one. Paul would screw over his own mother if it meant he made a killing on a property.'

'Sounds a real catch. I'm amazed you didn't hold onto him.'

I let out a hollow huff of laughter.

Jesse sighed. 'Look, I'm sorry you had to see that but I got the feeling you weren't going to give up until I told you.' He gave me a look and I gave a brief lift of my eyebrows, signalling that he'd had it right. 'For what it's worth, I apologise for the part my family has played in all this. Had I known...'

'You didn't and that's it. I'm here now so the only thing is to make the best of it,' I said, looking out of the window.

'Don't sound *too* thrilled about it.'

I turned to reply, my tone preset to 'sharp', but I stopped, seeing the grin on Jesse's face. He watched me, clearly prepared for a barrage but, just as he had surprised me, I then surprised myself as a laugh snuck its way up and through my usual defences. With my life in tatters, silence from my so-called friends and being the not so proud owner of the ironically named 'Paradise Farm', a place that most estate agents would describe as 'perfect for a new owner to put their own stamp on', plus the addition of its very own integral tree, laughter was the last thing on my mind. But for the first time in what felt like a very long while, a full, genuine belly laugh burst forth and, if I was honest, it felt great!

'I think that's the first time I've heard you really laugh,' Jesse noted, still smiling.

'Looking at the state of things, I have no idea why I'm laughing now. I'm pretty sure my mind was having a toss-up between that and hysteria.'

'I'm glad it chose the right one.'

'I'm not so sure it did.'

'I am. Everything is fixable.'

'Is it?' I batted back, half in jest but, as I did, a shadow flitted across his face.

'Almost everything.' Before either of us could say anything else, his phone burst into life with a jazzed-up version of 'Moonlight Sonata' by Beethoven. Had I heard this in town on a night out, I knew for a fact that my friends would have subtly sneered and, with an uncomfortable flush, I suspected I'd have joined them. But actually it sounded pretty cool.

'Frank, thanks for calling me back.' He paused for a few moments. 'Yeah, I know. She's fine, thank God.' Another pause. 'That'd be great. OK. See you soon.' Jesse hung up and turned back towards me. 'Frank will be here shortly to get the tree removed.'

'Thank you.'

'You're welcome.'

'What happens after that? Who do I need to contact?'

'It's all in hand.'

'You really don't need to do all this. If you can just let me know the names of some tradespeople you recommend, I can take over. I'm sure you have plenty of things you ought to be doing instead of flitting around solving my problems.'

His laugh was warm, rich and deep and my own lips tipped up into a smile without asking permission.

'Do I look like a flitter?'

He had a point. Built like the brick outbuilding in the garden, Jesse Woods was definitely not the most obvious type to associate with the word.

'Point taken. But you know what I mean.'

He turned towards me, arms folded across his chest. 'You're *really* not good at accepting help, are you?'

'I've always found it better to do things myself. That way, there's no one to let you down.'

'Bit of a cynical view.'

'Merely a realistic one.'

He studied me and I turned away, back to face the garden. For some reason, when Jesse looked at me, it felt as if he could see deep into my soul and that was somewhere I didn't want anyone to see, and certainly not this man.

'So what did you do, back in London?'

I was grateful for the change in subject and felt a layer of defence drop as I stepped back onto firmer conversational ground.

'I was an interiors stylist and house stager.'

'Is that how you met the estate agent with the impeccable ethics?'

I gave him a look.

'I'll take that as a yes.'

I stayed silent.

'So what are you going to do now?'

Good question.

'I... haven't exactly decided.'

'Bit of a sudden decision, was it, then, moving here?'

I had no intention of discussing my decisions and motives with him. Back in my London life, he wasn't someone I'd have looked twice at. Well, OK, yes, I would have looked twice. Maybe three times. But he wasn't my type. I was used to men who had a skin-care regime, wore Savile Row three-piece suits and watches one bought as investment pieces, and drove sleek, expensive cars. I'd never seen Jesse in anything other than beaten-up Levi's and he drove a pick-up. When I'd paid three thousand pounds for a dress, that was not the vehicle I would expect to be picked up in.

Not that there was likely to be any reason to dig out those clothes any time soon, or indeed be picked up by any man, let alone this one. I was done with men. My fiancé had dumped me, and another ex, with whom I was supposedly friends, had sold me out to land me with this potential money pit. I'd had issues with trust since I was a teenager and no one I met had seemed to do anything to dispel them. Until now.

But this man, who didn't know me from Adam, had come out in the middle of a raging storm to check on me and was calling in favours to make my home watertight and habitable because he felt bad that his cousin had sold me a lemon. It wasn't his responsibility. There was nothing in it for him and yet he continued to help. It was an uncommon situation to me and I was still getting used to it.

'You could say that,' I replied.

'That sounds like a story.'

'Not a very interesting one, I'm afraid.'

He quirked a dark brow at me, hinting at disagreement.

'I assume it's safe to be in here?' I asked suddenly. 'I mean, it's structurally sound and everything?'

'Do you think I'd have let you stay in here, let alone stay in here myself, if it wasn't?' The smile morphed into a frown and he studied me. I shifted my weight under the intense gaze.

'No. I suppose not.'

'I wouldn't. But we need to get it checked by an expert.' And the strange thing was, I believed him. This man I hardly knew had something about him that told me his word meant something. Then I gave myself a mental kick. I was being fanciful. He just had one of those kinds of faces. One of those kinds of bodies…

I turned away again as his phone beeped with a message.

'Some more of the blokes are on their way.'

'More? For what?'

'That bedroom is going to need stripping out. I'm hoping there wasn't anything valuable in there, but if there was, I know a good furniture restorer who'd be able to take a look at it.'

'Is there anyone you don't know?' I asked, half smiling.

His wide shoulders gave a shrug.

'Should I go and start clearing some stuff out of there, then?' I took a step towards the stairs, but Jesse caught my wrist, the slightly calloused hand strong but gentle on my skin.

'Wait.' He looked down and met my eyes. 'Please. I want to get that tree moved and check that it's all secure first before you spend any time in there. Just to be safe.'

'We were up there this morning.' I frowned.

'And I was ready to move extremely quickly if I needed to, taking you with me.'

'Is that right?' I asked, putting my free hand on my hip. It didn't quite have the full effect, bearing in mind his hand still circled my other wrist, but, for some reason, I wasn't quite ready to shake that off just yet.

'Yep.'

'You seem very sure I'd have obeyed you.'

A smile lifted his dark features. 'Even from the little time I've spent with you, I already know you're not a pushover so, no, I don't necessarily think you would obey me, or anyone. But you're little so slinging you over my shoulder in an emergency wouldn't be an issue.'

This time, I did shake his hand off. 'I'm not a sack of potatoes!'

'That wasn't what I was implying. All I meant was that, in some cases, there's little time for niceties and, other times, I'd be more interested in getting you out of danger than following the laws of etiquette.'

'Right. Well. Luckily, that wasn't needed.' I stepped away and put a little more space between us. It had been an eventful night, an eventful few weeks, and that was the only possible reason my heart was currently doing the rumba. Absolutely nothing to do with the thought of Jesse Woods wrapping his arms around me, protecting me. I gave myself a mental kick and told my heart to stop being so stupid. Those things happened in romance books and films. Not in real life. In real life, people looked after number one.

'How are you doing?' His deep voice wound itself around me, warm and solid, just as he'd felt last night as we got out of the damaged house, the storm howling around us.

'I'm fine,' I said, keeping my face away from him as I blinked away the tears that threatened to form in my eyes. Weaknesses were not to be shown. Weakness was what people looked for, what they used against you, however well you thought you knew them. It was only by being strong you survived. 'And just for reference,' I said, turning back towards him, my chin tilted up just enough, 'should there have been an incident, I can run just as fast as you. I don't need to be saved like some heroine in an old fairy tale.'

He waited a beat, the silence hanging between us before he replied with a single word.

'Noted.' His eyes remained on me but his expression was unreadable.

'Good,' I said, needing to break the moment. 'Are these your men?' I asked, going up on tiptoe to see a small fleet of vehicles approaching the house down the rutted driveway – yet something else that needed attention.

'Nope.'

I glanced up.

'But they're here for this job.'

'What?' I asked, catching his arm as he turned away. It was like trying to move a glacial boulder. I scooted round in front of him and he tilted his head down as if to see what gnat was bothering him.

'I don't know what it's like where you were before, but here we don't act like we own anyone. We've moved on from playing lord of the manor.'

His phrasing hit a nerve and I pulled my hand back as if burned.

'I didn't mean it like that.'

'Are you sure?'

'Yes!' I snapped. 'You don't know anything about me.'

'True. And I get the feeling you like things that way.'

'What's that supposed to mean?'

'It means it feels as if you don't like people knowing you too well.'

'I'm private. There's nothing wrong with that, or is that illegal in these parts?'

'No. But if you're planning to stay, you might want to consider being a little bit less—' He bit off the rest of the sentence.

'Less what?' I prompted him.

'It doesn't matter. I need to go and see the blokes and make a plan.' He took a step to the side to go around me and I matched it. 'Felicity...'

'I'm waiting for an answer.'

'It doesn't matter.'

'It does to me. I like to know where I stand with people.'

'Right now, you're standing in my way.'

'And I have no intention of moving until you finish your sentence.'

The idea that I was holding Jesse up was laughable. As he'd already pointed out, he could in fact have swung me over his shoulder with very little effort. For a moment, I'd lowered my guard but now it was securely back in place. I had a pretty good idea what the man actually thought about me, but I wanted him to have the balls to actually say it.

He gave a heartfelt sigh.

'Jesse? You there, mate?' A call came from outside.

He looked down at me. I raised a brow and stayed in place.

'Reserved. OK? A bit less reserved.'

'Is that a polite way of saying stuck up?'

His brows quickly drew together. 'No.' And with that, he stepped around me before I could block him again and pulled open the front door.

'Frank.' I heard him greet the other man. 'Thanks for coming so quickly.'

I shook off my surprise and hurried to the front door to follow Jesse out.

'Hello.' I raised a hand in greeting, suddenly feeling very much the outsider as I took in the faces of several men who had all been looking up at my roof. 'I'm Felicity. Thank you all for coming.'

'No problem. Jesse's always doing stuff for other people and it's rare he ever calls in his favours so our pleasure, love.'

Jesse was squinting at the roof and determinedly not joining in the conversation or looking at me.

'I'm Frank.' The man stepped forward, holding out a meaty hand, which I shook. 'Sorry. Probably not supposed to call people "love" these days. Old habits die hard.'

'It's fine.' I waved it away. And it was. Let's face it, I'd been called far worse than that in my time.

He smiled and began introducing me to the other men.

'Not the greatest welcome to the area, was it?' one of the men said, indicating the rogue tree with a side tilt of his head. 'Hope it's not put you off us?' he added with a wide, cheeky smile.

His mate gave him a shove. 'Ignore Romeo here. Thinks he's God's gift to women, he does. But we're glad you're all right.'

'Thank you. Me too, although I think that most of the credit goes to Jesse.'

Jesse shook his head. 'Not at all.' My words were instantly dismissed. 'Right, shall we get on with this, then?'

'Would anyone like a coffee or tea first?' I asked, standing my ground against Jesse, his words about being reserved still floating around in my mind.

A series of positive replies followed and I mentally took a note of the orders and headed back into the kitchen to make the drinks. Digging about in the cupboards, I found a packet of unopened Hobnobs and placed some on a plate before loading the lot onto a tray and heading back outside.

'Ooh lovely, thanks, Felicity.' The man they'd called Romeo lingered as he took the penultimate drink. 'No biscuits for me.'

He patted what looked like an already flat set of abs. 'Gym night tonight.'

A groan went around the group.

Jesse stepped closer and took the last drink, and, with a glance at Romeo, took two biscuits. 'I'll have yours, then.' From the brief flash of stomach I'd seen when I'd knocked the man on his arse with a plank of wood, Jesse was not someone who needed to worry about calories. Lucky bugger.

'What's the verdict, then?'

'You've got a bloody great tree house, love.'

'Shut up, Nobby,' Frank called before turning back towards me. 'You can see why we call him Nobby.' He rolled his eyes and I laughed, in turn causing the older man to smile. This type of banter was new to me. In my world, comments were made but one could never be entirely sure that there wasn't an element of underlying truth, a barely concealed dig veiled with a fake smile. But this was different and I liked it. I thought again back to my old life and what the people I'd once called friends would think now as I stood here sharing refreshments I'd prepared myself with a collection of tradesmen. I could almost picture their horrified faces, which made me smile even more. I hid it behind the mug as I took another sip.

'First things first, check for any other obvious damage. Jesse's done a recce already, that right?'

Jesse nodded.

'Then once we're sure there's no extra risk, we'll get that tree lifted, get some measurements taken and materials ordered, as well as covering the hole with a tarp and—'

'A what?' I asked.

'Tarp. Tarpaulin.' He pointed to something large and blue on the ground nearby before continuing. 'That'll keep the roof protected from any more weather. From what Jesse's said, it sounds like the room's going to need to be gutted.'

'Yes, so he said this morning. Naturally, seeing that it was the only room that was closest to being finished.'

Frank screwed up his nose. 'Yeah, I heard you got stuffed a bit with the sale. Sorry about that, love. The owner wasn't using local people, so none of us knew what it was like inside and could only go on the photos online. Sounds like old Joe used a bit of poetic licence on those. I take it you didn't view it beforehand, then?'

'We'd probably better get on,' Jesse said, taking a step closer.

'No, I didn't,' I replied to Frank, sharing a momentary glance with Jesse to thank him for his attempt at diverting the conversation. 'Not my finest decision but there we are. It's certainly been a lively introduction to living in the countryside, that's for sure.'

Now who's being reserved?

Frank gave my shoulder a brief pat. 'You've got a good attitude there, Felicity. When it comes down to it, the important thing is that you're here at all.' He eyed the sharp spikes of the trunk where the tree had snapped and fallen. 'Things could have been a lot worse.'

All eyes looked up.

'That's very true. So, is there anything I need to do? Any way I can help?'

'Nope. All under control here, isn't that right, Jesse?' Frank looked across.

'Frank's right. There's nothing you can do here right now.'

'OK.' Suddenly, I felt useless. No longer part of this little band as I had been moments ago, but then that was ridiculous too. They probably hadn't thought I was part of anything. More likely the dopey posh girl who'd bought a house in the middle of nowhere without even going to see it first. Maybe they thought I deserved everything I was getting. Certainly, some of my acquaintances – calling them friends any longer seemed pointless – had encountered difficulties in some places with their second – or third, or occasionally fourth – homes, where the locals had been far less friendly than I'd so far experienced. But then some of their own manners, I realised now, left a lot to be desired so perhaps there was more to their stories of 'ghastly locals' than I'd been led to believe.

Then Jesse's arm was around my shoulders, giving the briefest squeeze.

'Don't look so worried. We'll get it sorted.'

I looked up, met the concerned face and smiled. 'Thank you,' I replied, my voice, to my horror, breaking on the second word, tears threatening in my eyes. What was wrong with me? I didn't cry. I kept emotions in general to a minimum if I could. That had been my modus operandi for more years than I cared to remember. It kept a carapace around me. It didn't necessarily protect me from hurt but it did stop others seeing that hurt, which was the next best thing. But since I'd got to this most ironically named Paradise Farm, everything was changing and I seemed to have little say in the matter.

8

Jesse's arm rested a moment longer as he turned his back to the rest of the crew, his size effectively blocking me from their view.

'It's going to be fine.'

'I know,' I replied with a broad smile. The facial movement dislodging a tear, which made a beeline down my cheek and did nothing to back up my words.

'Do you want to start, Frank? I'll be there in a sec,' Jesse called.

Frank began giving the other men instructions as Jesse's hand wrapped gently around my biceps and led me round the corner of the nearby outbuilding, out of sight of the others.

'What's up?' I asked.

'Nothing, but I'm worried about you,' Jesse replied.

'Honestly, you really don't need to be. I'm tough as old boots. I think that was probably allergies actually, the more I think about it.'

His expression told me he smelled something and it wasn't coming from the countryside. 'It's OK not to be invincible – or be seen to be invincible – all the time, Felicity.'

I looked up at him, 'Is that what you think I'm trying to do?'

'Yes.'

'Well, I'm not. And I'm not sure you know me well enough to make a judgement like that just yet.'

'It's not always about the length of time you've known someone. You can know someone for years and still not have a clue what's going on with them. Alternatively, you can be minding your own business getting building supplies and get knocked on your arse by some random woman in a hazmat suit and a short time later, feel like you've known her for a lot longer than a few hours.'

'Is that how you feel?' I asked, surprise filling my voice, replacing the defensive tone completely.

'Kind of. It's hard to explain.'

'You looked like you were feeling mad as hell, if I'm honest,' I said with a grin.

'I was too busy seeing stars to think much at all!' The corners of his mouth tipped up and his eyes glittered with amusement.

'Oh, come on,' I teased back. 'I barely tapped you.'

The laugh this time was full and rich. 'Barely tapped me? You knocked me on my backside and drew blood!'

'Such a drama queen. I'm sure you could have steadied yourself better. There's quite the difference in our size, in case you hadn't noticed.'

'I'd definitely noticed,' Jesse replied, looking down at me from his significant height advantage. 'But the added lumber made a hell of a lever to add force.'

I put my hand to my cheek. 'I still can't believe I did that.'

'Me neither.' He grinned. 'But I'm kind of glad you did.'

'You are?' The faintest flutter of butterflies in my stomach took flight.

'Yeah.' He paused. 'Julie's not stopped talking about you since she met you, especially as you tagged her café in a social media post. I don't know how you did it, but it's certainly brought in new custom and boosted her figures. She's a worrier when it comes to the bottom line so anything that helps with that, I'm really grateful for.'

The butterflies fled back into the shadows.

'Oh. Yes! Of course. I really like her too. She's lovely! I hope we'll get to spend more time together. The post was nothing. Social media was part of my job before so I've just got good about knowing how and what to do to catch people's attention. I'm glad it's had a good effect. The café's a great place so it deserves to be known.'

Jesse made a sound of agreement as he pinned me with a look. 'What just happened?'

'Sorry?'

'You shut down. One minute, we were talking and opening up and the next moment, all the barriers were right back in place.'

'I really don't know what you're talking about,' I replied, a tad more coldly than I'd meant.

Jesse didn't flinch.

'Look. It's been a hell of a night and, as Frank pointed out, albeit politely, I'm in the way here, so I'm going to go and look at the garden room in the back and see about tackling that. If you need me, just call. Is that all right? Also,' I continued without giving him a chance to reply, 'even for a novice like me, it's obvious that there's a lot of work to be done, and I know they're all saying they owe you favours but, as I've said, those are your favours, not mine. I have some money, but I need estimates so that I can plan and budget.'

'I'm not using the favours so you may as well have them.'

'But you might need them in the future.'

He drew himself up, planted his feet squarely and crossed his arms. 'Then I'll deal with that when and if it happens. I'm not arguing with you about this. Right now, your bloody roof is falling in so that's what we need to focus on.' He turned away.

'Jesse!'

'Felicity.' He looked back towards me. 'Could you for once just accept some help? You don't and won't owe me anything. There's no worry that I'm going to think you're beholden to me. Like I said, it's what we do around here.' His boots crunched on the gravel as he strode back to where there was a hive of activity buzzing around my house, including an operator climbing into the cab of a small crane that had trundled up and was now secured in place. Jesse really did seem to know everyone.

I was left standing with my mouth open, catching flies, as Nanny would have said. Hearing those long-ago tones in my head, I snapped it shut and stomped off towards the garden room.

On my way, I stopped at the chicken coop, hooking my fingers in the diamonds of the wire fence that surrounded it, watching as the hens scurried around, their sharp beaks contrasting with their fluffy, feathered legs. Their soft clucking and mumbling sounds soon began to soothe me, my anger scale sliding back down as I observed them scuttling about, pecking and hurrying over towards me to see if I had goodies for them.

'No food, I'm afraid.' I crouched down on a level with them. 'I fed you earlier, if you remember.' They continued to blink at me with their dark and beady eyes. 'I'll be back later with something, all right?'

They studied me a little longer, realised I wasn't offering anything of interest after all and toddled off back to their pecking. I watched them go, feeling oddly thankful for their strangely calming presence. Prior to my arrival here, had anyone even suggested that I even be in the vicinity of a hen coop, let alone crouched down having a conversation with the inhabitants, albeit a one-way one, I would have thought they'd quite lost their marbles. But the strange thing was, having previously been almost laser focused on doing what people would approve of and disapproving of the same as all my peers, I was surprised at how quickly the wish to do that was fading. And how much easier life was when I wasn't second-guessing everything I said, did or wore.

I looked down at the wellies a size too big for me as I plodded through the squelchy grass that was in need of a mow, but that Jesse had said was still too wet to cut, and began laughing quietly to myself. Prior to my arrival at Paradise Farm, the thought of wearing anything other than my Le Chameau wellington boots was something not to be even contemplated. Hunters at a push. But this? Shoving my thrice-besocked feet into the found wellies – because I was yet to unearth my own from the boxes piled in one of the spare rooms – was beyond comprehension. Admittedly, it still wouldn't be my first choice, but I could hardly step out into the mud that was apparently my driveway and hand over drinks in my five-inch Dior stiletto shoe boots. Not that I knew where they were right now either.

I reached the garden room, reeled in my giggles – it was possibly on the point of turning hysterical, so definitely was best to rein it in – and pulled open the unlocked door. Peering inside, I thought perhaps leaving it unlocked was a good strategy. With a bit of luck, someone might actually steal the contents. I could live in hope. I looked around. Where the hell did I start?

* * *

'Hiya!' The cheery voice made me start and I tripped over my oversized boots as I turned and landed in an undignified heap on the ground.

Julie rushed towards me, holding out her hands to help. 'Oh

God, sorry! I didn't mean to make you jump! Here.' She helped haul me up. 'Are you all right?'

'Fine.' I smiled, brushing myself off as I stood. 'Don't tell me Jesse's roped you in too?'

'Marjorie's filling in at the café. She's got her sister staying with her and although they're close, I think she needs some breathing space. She rang up earlier practically begging me for a shift so I thought I'd pop over and see how things were going here. What you up to?'

'Staying as far out of the way of the house as possible.'

'Not a bad idea.'

As she spoke, the roar of a diesel engine chugging into life followed shortly by the raising of the crane arm made us turn.

'Oh God. What if it goes through the rest of the house?'

'It won't. Jesse won't let it. He trusts those blokes. He wouldn't use them if he didn't. Come on.' She turned me around by the shoulders, away from the house. 'What are we doing here?'

'We?'

Julie shrugged. 'I've nothing better to do and it'll be a good way to get to know you more. If you don't mind the help?'

'Mind? Why would I mind?' I asked.

She screwed her nose up a little. 'Jesse said you're very private and warned me not to come charging in but what can I say? I'm nosy.' When she smiled, dimples appeared in her cheeks and her grey eyes, copies of her brother's, sparkled with mischief. 'And,' she poked her head in the garden room, 'it looks like you could do with a hand.'

Once again, in an action the complete opposite to my standard response, I told Julie that some help would be brilliant as I hadn't a clue where to even start.

Over two hours later, everything that had been stuffed into the garden room – which sounded grander than it currently looked – was surrounding it. Thanks to teamwork – something which up until now hadn't exactly been my first choice – the job had gone far quicker and been a lot more fun than it would have been had I been on my own. Julie was great company, always ready to laugh, and as open a person as I was closed off. But in her company, it felt much easier to crack open that door in my defences and peer out. The only blip in the proceedings was coming across a large, hairy spider the size of Jesse's dog, which had us both tripping over one another to get out of the door.

At the sound of screaming, Jesse and another man came running over, their faces grim, but their pace slowed as they saw us clinging to each other in fits of laughter.

'What the hell?' Jesse asked.

'Massive... spider!' Julie forced out in between giggles.

He rolled his eyes and mumbled a couple of choice expletives.

'Still in there?' The other chap stepped past him.

Julie nodded. Was that a faint blush I detected on her cheeks? It looked as if there was a story here.

'Want to show me where, Jules?'

Behind him, Jesse glanced up at the sky.

'That'd be great, Pete, if you don't mind? Although I'm going to stay close to the door!' She giggled again and Pete grinned.

'No problem. Come on, then.' And they disappeared into the building together.

'What are you shaking your head about?' I asked in a whisper, coming to stand next to Jesse. 'It was huge!'

'I'm sure. You're in the countryside. It won't eat you though.'

I gave him a Paddington stare. Wait, was that a smile? I deepened my frown. 'I'm well aware of that, but I paid for this place and inherited some animals I'm desperately trying to keep happy and alive but I'm not prepared to cohabit with an eight-legged monster. That wasn't part of the deal.'

'You're doing great. Better than you think.'

'Apart from opening the tin of paint with a tin opener?'

His mouth twitched.

'Bloody hell!' Pete's exclamation interrupted us.

My hands went to my hips. 'Told you.'

'He's just going along with it because he fancies my sister.'

'Ooh! Does she know?'

'Nope.'

'She clearly likes him though.'

'Yep.'

I let out a frustrated huff of air. 'Well? Is he single?'

'Yep.'

'Then why don't you say something? It's obvious to everyone else that there's a spark there.'

'A spark?'

'Yes.'

He checked his watch. 'None of my business. They'll work it out sooner or later.'

I looked back towards where the two were now exiting back into the bright light of the midday sunshine, squinting and laughing as they did so, Pete's hands cupped around what I certainly hoped was the monster that had been within.

'And don't you say anything either,' Jesse whispered hurriedly to me before they reached us. 'People will work it out or they won't. The last thing anyone needs is others telling them what they should and shouldn't do about their love life. All right?' His eyes were fixed on me.

'All right! No need to get uppity.'

'I'm not uppity.'

'Could have fooled me,' I whispered back and turned to smile at the approaching couple.

'They weren't joking! It's a big bugger. Want to see?' Pete held out his hands towards Jesse and I did a six-foot leap in the other direction in case the arachnid made a bid for freedom.

'Not particularly.'

'Show him, Pete,' Julie insisted. 'He'll never believe us otherwise.'

Pete did as he was asked and Jesse's eyebrows lifted.

'See?' It was now Julie's turn to stand hand on hips and stare down her brother in a game of I told you so.

'Admittedly, it is rather large.' Jesse's eyes turned towards me. 'It's still not going to eat you.'

'Would you mind getting rid of it for us, Pete?' I asked.

Pete nodded, smiled again at Julie and began walking towards the house.

'Not near the house!' I squeaked.

Pete spun on his heel and marched towards the woods on the other side of the field.

'Thank you,' I called after him.

'I'll go and make sure he chucks it far enough away,' Julie said and jogged to catch him up.

As I turned back, Jesse was smiling.

'Now what?' I asked.

'You.'

'Me what?'

'You're quite the contradiction.'

'What does that mean?'

'It means you're never boring.'

'My ex-fiancé would likely disagree.' The words tumbled out unexpectedly and I fixed a smile in place before turning away and pretending to study all the junk we'd hauled out.

'Then your ex-fiancé and I would disagree.'

I swallowed at the lump that had unexpectedly formed in my throat.

'I think that's possibly the nicest thing you've ever said to me.'

Actually it was possibly the nicest thing anyone had ever said to me but he didn't have to know that.

'Then you're welcome.'

I cleared my throat. 'How are things going over there? I've done my best to keep my back turned. Felt it was better that way. Ignorance is bliss and all that.'

'Nothing to worry about. Tree's removed and the good news is you'll have plenty of firewood once that's all seasoned.'

'I can think of less dramatic ways to get firewood.'

'True. But it's a plus point. Wood's not cheap.'

I thought of my super-insulated, always warm, centrally heated apartment in London with a pang.

'The roofers have been up and taken a look. They're not worried about anything: fairly straightforward job as far as they're concerned.'

'Deal with trees falling in on houses every day, do they?'

'Hopefully not, but they've done more than you'd think.'

'Right.' I paused. 'I'd say good but that doesn't seem appropriate.'

The hard planes of his face softened. 'I know what you mean.'

'Is it safe though? I mean, the walls and stuff?'

'Yep. Looks like it. but the structural engineer is going to come up in a couple of days and go through just to make sure.'

'A couple of days?'

'What's a couple of days?' Julie asked as the two of them approached us. 'The mutant spider is well away now.' She thumbed towards the woods behind.

'Thanks. That is good news.' Unlike what I'd just heard.

'The structural check on Felicity's house.'

'Anyone know a good hotel around here?' I asked.

'You don't need a hotel,' Julie said. 'You stayed at Jesse's last night. I'm sure he wouldn't mind putting you up for a couple more nights.' She ended the statement with a simple shrug.

'Oh no, I couldn't possibly!' I replied, hastily, and did my best to communicate with my eyes to my new friend that that was a very bad idea. Now, I know people toss out this phrase when they fully intend to take up the offer of another glass of wine/a second helping of pudding/the last roast potato, but in this instance, the words had full meaning behind them. Yesterday had been an emergency. Now I at least had the opportunity to make other arrangements.

'Rubbish. It's ideal. You don't need to waste your money on a hotel, does she, Jesse?'

I steadfastly refused to look at him. I'd briefly caught his look of horror, likely similar to my own, when Julie had first posited the idea, and I wasn't about to add to either of our embarrassment now.

'Really, it's fine. I love a hotel anyway. It'll be a nice break from ill-fitting windows and clanking pipes.'

'You'll have to go a way to find a hotel. I mean, the pub does B&B but it's hardly The Ritz.'

'That's OK. I'm not fussed about it being anything fancy.'

'Says the woman wearing an Armani jacket to clear out the garden shed.' Julie grinned and the two men looked at me. I could practically hear Jesse revving up for an eye roll. I'd just grabbed what was nearest on the hallway coat rack this morning so as not to mess up the jacket Julie had lent me.

Julie wrapped an arm around one of mine. 'No judgement here. I've just been eyeing it up all morning. It's just that one look at you shouts "fancy".'

'No, it doesn't,' I reassured her. 'It really doesn't.'

Julie grinned at me. 'There's no denying it. You stand out like a sore thumb here.'

I felt the smile on my face morph into a rictus and clearly the others saw it too.

'I mean that in a good way!' Julie hurried on. 'In that you just ooze "classy".'

Jesse scratched his cheek. 'You wouldn't have said that the first time I saw her.'

I met his eyes as my mind helpfully went and fetched those mortifying images for me and held them up. *Ta dah!*

'I find that hard to believe.' Julie frowned at her brother, then looked at me. 'Why?'

I locked eyes with Jesse. 'If you tell her, I will kill you and make it look like an accident.'

The smile flickered. 'Nah,' he said after a moment. 'But I reckon you'd hire someone to.'

'You're hilarious.'

'Come on-n-n-n-n-n!' Julie begged. 'You have to tell us now, don't they, Pete?'

'I'm not sure I want to get dragged into this.' He laughed. Pete was clearly a wise man.

'Jules is right, though. The B&B's a bit... rustic.'

I pointed to my house. 'I'm getting pretty used to rustic.'

'My point exactly. Thought you might want a break from that. In which case, the best hotel is about forty minutes' drive away.'

'That's not so far.'

Jesse folded his arms. 'And what, exactly, are you going to drive?'

I closed my eyes. 'Shit.' Opening them again, I found all three looking at me. Julie and Pete looked sympathetic. Jesse merely looked curious. 'I forgot my car got pancaked as well as my house.'

'That's settled, then. You can stay at Jesse's until things are sorted here,' Julie said. 'I'm going to make some teas. Anyone want one?' she asked, already striding towards the outbuilding near the house where we'd moved the essentials like the kettle and mugs earlier to avoid traipsing mud in and out.

'Sounds great. I'll come with you,' Pete offered, his longer strides soon catching her up, leaving the two of us alone.

'Sorry about that.' We both spoke the same words and the surprise burst the thin bubble of tension that hovered around us.

'There's nothing for you to apologise for. My sister however...' He made a strangling motion with his shovel-sized hands, the corner of his mouth tilted up one side.

'I'm sorry she put you on the spot.'

'Not at all. I was going to offer anyway.'

'Your face when she first suggested the idea would contradict that.'

'No, no, no.' He held up his hands, moving them slightly to and fro, the atmosphere relaxed now as we united in our mutual embarrassment. 'That was due to Jules springing it on you like that. And in front of Pete too. I knew you'd feel awkward.'

'I just feel like I'm imposing. You've already done so much. Honestly, if it hadn't been for you, I'd probably still be sitting up there,' I waved towards the area where a blue tarpaulin now covered the large hole in the roof, 'hoping the tree would finish the job off.'

The smile fell away. 'Don't say that.' His words were soft but I felt the full meaning of them.

'I just meant—'

'I know.'

The silence hung between us for a moment, broken only by the sound of birdsong and the odd burst of laughter coming from where the men were now gathered around waiting for the refreshments to brew.

'Let's go and get a drink.' Jesse tossed a look at the garden room. 'Looks like you deserve it. You've certainly been cracking on with that. Unearthed anything other than monster-sized spiders?'

We fell into step as we walked back towards the others and I told him about one possible piece of treasure but that, for the most part, it was all going to have to be got rid of. Once I got myself some wheels again, of course.

'I can give you a hand until you do, especially if it's big stuff.'

'I'm quite capable of lifting things, you know. I went to the gym at 5 a.m. four times a week religiously.'

'God!' His expression was something between horror and impressed. 'That sounds awful.'

'Thanks!' I replied, a little confused. From the look of him, Jesse was certainly no stranger to the gym.

'I couldn't do that.'

'What do you mean? You're hardly out of shape,' I said, hoping that my words landed the right tone of telling him he looked fit without sounding like I was hitting on him.

'Not from a gym. I mean, I have done all that in the past. But, honestly, it's not for me. The noise, the poseurs, the... I don't know... fakeness of it all.' He shook his head. 'Just not for me.'

'You could have worn headphones.'

'Or I could lift weights in my garden and listen to birdsong.'

'Not everyone has that luxury.'

'Nope. You're absolutely right and I'm well aware that I'm lucky to be able to.'

'I didn't make you anything yet,' Julie called as we approached. 'Wasn't sure how long you were going to be.'

I pretended not to notice the cheeky look she threw her brother and the mutinous one he tossed back.

'That's OK. I'll do it. You have a sit down.' I indicated where the others had now gathered nearby. 'What would you like?' I asked Jesse, walking into the building and flicking on the kettle.

'I can do it.' He reached past me for the coffee tin.

'I'm sure you can but I offered. Quite frankly, it's the least I can do.'

Jesse stood back, his feet planted apart, the strong arms crossing on the broad chest.

'Uh-oh.'

'Uh-oh, what?'

'Whenever you stand like that, you're usually about to tell me something else I've done wrong.'

He stared at me for a moment, then let out a bark of laughter. For a second, the sounds of chatter outside silenced. Jesse ignored it.

'You're a quick learner.'

The mouth curved up both sides this time. The kettle reaching boiling point gave me the opportunity to turn away, which was just as well. The last thing I needed right now – or at all – was to crush on Jesse Woods.

9

'How do you take your coffee?' I asked, pulling across two mugs. Neither were mine. Someone must have brought extra supplies.

'Strong, no sugar.'

'Milk?'

'Just a drop.'

'Is it worth it?'

'I think so.'

I smiled but didn't turn around.

'So what was it?' I asked, adding the requested drop of milk to his drink.

'What's that?' he asked, coming to lean on the wall beside me.

I handed him the mug. 'What you were about to have a go at me for this time?'

He looked down at me with those storm-cloud, impenetrable eyes.

'You don't frighten me, Mr Woods.'

'I have no intention of frightening you. One, because, why would I? And two, I'm pretty sure you'd kick my arse.'

Now it was my turn to laugh and, I had to admit, it felt good.

In these most unlikely of circumstances, with my car thinner than an After Eight and my house given extra ventilation I didn't ask for, I'd laughed more since I came to this place than I had in what seemed a very long time. I wasn't entirely sure what that said about my life, but I didn't think it was anything good.

As we walked out into the sunlight, it was impossible not to notice the furtive glances thrown our way but I did my best to ignore them. Julie hadn't mentioned a partner when it came to her brother and I'd assumed the fact she was so quick to offer me use of his house meant it was unlikely that there was one on scene. But with him looking like he did, and apparently being a decent man, there was no way that situation would last long. However, it wouldn't be me filling that particular vacancy. Jesse did seem a good man, but then I'd thought that about previous men too. But I was too cynical to think it would last. At some point, the other shoe would drop and I wasn't going to be the one it landed on this time. Been there. Done that. More than once and I was not about to set myself up for another disaster. Even when the man was hotter than a white flame.

We drifted into a conversation with Pete and Julie and I smiled privately at the glances he stole at my friend. As she was talking, I accidentally locked eyes with Jesse and he returned the smile. Clearly he'd noticed too. But had Julie? And did she care?

'So what are you planning to do with that shed now you've cleared it all out?' Pete asked.

'It's not a shed.' Julie turned to him with a fake haughty expression. 'It's a garden room.'

Pete pulled a 'ooooh' face and they both laughed. Oh yeah, she cared.

'What *are* you going to do with it?' Jesse asked.

'Honestly? I don't even know.'

'It'd make a perfect office,' his sister offered. 'You could sit and look out at the garden.' All four of us turned to take in the unkempt grass – calling it a lawn would be stretching the truth. 'I mean, if you planted one.'

'That is a great idea,' I agreed. The only teeny problem was that I didn't actually have a job for which I needed an office. At present, I was living off the savings I'd built up. Savings I'd stupidly thought I'd be spending on a house with Adrian but now that that possibility was firmly off the agenda, they were free to be used here. My flat had sold substantially over the asking price so I'd made a pretty hefty profit on my investment there too, which was just as well. Together, those would be enough for a while but at some point, I needed to sort out the chaos that was now my life.

I looked back at the house and then the cluster of men laughing, chatting and joking, all of whom had come to help without even knowing me. It was obvious Jesse was well respected by them, and also well liked. But there was more to it. A sense of community that I'd never been privy to before. I'd been part of clubs and cliques, that was for sure. But this was different and far, far better. Would my previous circle have banded together for a stranger? Unlikely. Unless it meant an invitation to a heretofore unavailable gala or society event.

I was brought back to the present by a gentle nudge from Jesse.

'You look miles away.'

'Oh!' I shook my head. 'No, just...' Suddenly, the words wouldn't form. What was I supposed to say? *Sorry, I was just comparing you and your friends to the shallow society I've been used to.*

'It's a lot,' he said, looking down at me as Pete stole Julie's attention once more. 'Honestly, you're handling it a lot better than many would.'

'I'm not so sure about that.'

'I am. You're being a real trooper, if you ask me.'

'That's because I run screaming into the woods at night when no one's looking.' I meant it as a joke but a frown wrinkled Jesse's brow.

'You're not on your own here, Fliss.' He stopped himself immediately. 'Felicity. Sorry, that slipped out. I've got an old school friend with the same name and we always called her that. Habit.' He held up his hand.

'It's fine, really. Actually, I quite like it.'

'Is that what people call you?'

'No, not generally but,' I carried on before he could interrupt, 'as it appears I'm making a new start here, perhaps I need to reconsider other things too.'

'Anything else on that list?'

I wrinkled my nose. 'I'm not sure yet.'

'Well, you've got all the time in the world.'

'All the time in the world until I run out of money. The only reason I still have any left is because you've all been so kind in helping and organising all this. Thank goodness for you!'

Jesse's eyes seemed to darken just that little bit more and I felt a flare inside me shoot off in myriad directions like an out-of-control firework.

'All of you!' I mean, I blurted in a higher pitch than I'd have liked. 'Everyone. Of course.' I cleared my throat and straightened my spine and tried not to notice that Jesse Woods' very attractive mouth was now tipped into a smile.

'Of course,' he repeated.

'Right!' Frank called, pushing himself up from where he'd been perched on a stone bench. 'Think that's probably all we can do for now, Jesse. Unless there's anything else?'

'No, that's it until the surveyor gets out here. Thanks, Frank.'

Jesse stepped across and shook the man's hand. 'It's really appreciated.'

'No problem at all. Just glad everyone was all right.' He gave a glance towards my pancaked car, from which they had now also removed the tree. Jesse had taken some more photos showing the full impact for the insurance and forwarded them on to me while Julie and I had been burrowing away to Narnia in the garden room.

'Thanks so much,' I said, taking the small group in. 'To all of you. It sounds very inadequate considering all the time you've given up and how hard you've all worked for someone you don't even know.'

'Now, now, none of that,' Frank replied, a kindly smile on his weather-worn face. 'You're a local now and we help each other out here.' His words echoed what Jesse had told me and I flicked a glance at him, leaning against the warm brick wall of the outbuilding, watching with an air of amusement on his face that said *told you*.

'Well, considering I've barely been here a few weeks, I think it's very generous of you to include me as a local so soon.'

'No time limit, love. It is what it is and that's that.'

I didn't have an answer for that, which in itself was unusual and the most I could come up with was 'Oh', which made Frank laugh, and his smile was so infectious, I found myself doing the same.

The men filed out, got into their respective vehicles and drove away. I waved as they did so, trying to swallow down the shame I felt at the snobbish way I'd likely come across to tradesmen in the past. I'd never been intentionally rude but now, I realised, I'd never really considered them at all. They would be there to do a job and that was it. Would it have hurt to have made a little small talk? Asked them if they wanted a drink every so often? But I hadn't. I'd left them in the care of the housekeeper and not thought twice about it. It was what I'd known and I had never considered there might be a different way.

One man hung back and then hesitantly approached me. Julie was sitting on the stone bench that Frank had vacated and Pete was leaning against the dry stone wall next to it, chatting away to her.

'Everything all right, Pat?' Jesse asked.

'Yeah, yeah.' He nodded and his cheeks gained a little pink. 'It's just that I was wondering, Miss DeVere...'

'It's Felicity,' I said quickly with a smile. Fliss felt right from Jesse but one step at a time.

Pat nodded with a brief smile. 'Felicity. Well, we were just thinking, I mean, me and the wife, whether you'd had any thoughts about what you were going to do with the lower paddock yet.'

Before I could answer, Pat rushed on. 'I know this probably isn't the right time to ask, I mean what with the storm and your house and all, but it's just that, as I was here, I thought... well, we thought...' He ended the sentence with a slight jiggle of his head.

'The lower paddock?' I asked.

'Yes. Just if you'd had any thoughts, like.'

I turned to Jesse. 'Umm...'

He pointed. 'Over down that way, behind this field here.'

'Oh, that one,' I replied in a knowledgeable tone despite the fact I still had no idea. Honest to God. I used to be a sensible, highly organised person and now I didn't even know what land I owned.

'Didn't Maisie used to stable her pony there?' Jesse asked.

'Yeah,' Pat replied. 'But then the place went up for sale. We got a call to say we had to get the pony out the next day or Joe would let it out himself. Maisie heard the call and was beside herself. In floods, she was.'

'I'm sorry,' Jesse said, the muscles in his jaw tight and the hands that had been relaxed moments ago now gripped into fists.

'Oh no, nothing on you, mate. None of us can help who we're related to. Luckily, having the same blood doesn't mean anything. Different as chalk and cheese, you and your cousin are.'

'And Maisie is...?' I asked.

'My daughter. She's ten, going on thirty.' His face lit up at the mention of her name.

'Keen rider, then?'

'Horse mad!' He laughed now. 'Always has been.'

'I can understand that,' I replied. 'I was the same many years ago.'

He nodded and seemed to relax a little at this shared situation.

'And where is the pony being kept at the moment?'

Pat pulled a face. 'In a stables about half an hour away but it's costing us a fortune and trying to get Maisie there in the morning and evening before school and work and then ride and muck out at weekends...' His words tailed off and he heaved a deep breath.

'How soon can you get the pony over here?'

He hesitated. 'Ummm... I don't know. I'd have to ring them and see when they'd let us. My wife arranged it so I don't know if there's a notice period.'

'OK. You find out and then just bring him... her?'

'Her. Honey, her name is, on account of her colouring.'

'Then you bring Honey round any time you like. You probably know the way better than I do.'

'Are you sure, Miss... Felicity?'

'Absolutely.'

'We can pay you what we were paying the previous owner,

probably a bit more.' His features were more animated now and it was easy to see just how much of a problem the current situation was causing his family.

I shook my head. 'You won't be paying me anything, Pat.'

He looked at me and blinked. 'I don't understand.'

'You came here today to help.'

'Yeah, but that's different.'

'No, it's not. The paddock is land that's not being used and if I can be of help to you and your family, then that seems like a fair trade.'

'I'm not sure about this, though. It doesn't seem right.'

'OK. Let's say free stabling for six months in return for what you've done today and what I'm sure Jesse will probably rope you in for in the future as this mess gets tidied up. Then we can review after that. How does that sound?'

He nodded. 'OK.'

'And if there's any difficulties getting here at any time, just message or call me. Jesse has my number, and I can go and see to Honey. It's been a while since I had a pony but I'm pretty sure I can manage.'

'I don't know what to say. That's really kind of you.'

'You can say we have a deal.' I held out a hand and after a moment's hesitation, he shook it and the smile spread slowly over his long features.

'Maisie is going to be over the moon.'

'Hopefully, I'll get to meet her and Honey soon.'

'Definitely. Especially if you like horses. She'll talk the hind legs off a donkey about them to anyone who'll listen.' He checked his watch. 'I'd better get on, but thanks again for this. We really appreciate it.'

'You're very welcome. Thank you for everything you did today.'

Pat nodded and did a fast walk back to his car, his phone already to his ear as he did so.

Jesse looked down at me. 'Fancy a walk around so you can familiarise yourself with what you actually own?'

'Do you have time?'

'Plenty. Come on, Ned.' The dog who'd been curled on the front seat of Jesse's truck while the work went on was now hoovering up biscuit crumbs, but at his owner's call, he zoomed to Jesse's side and began trotting happily along beside us.

This was another difference I'd noticed from the short while I'd been down here. Life was lived at a different pace from the hectic frenzy of the city. I'm sure in some of the bigger towns nearby, things were more amped up but in the pretty hamlet in which Paradise Farm sat, it was as though time moved slower and no one was in any particular rush. Jesse gave off the same vibe. He was calm and steady at the same time as getting things done, the perfect examples being last night and then organising everyone today. Even being in his presence had a calming effect.

'That was a good thing you just did,' he said, then turned to look at me. 'I'm not sure if that came out as patronising. If it did, then it was unintentional.'

'I don't know you very well, but I think I've already grasped that's not your style and not only because your sister would totally kick your arse if you tried it.'

His laugh was full and deep as he tipped his head to the clear blue sky above, his eyes closed, the enviable long lashes resting momentarily on his cheeks. 'That is very true.'

'But thank you for checking. I'm glad you felt it was the right thing to do. I'll admit I was totally winging it!'

'Then you should do that more often.'

'That's what landed me here in the first place!'

He turned his head. 'And you think that's a bad thing?'

'Honestly, I'm still trying to work that out. It's been... interesting so far, I can certainly say that.'

'Yeah. You certainly know how to bring the drama.'

'Not intentionally!' I bristled.

His hand was on my arm, gentle. 'It was a joke.'

'Oh... right. Yes.' I looked away from him and continued walking, annoyed with myself for bursting the bubble of easiness that had surrounded us, but something about the words had rankled.

Don't be such a drama queen, Felicity! It's not always about you! I'm far more the injured party here. How on earth will I ever be able to face anyone again! Your father's ruined my life!

'Hey.' The deep voice prodded me back to reality.

'Sorry, miles away.'

Jesse stopped and after a few more steps, I realised and stopped too.

'What is it?' I asked.

'You.'

'Me?'

'Yeah. You've been like a different person all morning and whatever I just said was me putting my size fourteen right in the middle of something because now you're back being as tightly wound as a roll of baling wire.'

'Really, it's nothing.'

He shoved a hand in his jeans pocket and studied me for a moment. 'OK. But when you're ready, I'm happy to listen.'

Jesse walked on.

* * *

'This is the lower paddock.' Jesse looked at the huge padlock that was looped on the end of an equally huge chain keeping the gate closed. 'I'm guessing one of the keys you have up at the house fits that.'

'That's a fun job for later, then. Guess the key! Is that the stabling over there?' I asked, my hand shading my eyes from the sun and pointing to a small block in the corner of the field.

'That's it.'

'Do you mind if we take a look?'

'Not at all,' Jesse replied and we began climbing over the gate. This task was obviously a lot easier when you had long legs. At nearly a foot shorter, I was taking a little longer.

'Gosh, it's a long time since I've done this sort of— aaar-rggghhhhhh!'

The mud was cold, thick and dark. Luckily, my ears were still exposed enough for me to hear Jesse's, 'Oh, shit!' and I desperately hoped that the words were merely a cry of surprise rather than factual observation.

'Pfffffffffffffffffftttttttttttttttttttt!' I spat out as I was lifted by two large, strong arms and stood back upright, minus one slightly too large wellington boot.

'Are you all right?'

I didn't answer immediately as I yanked a tissue from my pocket and wiped away what mud I could from my eyes so that I could at least see. Although the thought of facing anyone, let alone Jesse Woods, in my current state, made me briefly wonder whether I should bother. Then I remembered he'd already pretty much seen me at my worst, so the point was probably moot.

Suddenly, something occurred to me.

'Why do I always make a fool of myself when you're around?'

'You what now?'

'It's you!' I said, pointing at him.

'What's me?'

'Something about you. Until I came here, I was quite capable of conducting myself in an appropriate manner without injuring either my pride or anyone else in the process. Within days, all that had gone out of my completely rotten windows!'

'So, it's my fault?'

'You seem to be the common denominator.'

'Right.' He nodded and didn't disagree, just rumpled his brow and appeared to be thinking about it.

'I take it there's running water in the stables?' I asked.

Jesse gave a shrug. 'Not entirely sure, I'm afraid. None of us have been up here for years. As you might have guessed, Joe was kind of the black sheep of the family and we all kept apart by silent but mutual agreement.'

'There must be a tap, especially if you're charging people money to stable their animal there.'

We got closer to the building and I looked around. Surely this couldn't be it? But there was nothing else in sight.

'This is it?'

Jesse shrugged.

A ramshackle outbuilding with a patched-up door and, as we soon discovered, nowhere to get fresh water for the horses.

'Pat must have brought everything they needed each time.'

'That's ridiculous. I need to make this more suitable for Maisie and Honey.'

Jesse leant against the door jamb, the low afternoon sun slanting light across his face, highlighting his sharp cheekbones and defined jaw. He pulled his cap down a little more to shade his eyes.

'What do you need done?'

I proceeded to give a quick overview of the alterations needed. 'Obviously there's no mains water out here but a bowser would at least provide fresh water if I get it refreshed every couple of days.'

'Mmm-hmm.'

I waited a beat. 'Your expression says you have other ideas.'
'What expression?'
'The face you pull when you're thinking.'
'I wasn't aware I had one.'
'Oh, you do. Very much so.'

He straightened away from the door, his eyes now crinkling at the corners with amusement. 'Is that right? So how come nobody else has ever mentioned this?'

'I have no idea. Probably they're a little scared of you. You can look quite intimidating, even though I'm sure they all know you wouldn't hurt a fly.'

'Actually, flies have an incredible ability to piss me off.'

'Well, yes. Me too. Bad example. Anyway. I have no idea why it's not come up before but, as you don't scare me, I can mention it. Now, what's your idea?'

'First off, I'm glad you're not scared of me. I'd feel like a shit if you were, but also it doesn't surprise me because despite appearances, you're tougher than some blokes I've known. Probably not supposed to say that these days either, but I've said it now.'

'Despite appearances?' I prompted.

'You're very ladylike.' He took in the mud currently plastered over me. 'Usually.'

'And ladylike can't be tough?'

'Not what I said. At least not what I meant.'

I tilted my head at him in question.

'I'm kind of wishing I'd kept my mouth shut now.'

I took a step towards him. 'Aha, but you didn't so now you have to explain.'

He closed his eyes and tipped his head back. 'Can I have a guarantee that you won't take it the wrong way?'

'No.'

'Fine.' He crossed his arms, the shirtsleeves now rolled up to expose forearms with muscles like braided wire and dusted with dark hair. I tried to ignore them. What was it about forearms on blokes, especially good, strong ones like these? I raised my eyes and concentrated. Hard.

'OK. I won't take it wrong.'

'Can I have that in writing? Especially as we're going to be housemates for a few days. I don't have locks on my bedroom doors.'

'Funny.'

Jesse grinned. Great forearms and a killer smile. Quite the combination. One half of my brain was lighting a fire and the other side was rushing over and rugby-tackling the matches away.

'Go on, then.'

'Let's walk back up around the perimeter of the grounds. That way, I can show you the boundary properly and if we're walking, I'll feel less cornered than I do right now.'

I rolled my eyes as we fell into step beside each other.

As we walked, Jesse pointed out the boundaries, who they abutted and any significance of the views in the distance.

'You're stalling,' I said as he pointed out a hill, apparently called 'Bob's Knob'. A childish part of me wanted to snigger at that but adult me held it in.

'Not at all. Just giving you a chance to either giggle or make a comment about the name. You're clearly bursting to.'

'Rubbish. I don't know what you mean.'

'Well,' he said, looking at me and seeing straight through. 'That's disappointing. I'd hoped your humour was more puerile than that.'

My lips twitched, wanting to laugh. 'So,' I continued. 'You said I was ladylike, which apparently can't mean tough.'

'Nope. That's not what I said. You're really not going to let this drop, are you?' The glance at me as he spoke confirmed the question was rhetorical. 'From first glance, you're petite and slight and look like a strong gust of wind would blow you over, but,' he hurried on as he sussed I was about to interject, 'clearly none of that is true. I know from first-hand experience that you can swing a piece of timber with heft.' He touched the faint scar my unintentional swipe had left.

'I refuse to apologise for that again.'

Jesse grinned and this time, I turned away as my brain was once again waving the box of matches with enthusiasm, threatening to light a fire I was worried I might not be able to put out.

'But, seriously, the way you handled yourself the other day with the storm. That takes guts. And then today. You just got stuck in, hauling stuff out of that shed.'

'Garden room, please,' I teased.

'My point is,' he said, stopping and catching my arm, his touch gentle, 'that although coming here was clearly not a considered and thoroughly researched decision, you've taken it all in your stride, refusing to give in even when a ruddy great tree comes through your roof.'

'Thank you,' I replied, the sentiment genuine. 'You're very kind, but the truth is I've not really had much option but to get on with it. What choice do I have?'

'You could have sold the house the moment you got here. Developers are always keen for sites like this. From what I understood, my cousin was negotiating something, which is why all the stuff in the house was only half done. It was too much like hard work and he decided just to sell it on to builders. Obviously it fell through and by that time, he'd got bored, as is his way, and just sold it on. You could have done that.'

'To be honest, it didn't cross my mind that there may be that sort of opportunity available.'

He tilted his head. 'Is it one you're considering now?'

Was it?

'No. Although perhaps developers would find it difficult to get a change of use permission for the land anyway?'

'There's people around here who've got the money to make it happen if they want.' His expression had darkened as he spoke.

'That sounds like a story.'

He continued without elaborating. 'But what I am saying is that I'm glad you didn't decide to do that.'

'Don't like the thought of a swanky spa hotel in your neck of the woods? There's certainly plenty of mud available for their treatments.' I'd wiped the worst of it off but I was in no doubt I still looked a fright.

'It's not that. Sometimes, people get talked out of land, or into decisions that they aren't necessarily 100 per cent behind.'

'And you think I'm at risk of that?'

'God, no!' His laughter was sudden and rich, curling itself around me and teasing a smile onto my face with ease whether I wanted it to or not. Although, right now, I didn't mind in the slightest. 'I find it hard to believe anyone could talk you into doing anything you didn't want to.'

'I'm not entirely sure how to take that, bearing in mind how amusing you find it.' I tried to squash down the smile and give Jesse a considered look instead but my brain was having none of it. 'However, I'm going to take it as a compliment.'

'It was meant as one,' he replied, easily. With some others of my acquaintance, the smooth reply might have had me suspicious but, from the short time I'd known this man, it seemed that he had no issues about calling a spade a spade and no inclination to butter people up.

We walked on and as we got closer to the house, Jesse veered off, heading towards another gate into yet another field I apparently owned. He unhitched the latch and pushed it forward, closing it after me and giving it a little wiggle to make sure it was secure.

'Are there any animals in here that might get out?' I asked, watching his movements then casting an admittedly nervous glance back towards the field in case a herd of bulls – do bulls live in herds? – appeared on the horizon.

'Nope,' he replied, turning. 'You can relax.'

'I'm completely relaxed!' I batted back, in a very much not relaxed voice.

Jesse threw me a look that told me, even if there weren't bulls in the area, he could smell BS all the same.

'Fine.' I fell into step beside him. 'But you have to understand all this countryside stuff is new to me.'

'More croquet and Champagne on the lawn than heifers and sheep, eh?'

'I think that's what one would call reverse snobbery.'

'I think that's what this one would call a genuine question. You've not said much about your history other than having a flat and a life in London. Jules pointed out your expensive taste in clothes and you mentioned you went to an exclusive private school. Those things paint a certain type of picture,' he finished with a shrug.

'Yes. I suppose they do and, OK, yes, my experience of the country *has* been more croquet and Champagne, if you must know.' My hackles had raised, ready for a less than flattering comment about my previous lifestyle.

'Never got the hang of croquet. Played a few times and got utterly thrashed every time.'

'That's because you didn't have me on your team.'

He turned to face me as we came to another abandoned outbuilding, the small, red bricks of its walls suggesting it was Victorian in origin. The state of it also suggested that era was the last time it had been used. My eyes roamed the outside before settling back on my guide. The late-afternoon sun was doing amazing things for his skin and the contours of his face.

'Bit of a croquet ringer, are you?'

'You'd better believe it.'

'I'll have to remember that.'

I smiled up at him without thinking and the one I received in return sent a tingling and not unpleasant warmth throughout my body.

'So what's this building, then? Apart from in need of attention, like everything else here.'

'From what my gran had managed to find out digging through the family history, it's a shelter built to house donkeys the family had adopted. Pretty run-down at the moment, but,' he slapped the wall of it a couple of times with his large palm, 'it's solid.'

'Victorian?' I asked.

'Spot on. They knew how to build things back then.'

'So why are we here?'

'Apart from helping you familiarise yourself with what you paid good money for, I wanted to share a thought I'd had.'

'Oh, yes?'

'What about moving the stabling to this field? There's another entrance down there,' he pointed to a gate the other side, adjoining the long driveway, 'so anyone using it wouldn't need to come up to the house. And,' he walked to the other side of the building, 'there's this.'

'A tap!' Who'd have guessed just a few short weeks ago I'd have been so thrilled to see an outdoor tap?

Jesse turned it. Nothing.

'Oh.' The smile left.

'Probably just turned off at the mains. I can look at that if you want.'

'That'd be great. Just when you have time, of course.' I was suddenly aware that me and my house had taken up the best part of this man's day. 'I expect you want to be getting home.'

'Is that a hint for me to bugger off?'

'No! God, no!' *Oh, crap. Did that sound far too keen?* 'I mean... I'm... incredibly grateful for all the time you're spending helping me. I just thought you might need to get back... to something... someone...'

'Nope.' His answer was succinct and unbothered. 'But if you've had enough for today, that's totally understandable.'

'Not at all,' I replied, unexpected relief causing my shoulders to relinquish the tension I'd just put into them. 'This... all of it, it's been, well, you've been great.'

'It's nothing.'

'It's not nothing. And I definitely owe you dinner.'

I saw his back stiffen as he stepped inside the building.

Shit.

I followed him in. 'I'm sure you didn't think this, but, just to be clear, that wasn't me asking you out.'

'I know,' he said, without turning.

'Oh. Right. OK. So why do you look like a flagpole just got shoved somewhere unpleasant?'

'That expensive education certainly wasn't wasted, was it? You have a way with words.'

I pulled a face that suggested I disagreed.

'Do I make you nervous?' I crossed my arms in front of my chest.

The flicker of a smile teased his mouth and he did his best to hide it. 'No, Felicity, you don't make me nervous.'

'I didn't think so. I get the idea that's not a feeling you get too often.'

'You'd be right.'

'So why did you go rigid when I suggested dinner?'

'Because, although both you and I know that it wouldn't be a date, others would make up their own stories.'

'And that bothers you?' I asked.

'Would it bother you?'

'No. People write their own stories about you whatever. If they want to think that, there's nothing you or I could do to stop them. I have to say I'm surprised that's an issue for you, if I'm honest. We've already established you're not afraid to say what's what, so the fact that you'd be concerned about idle gossip is unexpected.'

'I'm not concerned,' he replied.

'Oh... Oh-h-h-h-h-h-h.'

He didn't care but someone else might, which meant me staying at his place was not ideal either.

He squinted down at me. 'Whatever you're thinking it is, I'm pretty sure I can guarantee it's not.'

'No, look. You've been amazing and I certainly don't want to get in the way of anything for you.'

'Felicity—'

I continued. 'I'm sure the local pub will be fine for a few days and if needs be, I can hire a car and go a bit further.'

'Felicity—'

Again, I carried on. 'Even a taxi. It's not like I need or can do much here until the surveyor's been so I can spend that time looking online for a car—'

'Felicity, stop!'

The words bounced off the brick walls and I jumped, swallowing the rest of the sentence, automatically stepping backwards unsteadily where the flooring had sunk. Jesse was across the space in three long-legged strides, his hands wrapping gently around my upper arms.

'Sorry. I didn't mean to make you jump.'

'I'm fine.'

But both of us could feel the tension.

I moved away, back towards the door and the lowering winter sun, Jesse's hands falling away as I did so.

'Felicity...'

'You don't have to explain.'

'What?' His forehead furrowed so deeply, the two dark brows were practically touching. 'Of course I do.'

'Jesse.' My arms were crossed but this time in an unconscious stance of defence.

'Felicity...' he replied, taking a step closer. 'Are you going to let me speak now?'

I gave a stiff-shouldered shrug and he tilted his head down, the peak of the cap shadowing his eyes from the sun but allowing me to see them in all their long-lashed glory.

'I'm sorry I snapped at you.'

'Apology accepted.' I went to move but Jesse shifted just enough to block me. I looked up at him with irritation.

'Thanks, but I'm not done. I'm not bothered what people think about me and if you're immune to gossip, that's good too. Best way to be, if you ask me. But there's someone I do need to make sure knows the situation.'

'Which is what I was trying to say!' I huffed out. 'If there's someone you like—'

'There isn't.' He cut across. 'Not like that. But I need to tell my wife's family what's going on.'

'Nothing's going on! Wait... what? You're married!' What the hell was Julie playing at with her hints and nudging me in her brother's direction all the time knowing that he was married? I strode past him outside, suddenly needing air.

'Yes. No,' he said, following me.

'It's usually one or the other when someone refers to their

wife.' I did my best to keep the sarcasm low level. There was nothing between Jesse and me. He'd had plenty of time to throw in a flirty move or two in the time we'd been together, but there'd been nothing. But this still felt like something I should have known, if not for any reason but to stop me making an idiot of myself!

'She died.'

And right then I felt like a total and utter shit.

10

'Please don't look at me like that,' he said.

'Like what?'

'Like you just kicked my puppy.'

I sucked in a breath. 'I would *never*!'

He shook his head. 'I know you wouldn't. It's just your expression...'

I met his eyes. 'I don't know what to say, Jesse. "I'm sorry for your loss" always seems such an insignificant thing to say to someone so I never know whether to say it or not.'

'Thanks. I know what you mean. But you feel you want to say something, right?'

'Exactly.'

We stood for a moment in silence, listening to birds who hadn't opted for a tropical winter holiday settling down to roost for the night.

'It's been nearly five years but, like I said before, this is a small community.'

'Surely they wouldn't begrudge you meeting someone?' My

brain caught up. 'Not that we're... you know. The offer of dinner was meant as a thank you, not a date.'

His smile spread slowly and I didn't know what to do with it so I shoved my hands into my pockets and waited.

'You know, you could really dent a man's ego.'

I arched an eyebrow. 'Somehow, I don't think that's a problem you've ever suffered from.'

He made no reply to that, returning instead to the previous question.

'And no. They wouldn't begrudge me anything, but it's not that simple. If it had been the other way around, I'd have wanted Alice to meet someone and be happy again as soon as possible.' He looked up at the noisy birds in the treetops, squinting at them, and I hazarded a guess that he wasn't seeing them at all. 'There's been plenty of times I've wished it was the other way around.'

'But it wasn't,' I said, my hand reaching up to touch his shoulder.

He looked round, the briefest hint of something like surprise to find me there.

'Sorry. Miles away.'

I nodded. What was there to say?

'I just... I've seen a few people since and, I don't know, it just feels like I'm duty-bound to tell her parents.'

'I'm sure they want you to be happy.'

He straightened slightly, as if snapping himself back to the present. 'Yeah. Sorry, you don't want to hear all this.'

I smiled but kept my thoughts to myself because, actually, I did want to hear it. This and so much more. And that was a problem.

'Let's get out of here. You're right. Dinner would be good, but not because you owe me anything. You don't.'

I opened my mouth to argue but Jesse was there before me.

'It's not open to debate.'

I closed my mouth.

'There's a great little pub a couple of villages over.'

'Sounds perfect.'

'And before you think of it, I'm not suggesting that one because I don't want to be seen with you.'

'It hadn't crossed my mind.'

'Fibber,' he said with a grin.

'It's a bit late anyway, as you've offered me a room for the next couple of nights. Or at least your sister did.'

'That's true. But like I said, it's not that I care what people think in general. It's just…'

'They've been through enough?'

'Yeah,' he said with a sigh. 'Exactly.'

'Sounds like you've not had it easy either.'

'I'm fine.'

I recognised the automatic response but let it go. If he wanted to tell me anything more, he would.

'So you think it'd be possible to make this into an alternative stable?' It seemed a good time for a change of subject.

'Yeah, I do. I mean, the other one is OK. Maisie's had Honey in there since she got her a couple of years ago, as far as I know.'

'Yes, but I'm here now and those facilities aren't good enough, if you ask me, especially when you're charging money for it.'

'Which you aren't,' Jesse reminded me.

'No. Not at the moment, but it looks like there's some making-up to Maisie to be done.'

'Which isn't your responsibility.'

'It's not yours either.'

Jesse pulled a face.

'Just because you're related to someone doesn't mean you're responsible for their actions or attitude. You're clearly very different from your cousin and it's obvious that people around here know it.'

'I hope so.'

'They do. Stop questioning it.'

Jesse looked down at me. 'You can be quite stroppy when you want, can't you?'

'That's not stroppy. That's assuredness. Believe me, if you think that's stroppy, you've led a very sheltered life.'

'That sounds ominous.'

I flung him a smile. 'Don't worry. I wasn't talking about me.'

He mock wiped his brow and we trudged back towards the house to lock up what it was possible to lock and head back to Jesse's.

* * *

An hour later, we were in Jesse's BMW coupé on the way to the pub. The pale-tan leather seats hugged me cosily and my bum was warming nicely thanks to them being heated. Although the car was swankier than the pick-up, Jesse himself looked much the same, only slightly upgraded. A casual shirt had replaced the long-sleeved tee he'd worn earlier and the jeans he wore now were dark indigo rather than the well-worn, faded working pair I'd seen him in prior to this evening. He rocked both looks pretty damn well.

The blue sky had turned hazy with the sunset and clouds bubbled up as darkness fell, bringing with them a fine, steady rain. I sent up my thanks once again that the roof was now covered although, after the storm, I wasn't sure there was anything in my room that could have possibly got any wetter than it already was. I looked out of the car window but all I saw was my own face reflected back at me. I'd taken my hair down for the evening and earlier, when Jesse hadn't been looking, I'd shot into the house and grabbed a few items of clothing that were thankfully still being stored in one of the spare rooms. Conversation was limited as we drove along the windy, wet back roads and I had to admit that I was having second thoughts about the evening. Earlier, when we'd been chatting and even got a bit of banter going, it had seemed like a good idea. But now I wasn't so sure.

'You OK?' Jesse glanced over for a fraction of a second before focusing back on the road.

'Me? Yes, fine, thanks. Lovely weather.'

Being British, I resorted back to the one topic anyone on these isles could be sure to have an opinion on.

To my surprise, Jesse's opinion was laughter. He paused at a shrinky-dink sized crossroads and looked over at me before pulling out and turning left.

'What's so funny?'

'You're pretty quiet. I was wondering if you were having second thoughts about wanting to go out tonight. And then you started talking about the weather and I knew for sure.' There was still amusement in his voice as he asked if I wanted him to turn back.

'No, of course not. If anything I thought you might be the one regretting agreeing.'

'Not at all. Just concentrating. There's a lot of deer around here and they have a tendency to just appear from the side of the road.'

'Oh!' I peered at the hedgerow suspiciously. 'Then, by all means, be as silent as you like.'

'It's fine. The pub's just down the road here.' He pointed by lifting one finger from the steering wheel towards where a cluster of warm white lights was illuminating a postcard-quaint, thatched-roofed building.

The gravel of the car park crunched beneath the tyres as Jesse pulled in and found a space.

I bent to pick up my clutch as Jesse got out and moments later, he was opening the passenger-side door. I took the hand he offered to exit the car onto the uneven ground and he pushed the door closed and, after two steps, offered his arm. The rain had just about stopped as we started towards the door.

'Thanks.' The last thing I needed was a broken ankle on top of a broken house and a broken car! 'I didn't realise it'd be uneven.'

'No, I should have mentioned it, sorry. I didn't realise Jules had lent you heels.' We both looked down at my feet as we entered the pool of light cast from the porch lamp.

'Umm... she didn't.'

I could feel Jesse's eyes burning into me even before I tilted my head to meet them. His arm had dropped away and, in a change from his usual annoyed-with-me stance, his hands were now rammed in his pockets.

'Please don't tell me you went back into that house to get shoes.'

'No, I didn't.'

He let out a breath of relief.

'I went in to get underwear and a few other clothes as well as shoes.'

'Felicity.' It was almost a growl. Before he could say anything else, another couple crunched their way up to the door and I hoped we might all enter together, but Jesse nodded to them as he moved us both to the side. The door closed on the cosy inn, the smell of woodsmoke teasing my nostrils. I wrapped my coat tighter and waited.

'I expressly told you not to go back in there until it's checked over. The whole bloody thing could have come down on you!'

'As it could have last night and you still charged in so I'm not sure you're in any position to lecture me.'

'That was different. You were in there!' He was still close and I could see the frustration boiling in his eyes.

'Then you could have called the fire brigade! Anyway, I would have got out. I was just... waiting for the right moment.'

His lips disappeared into a thin line and he tilted his head fractionally to the right. 'You must think I've just come up from nearest cabbage patch if you think I'm going to believe that one. And yes, maybe I should have called them, but I didn't think about it at the time. You had all day to think about going back in for...' he looked back down at my feet '...shoes.'

'Look. I'm sorry, OK? But as much as I like your sister, I'd really rather wear my own underwear! Surely you can understand that. You'd been banging on about the roof all morning and nothing had shifted so I thought it'd be OK just to grab a few things. I swear I wasn't more than three minutes. As reckless as you think I am, I don't actually want my house to fall on me either!' I let out a tense huff through my mouth, the breath turning into a cloud in the cold night air.

'I understand why you'd want to do that. Just, please, don't do it again until we know it's safe.' His voice was calmer now, deep and rich in the low light.

'I won't.'

Without replying, he placed a hand on the small of my back and guided me towards the door. 'Come on. Let's get inside. You're freezing. And as pretty as those shoes are, I imagine you've long since lost all feeling in your feet.'

We hurried in through the thick wooden door, and quickly closed it again to keep in the heat. I wrapped my arms around me and stamped my feet a couple of times in an effort to go home with the same amount of toes I arrived with.

Clearing a way through the surprisingly busy Sunday evening crowd in the bar area, Jesse took my hand and led me through in his wake, his fingers wrapped firmly around mine.

'Jesse, love!' the woman at the bar greeted him warmly. 'Lovely to see you, especially out in this weather.'

'Nothing stops me from coming here, Janet, you know that.'

'Ah, you're just saying that,' she teased.

'I'm here, aren't I?' He spread his hands as far as he could in the cramped space.

'You are, indeed. And what are you here for?' she asked, casting a smile and an interested glance in my direction.

'My neighbour's got some house problems so she could do with a decent meal. I knew just where to suggest.'

'Well, I'm sorry to hear that, love, but Jesse's right. If it's a good meal you need, then he's definitely brought you to the right place.' She gave us both a wide smile and I saw the twinkle in her eye. Time to quash that particular avenue of gossip.

'Jesse forgot to mention the storm also flattened my car, hence he was kind enough to be my taxi tonight.'

From the corner of my eye, I saw my neighbour's head turn towards me a fraction.

'Oh, goodness! You are in the wars, aren't you? Let's get you both sat down and warming up, then.' Janet came around from behind the bar and bustled us through under a low beam, which Jesse automatically ducked, into another room, quieter than the bar with tables laid more elegantly than I'd expected for a country pub, many of them already filled.

'This one here?' she asked.

'Perfect,' Jesse replied as I pulled out my chair and sat down.

'Right, here's your menus. Gabby will be your waitress tonight and she'll be along soon. Can I get you some drinks in the meantime?'

'I'd love a white wine, please. Whatever you recommend.'

Janet nodded at me, smiling, then looked expectantly at Jesse.

'A bottle of still water would be great. Thanks, Janet.'

And off she bustled back to the bar.

'You didn't have to do that, you know,' he said, once she was out of earshot.

'Do what?'

'Earlier. Making sure Janet knew this wasn't a date.'

'I don't know what you're talking about,' I replied, my focus now on the menu in front of me.

Jesse leant closer and, without consultation with my brain, my gaze raised to meet his.

'Remember,' he whispered. 'I grew up on a farm. I can smell bullshit three miles away.'

I looked back down and studied the options.

* * *

'You going to tell me this isn't as good as some of the places you've eaten in London?' Jesse asked. Gabby had just finished clearing the plates and had left us with the pudding menu, although there was no way I could find room for any more food.

'If I did, I'd be lying.'

He seemed pleased with the answer and returned his attention to the menu. 'Are you having anything?'

'I really don't have room.'

Jesse raised his head. 'You're missing out if you don't. Seriously, the sticky toffee pudding here is beyond anything you've ever tasted.'

'That's quite the claim.'

'And I stand by it.'

I closed the menu. 'Then I think we'd better order.'

Annoyingly, he was right and he knew it. 'The look on your face,' Jesse said, laughing. 'Don't even try to tell me I'm wrong now.'

'Have you ever heard of winning gracefully?'

'It's not about winning,' he said, taking a forkful of the heavenly pudding we were sharing. 'It's about showing you what you've been missing.'

'Smug isn't attractive, you know that, right?'

His mouth full of pudding, he laughed with his mouth closed, his eyes catching the light from the candle on our table, bright sparks reflected in the deep grey as they too crinkled with amusement. Smug might not be attractive but Jesse Woods definitely went in the 'hot as hell' pile.

The drive back to his house felt more relaxed. On my part that was probably due to the two glasses of wine I'd had. I wasn't sure what Jesse's reason was, although the sticky toffee pudding had been an almost spiritual experience so it might have been that.

'I am sorry that I went into the house again. I guess I wasn't really thinking.'

'That's OK. I get it and probably I'd be the same.'

'Partial to a Louboutin heel too, then? Not sure you need the height, to be honest.'

He tossed me a look in the low light of the car that told me not to be a smartass.

'Thanks for this.' I waved my hand around and the thought that I probably should have stopped at the one large glass flitted briefly through my brain but didn't pause to land. 'Taking me out tonight. I mean, not that you're taking me out, out. I just mean driving me – us – out tonight.' Another thought then flew in, this one roosting in my brain a little longer, that perhaps I should have waited for the food before downing nearly all the contents of the first glass. 'Why did you bring me those nails when I dropped them?'

'Huh?'

I shuffled my bum round in the seat. 'At the DIY shop? You didn't have to follow me.'

'It sounds creepy when you put it like that.'

'No-o-o-o-o. It was really kind. If I'd realised I'd left them behind at that point, I might have just lain in that mud and never got up again.'

'Then I'm glad I did what I did.'

'But why?'

'Honestly? I was kind of worried who else might get hurt with that timber. Let's just say you didn't look like a natural.'

'I dread to think what I looked like – don't remind me!'

'And secondly, probably a bit of basic nosiness. I knew who you were. At least, I knew you'd moved in and I hadn't been up here for years so I was interested to see what my cousin had done with the place. The fact you were buying wood made me wonder why. He'd been on about making it a turnkey property.'

'I might have been building something.'

'You might have,' Jesse replied without a hint of belief in his tone. 'Which reminds me,' he continued as we swung into his driveway. 'We need to sort out that entrance that I came through. It needs blocking off. The last thing you need is animals wandering in or out.'

Oh God, I never had this problem in London. I let out a groan and covered my face with my hands. 'What have I done?'

Jesse applied the handbrake and then gently curled his

fingers around the edges of mine and removed my hands from my face.

'We'll sort it. Don't worry.'

I let my head drop back against the headrest. 'This isn't your problem, Jesse. You've already done more than enough. Look, maybe you were right earlier. Maybe I should just have sold to someone. It doesn't have to be a golf club or whatever. Perhaps the agent can find someone who's looking for a project and can finish it to the level it should have been?' I pulled my head back up and faced him. 'We both know I don't really belong here.'

Jesse didn't say anything for a moment, then sat back and got out of the car. Yeah. Wine was definitely a bad idea. I closed my eyes.

The passenger door opened and I jumped. Jesse held out a hand and I took it. Suddenly everything, including me, was feeling a bit wobbly. I stood, my head closer to his chin with the heels I'd possibly risked my life to retrieve. I turned to close the door but he was there before me.

'Come on. Let's get inside. It's freezing out here.'

I held back. The wine had led me to look at things a little more deeply and the realisation of the current state of my life, combined with the sharp cold air of the night, had suddenly sobered me entirely.

'I'm going to call a taxi.'

'To where?' The planes of Jesse's face were all highlights and shadow from the porch light.

'A hotel.'

He let out a sigh. 'Felicity, we've been through this. Come on.'

'No. I'm leaving.' I took a step back. 'What the hell am I doing, Jesse? I don't belong here. I've been playing at fitting in and being part of the village but we both know I'm not. I made a stupid, stupid mistake and now I'm stuck in the middle of nowhere, on my own, with a disaster of an uninsured house, no job and, as much as I'd like them to be, my finances aren't bottomless. It's better for everyone if I leave now and sell it to someone who either knows what they're doing or can at least pay people to do the huge amount of work the house needs.'

'I already told you that's not an issue.'

'I'm not having you keep doing everything for free!'

'You really don't take help well, do you?'

'No, I probably don't. People can't let you down if you don't involve them.'

'I'm not going to let you down, Felicity.'

I looked down at my shoes then back up into his face. 'I liked it when you called me Fliss.' My voice was softer now.

His mouth flickered into a smile. 'Then Fliss it is,' he replied, his voice low and gentle.

I shook my head and to my horror, a tear freed itself and rolled down my cheek. I swiped it away. Crying in public was not the done thing. And certainly not *my* done thing.

'Do you still want that taxi, Fliss?'

'I'm a mess.'

'No, you're not. You've just hit a rough patch. Happens to the best of us.'

'Not to me, it doesn't. When I fall down, I get up, straighten my tiara and carry on. The problem is, right now, I don't even feel like I have a tiara to straighten any more. I've lost everything! I made an idiotic decision and ruined my life!'

Silence hung between us.

'You done with the dramatics now?'

My head snapped up, eyes narrowed. 'What?'

Jesse shrugged. 'You heard.'

My mouth dropped open. 'I can't believe you just said that. I poured out my heart to you, which, by the way,' I gave him a shove, 'is something I never do! And that's all you can say? Thanks for nothing. And yes! I do want that bloody taxi! As soon as possible, but don't bother putting yourself to any trouble. I'll call it myself on the way.'

'On the way to where?'

'On the way to wherever isn't here!' I shouted back and proceeded to stomp across his block-paved drive back up to the road. I had no idea where I was going but, right now, I was being fuelled by pure rage and embarrassment and that was enough.

'Fliss. Where are you going?'

'And don't call me Fliss!' I yelled back at him as I got to the electric gate at the boundary of his house. Beyond it, through the fence, the long driveway stretched out, puddles glinting like quicksilver as the moon darted in and out of clouds. 'Could you open this, please?' I snapped, still not turning.

'Nope.'

'Fine.' I started climbing it. Honest to God, six months ago, if you'd told me I'd be in the depths of the countryside, climbing an eight-foot-high gate in a Christian Dior dress and five-inch Louboutins, I'd have suggested a session with a therapist. But here I was.

'Fliss! What are you doing?'

'What the bloody hell does it look like I'm doing?'

'Get down!' Jesse's voice was closer now and, in my haste to get further up – inconveniently, he had not installed an easy-to-climb gate – I missed my footing and slid backwards, my hands and shoes scraping on the wood as I fell, trying to stop myself. His arms were around me long before I hit the ground. Jesse adjusted position so that I was now in his arms, one around my back and one hooked under my knees.

'You could have broken your bloody neck! What the hell were you thinking?'

'Put me down!'

My shoes had fallen off in the fall and he bent quickly to scoop them up with one hand as he balanced me in his arms. 'The ground's wet,' he said as he handed me the shoes. One no longer had a heel at all and both had huge scrapes down the sides, the leather shorn bare during their argument with the gate.

For a moment, I stared at the shoes I'd worked so hard for. The pair I had set as my goal, and had run in to fetch despite Jesse's warning to stay out of the farmhouse. They were just a pair of shoes. But they weren't. They were so much more.

The fight left me. Jesse felt it and began walking towards the house. Leaning us both towards the front door, he unlocked it and, moments later, having nudged the door closed with his hip, he gently put me down, his hands resting on me lightly until he was sure I was steady.

For a moment, we were both silent.

'Fliss, I'm really sorry.'

I nodded my acceptance, too exhausted to do anything else.

'Sorry about the shoes.' He pulled a face.

I shook my head. 'They're just shoes.'

'They're not though, are they? As obtuse as I've apparently been, even I can see that now.'

'It's nothing, Jesse. Honestly.'

He didn't push and for that I was grateful. 'You know where everything is and you're welcome to go up if you want. I was going to make a hot chocolate. It might warm you up?' His fingers wrapped briefly around mine. 'You're freezing and that's my fault.'

My laugh was tired but genuine. 'You're not responsible for the weather, Jesse.'

'No, but I'm responsible for keeping you out in it and making you angry enough to start climbing an eight-foot gate in five-inch heels!'

I looked up at him and from somewhere deep inside a bubble of exhausted, part-hysterical laughter rose up.

'What the hell was I thinking?'

'I'm not sure you were. From the look on your face, you were so mad with me, the most important thing was to get as far away as possible.'

'True.'

'Sorry. Again.'

I sighed. 'Hot chocolate sounds great, if you don't mind?'

'Not at all.'

'I think I'll get ready for bed while you're doing that?'

His smile was soft. 'You look fit to drop. Go get into your jammies and I'll see you in a minute.'

I turned and plodded, barefoot, up the pale-grey, carpeted stairs.

Ten minutes later, I'd scrubbed the make-up from my face, rubbed in some moisturiser, brushed my hair back into a plait and got into the pyjamas that Julie had kindly lent me. Soft brushed cotton in a cosy red check, they weren't something I'd ordinarily have worn and definitely not bought. Not stylish enough, I'd have told myself. But I'd clearly been missing out. They were snuggly and warm and cute. Chic was overrated when it came to bedtime.

Wrapping the guest robe around me, I tied the waist, slid my feet into the guest-room slippers and headed downstairs.

'Just in time,' Jesse said as he lifted a tray with two drinks and a small plate of biscuits on it. 'I was going to go and sit in the snug but you're welcome to take yours upstairs if you'd prefer.'

'No, I'll come with you, if that's OK?'

'Of course it is.' He indicated with a nod of his head. 'After you.'

Having placed the tray down on the coffee table, Jesse stepped across the small room to the log burner and, a minute later, flames began licking around the prepped kindling and the log resting on top of it. He took a seat next to me on the chesterfield. Rich velvet in a hunter green with gold studding, it suited the room perfectly. Bookshelves lined one wall and heavy, padded silk curtains were drawn across the window. An Indian silk rug was laid over the carpet and under the coffee table, and the whole room was lit by one lamp, giving it an appropriately snug feel.

I took a sip of the salted caramel hot chocolate Jesse had prepared. Not too sweet, it was impossibly smooth and comforting. Exactly what I needed.

'This room is gorgeous. I mean, your whole house is perfectly styled.' I hesitated for a moment then spoke again. 'Did you design it or did your wife? If you don't mind me asking, of course.'

He sipped his own drink and rested it on his lap. 'Neither. We didn't live here when she was alive. I moved here a while after Alice died. I'd always liked the place but it was in a bit of a state so when it came up for sale I took it on. Having a project gave me something to get up for and I was struggling in the old house. Too many memories.'

'I don't pretend to understand but I can see how that could be. You've done a wonderful job and the styling is gorgeous.'

'That's down to the interiors specialist I used to work with. I gave her some thoughts of what I'd like and then let her get on with it. She'd done work on other projects I'd been involved with so I knew she was good.'

'Used to work with?'

'Yeah. Her and her husband have just moved to New Zealand, which is where he's from originally.'

'Oh! Yes, that would be quite the commute.'

'Yeah.' He laughed. 'She gave me a couple of names but I've looked up some of their work and, while they're obviously good at their jobs, neither of them have got quite the style I'm looking for.'

'Oh.'

The room fell quiet again, the logs catching in the burner the only sound. Both of us sipped at our drinks before Jesse spoke again.

'What was it you said you did before you came here?'

'I'm not taking a pity job, if that's what you're thinking.'

Jesse tipped his head back, then looked at me. 'You are impossible, woman. You do know that, don't you?'

I gave him a look over the rim of my cup before I took another sip.

'You're an interior designer, right?' he persisted.

'I *was* a home stager.'

'So you *are* a stylist.'

'And you say I'm impossible.'

'Did you enjoy it?'

I was too tired to argue. 'Yes, I loved it, actually. But I well and truly burned my bridges with my employer.' I felt the blush creep up my chest as I thought back to that day.

'That bad, eh?' Jesse pulled a face.

'Let's say I certainly don't do things by halves.'

'No, I got that impression pretty quickly.'

'I cocked up on an important meeting and when they, quite rightly, took me to task about it, I announced I didn't need their bloody job anyway as I was moving to the countryside to "lose myself in nature as that was where I truly belonged!".'

'That told them.'

'As you have probably realised by now, I've made some very poor life decisions in recent months.'

'Maybe. Maybe not.'

'You were there tonight, right?'

'OK. Fair enough, I'll grant that attempting to scale the gate tonight probably wasn't the best decision, but then part of that was on me and I'm pretty sure I owe you a pair of shoes.'

'Don't be silly.'

'I may not be a fashionista, but I know those shoes are pricey and, even if I hadn't, your face when you realised they were ruined told me as much.'

'It wasn't that.' I finished my drink and placed the empty Emma Bridgewater mug down on the coffee table.

'I grew up rich. Anything I wanted, I got. Money was literally no object. I was, admittedly, very spoiled.'

I glanced at him and he was watching me, listening.

'I'm pretty sure you already guessed that.'

'Carry on,' he encouraged gently without answering the question.

'When I was fifteen, everything fell apart. My mother died when I was three and my father remarried quite quickly. It's funny how sometimes, people choose the same sort of person for their partners and sometimes they go for the opposite. My father definitely went for the opposite this time. Estelle was nineteen years his junior.' I glanced across at Jesse. 'Very much a trophy wife. They were out a lot of the time, either at events or shopping or travelling.'

'Do you have any siblings?'

'No, just me. I think there were plans but then Mother died and...' I paused. 'The new wife wasn't interested in having children. Didn't want to ruin her body, apparently. She spent enough of my father's money on it, that was for sure. Anyway, I was at school one day and got called into the headmistress' office. The school had been trying to get hold of my father for some time without success. Apparently, none of the fees had been paid and they were, as politely as they could, telling me unless the bill was settled imminently, I would have to leave. I don't know what sort of school you went to, but secrets rarely stay secret in private school and by the end of the morning, the word was out and my so-called friends had already dropped me in case my apparent penury was catching.'

Jesse shifted in his seat, his body turning to face me a little more. 'That's harsh.'

'Had the shoe been on another foot, I'm ashamed to say I probably would have done the same.'

'Kids can be cruel, that's for sure.'

I appreciated his diplomacy but, while that was true, it didn't excuse what my behaviour might have been.

'I skipped the rest of the day and went home. I could hear my stepmother wailing the moment I got in the door and my father pleading with her. It took them several minutes to even notice I was there. Not that that was particularly unusual.' I shifted my gaze briefly from the fire to Jesse, pulled a face and returned my concentration to the flames. Beside me, Jesse's hand moved, his little finger now resting against mine, the briefest of touches but it was enough. I swallowed and carried on.

'Eventually, my father noticed me and asked me what I was doing home. I told him what the headmistress had said. Even then, I was hoping it was all a misunderstanding, a mistake by the bank. The fact that Estelle was having hysterics was neither here nor there. She always did that when she wanted her way. But I could tell by his face this time, it was different. There was no mistake.'

'Did he say anything?'

'He said sorry. That was it. Just one word. Although, to be fair, he didn't get much of a chance to say a lot else as Estelle kicked off again about how I wasn't the one that he should be apologising to, that it would barely affect me and that it was *her* life that was ruined, and how was she ever supposed to face any of her friends again, blah blah blah.'

'She sounds a delight.'

'Oh yes, a real treasure.'

'So, the money was all gone?'

'Yes. Despite the drama, Estelle was a large part of the reason. My father had always had a tendency to live beyond his means, despite those means being substantial, but, from what I understood from Nanny, Mother had always been the sensible one. Reined things in when they were in danger of spiralling, but with her gone, Father spent more freely and then once Estelle came on the scene, it was a constant merry-go-round of parties, the races, shopping, travel and more shopping.'

'What did, or does, your father do?'

'He inherited his wealth but was wise with investments, again thanks to my mother. Those made him a lot more but after Mother...' I swallowed. 'He took his eye off the ball, ignored advice from the right people and listened to the wrong ones. Eventually, the entire piggy bank was empty.'

'So what happened? Where did you live?'

A log shifted suddenly in the heat of the wood burner and brought me back to the moment.

'Gosh. Listen to me waffling on. I'm sure you don't want to hear all this. I'd better be heading up to bed.'

Jesse's hand moved to cover mine. 'I do want to hear it. If you want to tell me.'

My eyes focused on his hand. Large with strong but slim fingers, the thin, silvery trace of a scar stretching from his index finger almost to his wrist. I had a sudden desire to run my finger along that scar. Instead, I tucked my hands under my thighs.

'I never do this.'

'Do what?'

'Tell people about... everything.'

'Then I'm glad I'm the one you chose to tell.'

'I'm not great with trust.'

'I'm beginning to see why.'

I raised my gaze and met his grey, unwavering one, but it was soft, understanding and, despite the drama of earlier, I realised that for the first time in a long time, for the first time I could remember if I was honest, I felt safe. That here with this man I barely knew, I felt more secure than I had with those I'd been the closest to. That alone probably said more about my previous relationships of all types than anything.

'An aunt took me in until I finished school.'

'You went back to school?'

'A different one. A local comprehensive.'

'How was that?'

'Awful. My aunt was rather fierce and if I hadn't been so scared of her, I'd have bunked off as much as I could. In hindsight, it's probably just as well that I didn't but at the time, I dreaded each day even to the point that I was throwing up most mornings.' I glanced up. 'Sorry. Too much information.'

'Not at all. I'm sorry you didn't enjoy the new school.'

'I hated it. And they hated me so at least it was even. Although I teased you about reverse snobbery, it definitely exists. As far as most of the other students were concerned, I'd come in with this posh accent and therefore thought I was above them. Actually, I was terrified and completely intimidated by them and the whole situation so they couldn't have been further from the truth. If I opened my mouth, they took the mickey out of my accent but if I kept silent, I was a snob and "too good to speak to them".' I wiggled my fingers to make bunny ears as I recounted those dreaded days. 'And of course, once they found out I was there because my father couldn't pay the private school bills, it just got worse.'

'How did they know that?'

'I guess word had got around about my family's fall from grace. However they found out, that provided extra ammunition.'

'I'm sorry you had to go through that.'

I shrugged. 'People go through worse. You, for example.'

'That doesn't take anything away from what you were dealing with.'

'No. I know, and thanks.'

'So what happened after that?'

'I went to sixth form at a different school two bus rides away to get as far away as I could from the school I'd been to. Got my head down. Got my A levels, took on three jobs to put myself through university and worked my arse off to get to where I was a couple of months ago. Then my fiancé dumped me for an heiress, I got absolutely blotto, made some very bad life decisions and ended up in a village deep in the countryside that I'm still not entirely sure I could give directions to!'

'I can help you with that if needs be.'

I gave him a tired smile. 'Thanks.'

'As much as I'm enjoying our conversation, you really do look fit to drop. Why don't you head up and get some rest?'

'Yes, I think that might be for the best.' I pushed myself up from the sofa. 'Are you coming?' I asked, then immediately felt a rush of blood to my face that had nothing to do with the heat of the room. 'I didn't mean—'

'I knew what you meant, don't worry. I'm just going to sit here for a little while longer.'

'OK. Thanks again for tonight and sorry about earlier. I promise I'm really not normally that much of a drama queen.'

He held up his hands, palms towards me. 'It was on me.'

'No, it wasn't.'

He stood and rested his hands on my shoulders. 'How about we talk about this tomorrow?'

I nodded, too tired now to even reply. 'Goodnight,' I managed, gave the dog a quick pat and headed upstairs.

Less than five minutes later, I was under the covers and dead to the world.

11

The following morning, Ned greeted me as if I'd been on a six-month trek to the Andes.

'Hello! Hello!' I laughed as I patted his side, which led him to flop down and expose his tummy to me, his whole body wiggling from side to side on the polished oak flooring. Crouching beside him, I gave him a thorough tickle as I chatted away quietly.

'That's you set for the day.'

'I can think of worse ways to spend my time,' I replied to Jesse as I straightened. He was leaning against the door jamb of the kitchen in faded jeans and a white T-shirt, mug in hand, hair damp from the shower and feet bare on the heated floor. There were also worse sights to wake up to.

'I'm just doing some breakfast. How did you sleep?' he asked as he stepped back for me to pass into the kitchen.

'Really well, thanks. I don't know what magic mattress you have, but I haven't slept this well in years. How about you?'

'Not bad, thanks. What would you like for breakfast?'

'You don't need to wait on me.'

'I know. So what would you like?'

I let out a sigh. 'What are you having?'

'I reckon scrambled eggs, with mushrooms and avocado.'

'Then that sounds perfect. Assuming you have enough?'

'I do.'

'What can I do to help?'

'I'm not going to get you to just sit down, am I?'

'No.'

'I didn't think so. OK.' He placed an avocado on a cutting mat in front of me, together with a knife, and turned away to get the eggs. When he turned back, I was attempting to copy what I'd seen on various reels and videos to prepare the fruit. Turned out it was harder than it looked and none of my cuts around the avocado were matching up with where I started.

'You all right there?'

'Do I need a map or something? Why are they going skew-whiff? It's not supposed to be this difficult.'

'Show me what you're doing.'

I picked up the fruit, which by now was beginning to look as if it had picked an unwise fight with a vegetable twice its size, placed the knife in one of the grooves and began sawing.

'OK, hang on a sec. Try and move round in a smooth action rather than sawing it and keep an eye on roughly where you started. That's it, but push the knife in a little deeper.'

'I thought I was doing that but I seem to have gone off-piste.'

'Don't worry. There, you've met up with the start now.'

'One of the starts.'

'Now give it a twist,' he said, ignoring my despondent tone.

I followed the instructions and to my amazement, the two halves came apart. Admittedly, there were very raggedy edges, but still. I grinned up at Jesse, ridiculously pleased with myself. On a roll now, I placed the concave side down and put the tip of the knife near the stone on the other half.

'Wait. I think you're best off doing that with a spoon. Less chance of injury.'

'It's almost like you don't trust me,' I replied, laying down the knife with an inner sense of relief.

'Not at all,' he said as he carefully watched me remove the stone without loss of blood or digits thanks to the bluntness of the utensil.

'I've seen chefs whack the stone with a knife and twist it to remove it.'

'Yep, that's an option, although from experience I've found that method a bit hit and miss but I'm no expert. I probably don't have the right technique.'

'This seems safer anyway.'

'Certainly good to start with. Do you mind chopping that?'

'No problem. Any tips for getting the flesh out you can show me or shall I just have a go?'

'It's pretty ripe so should just scoop out with that spoon easily. Some people score the flesh but whatever works best for you. I'm guessing none of those three jobs you had at uni were kitchen based?' he said as we worked alongside one another.

'How did you know?' I said, not taking offence. I was the first to admit I couldn't even boil an egg. Once I'd no longer had access to a private chef, I'd lived on takeaways, ready meals and then, as I'd earned more, restaurants.

* * *

'That was delicious, thanks,' I said, placing my knife and fork together on my plate, the linen napkin still resting on my lap.

'Glad you enjoyed it.'

'You're a great cook.'

'Nah, not really. I've just picked bits up as I went along. Had to, really. Before Alice, I mostly lived on beans on toast and takeaways and once I met her, she cooked. And before you say anything, I did offer but she enjoyed it. Cooking was her way of relaxing and her hobby as well as a way to feed herself and anyone else who happened to be in the vicinity.'

'She sounds lovely.'

'She was. A generous soul, for sure.'

I gave him a smile, not sure what else to do.

'Not that she didn't have the odd paddy,' Jesse continued with a grin.

'Nobody can be expected to be a saint.'

'Very true. But it never lasted long and was usually when she was tired or hungry or just needed to get into the kitchen and destress. Which is what led to my misstep last night with you.' He had been studying the grain on the tabletop but at this, he gave a brief look up at me through the long, dark lashes.

'What do you mean?'

He straightened, tipped his head back and blew out a breath as he stared at the ceiling before looking back at me. 'When Alice got in a huff, I'd let her stomp about for a few minutes, then ask, like I did with you last night, if she was done with her tantrum. That broke the cycle and she'd look at me, burst into laughter and get on with whatever she needed to do to unwind. Partly out of habit and partly because I didn't know what else to do, I did the same last night, but I realise now that I misread the situation entirely. You were properly upset and, quite rightly, felt my comment was insensitive and uncalled for. Believe me, I feel awful about it now.'

'You weren't to know. Let's face it, we barely know each other.'

'True. But I reckon there's a story behind those shoes because, despite your protestations about them just being shoes, the look on your face said they mean a hell of a lot more to you than that and the fact I indirectly sent you climbing the gate, ruining them in the process, truly makes me feel like the biggest shit, if that makes it any better.'

I touched his hand briefly. 'Of course it doesn't. The last thing I want is for you to feel bad after everything you've done. You weren't to know I was going to try and scale the gate. To be fair, I didn't even know myself!'

We exchanged a smile, tentatively building on the fragile ground of understanding.

'Did they belong to someone special?'

I shook my head. 'No. I bought them.'

'But?'

'But what?'

He fixed me with his 'don't try that with me' look and waited.

'I bought them when I knew I could finally afford such an extravagance again. I'd set myself a goal of reaching a particular level of disposable income and that, when I did, I was going to buy myself this particular pair of shoes to celebrate. It sounds stupid now when I say it out loud...'

'No, it doesn't. Go on.'

I swallowed and looked away for a moment, my attention focused on Ned, who had now finished hoovering up any stray crumbs under the table and was sitting next to me in the hope that either more might miraculously appear or, failing that, he'd get attention. I gave him the latter. It was easier to talk when I was looking into the soft brown eyes of the dog rather than the unusual grey of his owner's.

'The shoes were a symbol. Like once I could buy high-end designer labels again without double-checking my bank balance every hour, I'd made it. I'd clawed my way back up to the level I'd been kicked out of years previously. That if I ever ran into any of those I'd been to school with, I would no longer be ashamed, or made to feel ashamed and worthless.'

'Money doesn't make people worth more or less, Fliss.'

'No, I know.' Automatically, my hand rested on his forearm for a moment and I felt the hairs tickle my palms, the corded muscles move and the warmth of his skin. Just as quickly, I removed it and let it rest on my lap. 'If I'm honest with you, at one time I did think money defined people because that was what I had been brought up to think. All my friends thought that. It's just how it was. Obviously, I know differently now.'

'Are these the same friends who set themselves apart from you when they found out your family was no longer monied?'

'Yes.'

'Sounds like you're better off without their influence.'

'I completely agree.' And I meant it. 'But I needed to prove something to them and to the pupils at the other school. At least, I thought I did.'

'Or was it more about proving something to yourself?'

'Quite possibly. I'm sure if I'd ever taken time to go to a therapist, all of this would have come out.'

'Never tried?'

'No. Not the done thing in my family.'

'But you're able to make your own rules now. And everyone knows bottling things up never works.'

'That's true. Otherwise you end up unwittingly buying a project house in the arse end of nowhere.' I blushed. 'No offence.'

Jesse wiggled his head. 'A little taken but we can work on that.'

The skin around his eyes was crinkled at the corners and amusement danced within the bewitching irises.

A ping from his phone broke the moment and he pulled it across the table then lifted it and typed a quick reply. 'Great. Dermot the surveyor is able to get here by half eight tomorrow morning. That's quicker than I'd expected.'

'Let me guess. Someone else that owes you a favour.'

He dismissed the comment, but it was obvious Jesse did a lot for others around here and they were keen to repay what I was beginning to get the impression were a lot of good turns.

'Which means we have today free.'

'We? Don't you have work to do?'

'I do, and I was serious about what I said last night. We really are in need of a designer to help with a property that's due to be put on the market.'

'Won't your boss want to interview me? I'm not sure he'd appreciate you hiring any old waifs and strays you find.'

'He trusts my judgement. I can show you the rates and terms we were paying the previous stager, let you see what you think?'

'If you're happy working for them it must be fair terms. Your boss trusts your judgement and so do I. I've got some photos of places I've styled.' I went to stand up and retrieve my phone from where I'd put it down on the console table back out in the hall when Ned had barrelled over to greet me, but was stopped by Jesse's hand on mine.

'I already know you're going to be great.'

I opened my mouth.

'And no, this is not a pity job. This is a feel-it's-right-in-my-gut job.'

'It'll be interesting seeing us have to explain that to the boss if he hates what I do.'

'He won't.' The words were definitive and signalled an end to the discussion, at least as far as Jesse was concerned.

'Then I'd better get ready.'

A smile spread across his face, making me happier than it should have done. That, however, was something I'd unpack another time. Right now, I had a job to do. The thought fired excitement through my veins and I realised how much I'd missed my career and the sense of satisfaction I'd gained from it.

12

The house was in a tiny village, down a winding road that felt far too small for the pick-up. When Jesse pulled onto the parking area beside the house, the gravel crunched beneath the tyres, but the moment he stopped, all that could be heard was birdsong and the sea. We both pressed the buttons to release the seat belts and, as I did, I caught sight of his expression.

'What?' I asked.

'You're practically fizzing.'

'Oh, I am not. You must have realised by now that I'm the cool and collected type.'

'See, that's what I thought, but you have a habit of constantly showing me I'm mistaken.'

'Yes, well. I was until I ended up here. I don't know whether it's in the water or the air but certainly something has sent my entire being off kilter. I can only hope it rectifies itself before long.'

Jesse got out then turned and bent to look in. 'I don't know. I kind of like this version of you.' And with that, he closed the door.

'The house was built four years ago, architect-designed with input from the current owner.' Jesse explained as we entered. 'He spends a lot of time out of the country, especially as he's now partially retired. Apparently, there's brilliant golf over in the US.' Jesse shrugged at this and I had to admit, I couldn't see the attraction either. 'So, it's going up for sale. The furniture has already been shipped out to a house he's bought in the States so he wants this one staged in order to get the best price.'

'That's a sensible decision. At any price band, you're selling a lifestyle, but especially once one's into the millions with this kind of property, then staging is definitely something to consider.'

'Exactly. Do you want to have a look around?'

'Please.'

* * *

The six-bedroom house overlooked the sea and was set in four acres with a high degree of privacy, professionally landscaped gardens and a private helipad. Inside there was a balconied master bedroom also overlooking the water, which included a large dressing room and en suite with a freestanding bath. The five other bedrooms were well proportioned, with floor-to-ceiling windows making it a wonderfully light and airy property. The kitchen was the stuff of culinary dreams and an indoor swimming pool with two tri-fold doors opening onto a patio area made the package complete in its luxury.

'What do you think?'

'I think, when can I move in?' I replied, only half joking.

'I know the feeling. It's stunning, isn't it?'

I walked to the window in the living area and looked out at the sea, turquoise in the sunshine and punctuated by the odd white horse as the wind began to whip a little more than it had been earlier. I'd always lived in London and holidays by the sea had meant a beach in Aruba or Nice. But there was something more raw, more vital – despite certainly being more cold – here than any of those exotic and lusted-after destinations had held.

'Do you mind if I make some notes and take some photos? I'll need a budget to work to, of course, and if there are any dos or don'ts I need to know about before we start.'

'Sure. There's a pad of paper in the truck. I'll grab that, and I printed out a contract too. Just in case you went for it.' He grinned. 'So you can read that through before you start.'

A couple of minutes later, Jesse was back with all the paperwork as well as a flask of coffee and a small tub of home-made goji-berry biscuits.

'New recipe Jules is trying out. I'm her go-to guinea pig,' he said, offering me one. 'She knows I'm honest enough to tell her the truth.'

'Where does that leave me?' I asked and took a bite. 'Ooh, never mind!' I said, covering my mouth with my hand. 'These are amazing!'

We were sitting on the patio steps, looking out to sea but sheltered from the wind by the clever planting of the hedges and trees that provided a wind break. The sea washed the shore then drew back and gulls swooped and dived in the blue, cloud-studded sky. I sipped on the dark, rich coffee and studied the contract Jesse had given me.

'J Woods Property Development.' I read the top of the contract.

'Mm-hmm.' His eyes were focused on the horizon.

'It's your company?'

'Mm-hmm.'

'And when were you going to tell me that?'

'I wasn't sure if you'd take the position if you knew it was working directly with me. You were already concerned it was a pity offer before I'd barely said anything.'

I didn't miss his use of the word *with* as opposed to *for*. Just as he'd corrected me when the trade guys had been arriving. He was certainly not a man who thought himself better, or less, than anyone else. And that was incredibly attractive.

Felicity. Focus!

Twenty minutes later, I was officially a contractor and in my element making notes in the fresh notepad I'd been handed and snapping photos of the rooms from all angles. Ideally, I liked to come back in the afternoon to see how the light changed and if that made any difference to the thoughts I was already having. I mentioned the possibility to Jesse.

'We can do that today if you want? There's a great restaurant not far from here. We could go there for lunch, discuss what you've already thought about and come back for another look later. If that works for you?'

'It does for me but I don't want to keep you from anything.'

'You're not. This is my main project at the moment so it's fine.'

'Then that sounds great,' I agreed, buzzing with the thoughts and ideas I'd already noted down.

'I've emailed Gina, the previous designer I worked with, and asked her to send over a list of contacts and places she recommends in the area. I'm sure you'll make your own but just to get you going, if you wanted. Obviously, you don't have to use them if you don't think they can offer what you want.'

'No, that'd be really helpful, thanks. I'm not familiar with anywhere around here so it'd be great to start with a base.'

* * *

The restaurant was, as Jesse had promised, excellent. With a table at the window, overlooking the turquoise sea, life, for this moment in time at least, felt pretty good.

'That was amazing!' I said, laying my cutlery on the plate and feeling more myself than I had in ages.

'Not bad, eh? This was one of the first places I ever worked on when I started my own business.'

'The restaurant?'

'Yeah. When the current owners bought it, it was in a right state. It was a case of ripping everything out and starting from scratch. Big job, but worth it. This window wasn't here at all.'

'That view was out there and people couldn't see it?'

'I know, right? That's what I thought.'

'Is that when you first worked with the interior designer you mentioned?'

'Yes. She was a perfect fit from the start. Really seemed to have the same vision.'

'That's great. It's certainly easier when that's the case.'

'What got you into design and staging, then?'

'I'd always liked interiors and I'd been lucky enough to have experience of quite a lot of luxury homes and hotels so when a position came up, I persuaded them to give it to me.'

'So you blagged it?'

I tried not to smile. 'Not at all. I was there for years and did an excellent job, so I was clearly the right person for the position.'

Jesse lifted his glass to his lips. 'You blagged it,' he said again, amusement in his eyes as he took a sip.

I gave him a snooty look as I reached for my own glass but I knew my eyes had a smile in them too, despite my best efforts. 'Yes. I blagged it. But I can show you pictures of my work to confirm I do actually know what I'm doing.'

'I don't doubt it. I know you'll be great for this property.'

'But you have no idea of my style.'

'I've seen your bedroom.'

A woman walking past as he said these words gave me a look and a private smile that indicated she thought I was a lucky woman. In another life, I might have agreed with her, but not this one.

'It looked a lot better before the roof fell in on it.'

'Even so.'

'Also, you might want to think about rephrasing how you approve of my style in future, in the event that someone asks. At present, it may give people the wrong idea. I'm sure quite a few people in the village already have a skewed version of the truth.'

He shrugged the wide shoulders. 'I've told Alice's parents the situation now. I'm not too fussed about what people in general think. Are you?' he asked, folding his arms across his chest.

'No. Not particularly. But also I don't want people to think I got the job by sleeping with you.'

'Believe me, nobody would think that. They know me too well.'

'What does that mean?'

'Can I get you anything else?' the waitress asked.

'Just the bill, please.'

'No problem. Two secs,' she replied and headed off to get the card machine.

I pulled my bag from the chair onto my lap.

'I hope you're not thinking of trying to pay.'

'Half. Yes.'

'No need. It's a business meeting.' He pulled a card from a slim metal wallet. 'Company credit card.'

The girl returned, he checked the bill, tapped on the screen a couple of times, I assumed to add a tip, and then held the card against it for a moment. The waitress smiled widely. I guessed she'd seen the tip now and handed him the paper receipt that chugged out from the machine.

'Thanks very much. Have a lovely afternoon.'

'Thanks,' Jesse replied as we prepared to leave.

'Jesse Woods, is that you?' a disembodied voice called, followed shortly by a tall, willowy brunette. 'I hope you weren't planning to visit and not stop to say hello.' Her hand went to her hip, but the smile was wide and dark eyes full of laughter.

'Marie! I didn't realise you were here. How are you?' Jesse's smile matched hers and his strong arms wrapped around her in a hug.

'I'm great, as you can see!' She laughed, her hand flowing down her body as she did so. And she was right. 'You're not looking too shabby yourself.' Her gaze moved to me. 'Is that because you're finally dating? Thank goodness for you!' she said, laying a hand on my arm. 'Such a waste of a good man otherwise, and God knows they don't come along that often. Am I right?'

'I... err...' I definitely agreed with her on the latter comment, but wasn't sure how to handle the first part. Luckily, Jesse took care of it.

'Nope. Business lunch.'

Marie took a considered look at the both of us. 'Shame.' She waved her finger between us. 'You look good together.' Her accent had a faint hint of Greece.

'I'm pretty sure you'd say that about anyone I brought in,' Jesse returned, a knowing smile teasing his lips.

'True. But happily this particular circumstance...' she waved between us again '...means I don't have to lie.' She tilted her head. 'Think about it at least.'

'Felicity is our new interior designer.'

'Oh, right! I heard Gina was emigrating. Has she left?'

'Yep. I had meetings with several other designers but none of them really clicked.'

'Until now?'

'Until now,' Jesse confirmed.

'Congratulations. He's a great guy to work with. Honestly, the job he did here was amazing.'

'Yes, he was just telling me about it. It sounds like it was quite a transformation from the old building.'

'You wouldn't recognise it! And Jesse kept it all under budget and within the original quote. Believe me, that can't be said for all property developers I've had dealings with.'

'No, I agree. It's very hit and miss. Like life, I suppose.'

'That's true!' Marie said, crossing her arms and giving me another wide smile. 'I like her,' she continued, turning to Jesse then back to me. 'Are you with someone? I don't see a wedding ring.'

'Marie.' Jesse's voice was low and the warning in it was unmistakable.

I liked this woman with her open and ready smile and forthright ways.

'No,' I said with a laugh. 'But I'm not looking for anyone either.'

'Some of the best things happen when we're not actively looking for them. Isn't that right, Jesse?'

Jesse was now standing with his feet planted apart, arms crossed – mentally and physically blocking what he clearly considered to be Marie's nonsense. At her question, one brow rose.

'He agrees,' she said, turning back to me. 'He just doesn't want to admit I'm right. Typical man, you know.'

'Are you done?' Jesse asked, but, as much as he tried to hide it, I could see the light of amusement dancing in his eyes.

'For the moment. Although I expect updates.'

'There won't be any updates. Now give me a hug so we can get on our way.'

Marie flung her arms out and they hugged once more.

'Lovely to meet you too,' she said, holding out her hand and taking mine, then laying her other on top of it. 'I'd say I hope you enjoy working with this one,' she tilted her head towards Jesse, 'but I already know the answer. He's one of the good guys.'

'Thanks,' I replied. 'I'm sure I will.'

'Sorry about all that,' Jesse said when we got outside, squinting against the bright, low light of the winter sun.

'Nothing to apologise for. She's lovely.'

'Yeah, she's great. Mad as a box of frogs, but great.'

I laughed at his choice of words.

'Tell me more about this project. You said it was the first you did on your own?'

'That's right,' he replied, beeping the doors to the pick-up unlocked and opening the passenger side for me.

'Thanks.'

He closed the door, and crossed to the driver's side, his long strides quickly covering the distance. Moments later, he was buckled in beside me and pulling out of the restaurant's driveway. 'Marie's family have owned the place for decades but when it was passed on to Marie and her partner, they had a completely different vision for it.'

'How did the family feel about that? Sometimes people like others to do what they've always done, something that's familiar. Although I can imagine, having met Marie now, she's a force to be reckoned with.'

'You're right about that. About both aspects. Marie and Yanis certainly wanted to do a lot to the restaurant, but I think the way she got through to the family in the end was to bring them onboard. Show them what the plans were. Having been present at a couple of those meetings, I'm not going to say that it was an easy process for her. I tell you,' he said, glancing across at me briefly before switching his concentration back to the road, 'that family can row!'

'Wasn't that uncomfortable for you, being caught in the middle of it all?'

'Absolutely! I tried to leave a couple of times, you know, just say, well, I'll leave you to discuss this amongst yourselves for a bit, but Marie was having none of that. She told me to keep my backside exactly where it was and, between you and me, I was too scared not to!'

It was hard not to laugh at the thought of this man with all his height and muscle being verbally pinned in place by his far smaller client, but I could understand what he meant. Just from the short interaction I'd had with her, it immediately came across that she wasn't one to take any crap and I liked that about her.

'So you didn't have any disagreements about the project?'

'There were a couple of heated discussions. Marie was adamant about one particular aspect of the design that the local council overruled. She was so mad, she wanted to go ahead and have the decked terrace put in anyway, but I refused. I knew there was every possibility that if we did that, they could turn round and say it had to be taken down again. That was a fun afternoon.' He turned and grinned.

'I can imagine.' I returned the smile.

'She told me she was going to get a new developer in. One who had more balls than me.'

'Oh, wow.'

'Yep. She was spitting nails.'

'So what happened? I mean, obviously she didn't go through with the threat.'

'I kept as calm as I could, although under the surface, I was panicking like hell. This was my first big job and it was quickly going pear-shaped. I'd given Marie a couple of alternative designs for the decking that would fall within the parameters the council had decreed so I told Marie to think it over that night and, in the morning, if she still wanted to part ways, then that's what we would do.'

'She changed her mind.'

'It was emotional. She had her heart set on this particular design for the deck but she and Yanis took a walk down by the sea that evening. She said they didn't even really talk that much. Just took in the view, listened to the waves, felt the sand under their feet then went home. The sea worked its magic because that night, I got a text and we were go for the next day.'

'That must have been a relief.'

'It really was.'

'Were you angry at all that you'd got the sharp end of the stick even though it wasn't your fault?'

'Honestly? No, not really. Alice was upset on my behalf. Told me I should tell them where to stick it and that I'd get more jobs.' He shook his head. 'She always was a firecracker.'

'I'm sure it was hard for her. When you see or hear about someone you care about being undervalued...' I gave a shrug. 'It just sounds like she was being protective.'

'Yeah, she was. Half my size and fierce as hell.'

I wasn't sure what to say. 'I'm sorry.' It sounded lame but it was also the truth.

'Thanks,' he said, a faint smile touching his lips as he looked over. The traffic light was red and for a moment, the silence was all-consuming. 'She'd have liked you.'

'Sorry?'

'Alice. She'd have liked you.'

'Are you sure?'

His laugh was easy and warm, perhaps the tensions loosened by the thoughts of his wife. 'Yeah, I'm sure. We were together over twenty years so I knew her pretty well.'

'Oh God, I didn't mean to suggest that—'

'I know you didn't.' His hand rested for barely a moment on my arm, interrupting me. 'And I know we don't know each other all that well yet but I get the feeling that you're not someone who takes shit from people either.'

'No, I don't. But from what I've heard, I'm also nothing like your wife. She had it all together and got herself a good man into the bargain.'

Jesse flexed his fingers on the wheel.

'Sorry. That came out a bit... weird.'

His laugh was easy. 'No, it didn't. And thanks, but there are those who'd argue she got herself a bloke she knocked into shape.'

'Let's go with fifty-fifty.'

'If Alice were here, she might say more like seventy-five twenty-five but I'll take that.'

'So you grew up here, then, I gather?'

'That's right. Born and bred with a few diversions in between.'

'And you met Alice here?'

'Known her since school. Annoyed the hell out of me back then, little pipsqueak.' Even from the side angle I had of him, it was easy to see the love in his eyes when he spoke about Alice. The tone of his voice confirmed it. Had I ever had that look on my face when I spoke about Adrian? Had he about me? The latter was pretty easy to answer and, if I dived deep enough, I had a feeling that the first might be just as easy to answer too.

'That obviously changed.'

'Yep.' He turned his head as he pulled back into the drive of the house I was due to style and the smile on his face was beautiful. I'd never been accused of being over-emotional – although the country air was certainly having some strange effects on me. But something in that smile pierced my heart. I couldn't name it. Whether it was sadness that Jesse had lost someone he loved so very much, or the knowledge I'd never come close to experiencing a love like that, I couldn't say. I squashed down the threat of tears and planned to resume the conversation, but Jesse's single-word answer appeared to have been the last one. He set the handbrake and turned off the engine and the only noise once more was the sound of birds tweeting and the calming waves.

'You OK?' he asked.

'Absolutely,' I replied, then pulled the handle of the door, slid out of the pick-up and headed back into the house to take another look.

13

By the time we got back to Jesse's house, it felt like the end of a long but great day. I thought back over our earlier conversations as we walked to the front door together in a companionable silence.

'Was it all right to talk about your wife? I never meant to say anything that might upset you.'

Jesse turned from where he'd been about to place the key in the lock and looked down, his gaze hooking onto mine.

'It was perfectly all right, Fliss. In fact, it was lovely. Sometimes, people don't want to mention those who've gone in case it's upsetting, even with me, five years on.' He gave the tiniest shake of his head. 'The truth is, it's the not mentioning them that's more upsetting. They've gone from our lives but they're never gone from our hearts and in the end, you can be treading on eggshells for others when all you want to do is just tell them to say her name. Talk about her, for God's sake! So yes, it was more than all right.' His eyes lingered on me a fraction longer before he plugged the key in the lock and twisted.

A bowling ball in the shape of Ned came hurtling down the hallway towards us.

'Ned! Calm,' Jesse said as he stepped across, placing himself between me and the dog.

Ned made a valiant effort at stopping, paws and claws sliding on the polished wood floor before he slid almost perfectly into place on his fuzzy bum to a halt in front of his owner, who greeted him. I moved past and gave Ned a pat on his side too.

'I don't need protecting,' I said, looking up at Jesse as we both straightened away from the dog. There was an edge to my voice that I hadn't intended.

'I know,' Jesse replied, his tone easy. 'But calming down his greeting ritual is currently a work in progress. I've been bowled down like a skittle before now and I've got a lot more weight to me than you. Ned might think he's a lap dog but the scales at the vet's beg to differ. I just didn't want him scoring a strike.'

'Oh. Right. I see.' I crossed my arms then uncrossed them then shoved my hands in the back pockets of my Prada jeans. 'Umm. Thank you, then.'

'No problem,' he replied.

'Are you smirking?'

'Nope.'

I planted myself in front of him and Ned rested against the side of my thigh. 'Yes, you are. What are you smirking about?'

Jesse mirrored my stance. 'You.'

'Why?' I felt the tension weave itself back into my muscles, back to how it had felt in London. But that had been normal in my busy, always on life. But here, gradually, I realised those knots had unfurled without me even noticing. But now they were snapping right back in place.

'I've never doubted your ability to take care of yourself. That much was obvious from the moment I met you.'

'Says the man who later found me flat on my back in a pool of mud.'

'We all have our moments. That's not the point.'

'What is the point?'

'That just because you *can* do something doesn't mean you always have to.'

I thought about that for a moment but before I could dissect it too much, Jesse spoke again.

'I'm a little old-fashioned, I guess, but don't get me wrong, I know for a fact that women are more than capable of taking care of themselves. Believe me, if I'd ever had any doubts about that, Alice and my sister, not to mention my mum, would have soon disavowed me of them. But that doesn't mean I'm not going to open a door for a woman.' He shot me a look. 'When she doesn't beat me to it. Not because I don't think she can do it herself. That's ridiculous. Of course you can. It's not about that. It's not a form of disrespect. In my eyes, it's the opposite. And blocking any potential collision between you and Ned in his excitement to see us is part of that. I'm sorry if it offended you but I'll tell you now, until he's got the hang of it a little more, I'll be doing the same next time too.'

'Right,' I said after a few moments of silence. It didn't appear that Jesse had been waiting for an answer. Once he'd finished talking, he'd slipped off his jacket and pulled off the peaked cap he'd worn and put them both in a downstairs cupboard before reaching out to take my coat.

'Thanks.'

'We OK?'

I nodded.

'Good. I've got a bit of work to do. Did you want to set up an office somewhere so you can get started?'

'Oh, no. That's fine. I can just sit in the kitchen.'

'You could. But even if the house is deemed safe tomorrow, there's nowhere suitable over there for you to set up an office. The one room that was closest to being finished is the one with the hole in the roof and, even if it wasn't, it's more ideal to separate work and home if you can.'

'I'd thought about possibly making one of the bedrooms into a home office, but the garden idea was good too if the outbuilding could be insulated and have power, and so on. Not that I have a business to run from it.'

'You do now.'

I let out a small, disbelieving laugh. 'One job does not make a business, Jesse.'

'True. But I know of a few properties under my business alone that will need interior skills shortly and I'm sure other work will come up pretty quickly. Gina left a pretty big gap in the market when she emigrated. I'm sure some of that has been filled but your style is elegant and timeless and that's what a lot of people, especially around here, want. They don't want outlandish schemes or colours that seemed like a good idea at the time but a fortnight in gives them a migraine every time they go into the room.'

'I can do bright and funky when it's needed.'

'I'm sure. I can already tell that you follow the brief you're given, whatever that is, but put your own spin on it. That much is obvious from the photos you showed me. But your natural style is what I'm after. The ideas you had at the house, the aesthetic that you naturally spoke about for it, are exactly what I'm looking for.'

My arms folded across my chest again.

'Uh-oh.'

'What?' I frowned.

'You've gone into defence mode.'

'I do not have any mode, defence or otherwise.'

'Yep, you do. So let's have it.'

'Have what?'

'Whatever's on your mind. Then we can straighten that out and get on with our work.' He hooked his thumbs onto the pockets of his jeans and waited.

'You can wait all day. You're wrong.'

'No, I'm not.' He looked at his watch and I felt my arms tense even more.

'You really are terribly annoying. You do know that, don't you?'

He sucked in a deep breath. 'I do,' was the reply as he released it.

'OK, fine. I'm still concerned that this is a pity job and I'm not comfortable with it. You've already done so much, and got others to do so much, for free and... I can't repay that. I never have, and never will, accept anyone's pity or charity. It just all seems very convenient that your favoured interiors contact left the same time as I arrived in the area.'

'We already went through this.'

'We did but, like I say, I don't buy it.'

'Do you believe that sometimes the only explanation for something tragic is that people were just in the wrong place at the wrong time? That as much as you try to find a reason for something bad happening, there's just no logic.'

I paused. 'Yes, I suppose so.'

'Then doesn't it follow that sometimes someone can be in the right place at the right time for good things to happen too?'

'Well, yes.'

'Then can't you accept that perhaps you just happened to be in the right place at the right time?'

I gave a dismissive snort. 'First time for everything.'

'There you go, then. Now, let's see about an office set up for you.' With that, he toed off his shoes and took the stairs two at a time, Ned at his heels.

I blew out a sigh and followed him up more slowly.

* * *

'Do you have a laptop?' Jesse asked as he entered one of the spare guest rooms.

'I do, but it's in the house.'

'Right. Well, we'll see tomorrow if that's accessible.'

'Jesse, it has to be. Even if they need to tear the whole bloody place down, I need some of my things.'

'Then maybe you should have grabbed that when you ignored my warning and sneaked back in.'

I looked up sharply, ready to engage. His smile took me off guard.

'That's a hell of a battle face.'

I tried not to smile back. 'And don't you forget it.'

'Believe me, even if I wanted to, I couldn't.'

For a moment, I wondered if there was another layer to that sentence, a deeper meaning, but then I gave myself a good kick up the arse back into reality. For one, it was obvious this man was still in love with his wife and, secondly, I did not need a man. Every crappy situation I'd ended up in in my life was as a direct result of a man – my father, my ex-fiancé, my ex-boyfriend. From the short time I'd known him, it was clear that Jesse was a way better man than any of those. He wasn't the type to let someone down, especially not someone he loved. I knew already that he'd walk through fire for his loved ones. The amount he'd done for me, a stranger, was beyond anything any of my so-called friends, and certainly my father, had ever done. But I had a feeling that being let down by this man would be worse than all the others put together.

'Hey?' He tilted his head to the left.

'Sorry, miles away.' I waved my hand.

'I know it's a lot but it's going to be OK. Anyone who's ever met you for like five seconds can tell you're someone who kicks arse. This is a minor setback, that's all.'

I stared at him for a second and then the laughter exploded, loud, easy and unrestrained.

'Buying a disaster zone of a house, having a tree total its roof and my car is a minor setback? I'd hate to hear what you call a major one.'

'Those are all things that can be fixed.'

'Yes. I suppose so.' Suddenly, I didn't feel like laughing any more. 'Sorry.'

But Jesse had already reached for my hand. 'No, don't be.' His smile was gentle as his fingers wrapped around mine and squeezed the tiniest amount. 'And now I'm sorry I said anything because it's so good to hear you laugh. You should do it more often.'

I pulled my hand away as gently as I could and shoved it in my back pocket.

'I think there's every chance it was hysteria rather than amusement, now I come to think about it,' I said.

He turned away and moved an ottoman that was sitting beneath the window to a space at the end of the bed. 'What do you think about that there?'

'It looks good. But why have you moved it?'

'This space would be perfect for a desk.'

'Jesse.'

'Felicity.'

'I can manage... somewhere. The bedroom I'm using, for example.'

'It doesn't have the room for a desk.'

'It could do. We could move the dressing table from there into this one and then put a desk in the same space.' I tilted my chin triumphantly.

'True. But then what happens when you want to close the door on work? Bedrooms are supposed to be room for rest and...' He hesitated. 'Not work.'

'I'm more than happy to work all hours right now, bearing in mind I might never get a job in that field again.'

'I'm sure you would have.'

'You don't know my old boss. He's not exactly the forgiving type and he has a *lot* of connections.'

'Then it sounds like you're best off out of it.'

'Hard to think that when your savings are draining every day.'

'Always hard to see the light when you're in the darkness. Right, the desk is going in here. I'm not having you sit up late into the night when you should be getting rest. Now, what style do you think will fit best in here?' He stood back, looking at the space he'd freed up.

I mirrored his stance. 'Something period to go with the house but not dark.'

'Exactly what I was thinking. The salvage yard down the road has some beautiful pieces.' Jesse checked his watch. 'Want to go and take a look now? We still have time but say no if you want. It's been a busy day already. We can always go after we see Dermot tomorrow.' He looked around. 'How do you feel about giving the whole room a bit of a refresh as you'll be spending time in here?'

Excitement bubbled within me and I knew Jesse saw it. The glint of humour in his eyes, the slow curve of his mouth. But I knew instinctively that he was laughing with me, not at me and never would.

'Let's go.'

* * *

A couple of hours later, an antique limed-oak roll-top desk sat neatly bathed in the final rays of evening light from the window. Added to that was a powder-blue dressing-table chair, which toned perfectly with the new toile de jouy curtains and throw cushions. We'd compromised on getting this one by literally pinkie-promising in the shop that if I got neck or back or anything else ache from sitting working on it, it would be changed for a more ergonomic one. A 1930s brass, shell-shaped lamp stood on top, adding a soft pool of light. It was perfect.

'What do you think?' I stuck my head out of the door and called to Jesse. I'd just finished styling a couple of other bits I'd picked up together with a bunch of fresh flowers I'd bought from a stall we'd passed on the road.

A couple of moments later, he was jogging up the stairs. I stood in front of the door, aware that I was really no obstacle, but it was the principle.

'If you don't like it, you have to tell me, OK?'

'I will.'

'It's your house so you need to be 100 per cent, even though we can move it out again once I'm gone.'

'I might keep it there for a while. It looked pretty good when we positioned it earlier.'

'Hopefully, you'll think it looks even better now.'

'Can I come in yet?' he asked, his expression a mixture of exasperation and amusement. I didn't know him well enough yet to be able to tell which one was winning but if I'd had to put money on it, I'd have gone with exasperation.

I stepped back and opened the door. The bedside lights were lit, along with the one on the bureau, casting a soft, ambient light over the whole scene. It was the first time I'd styled anything other than my half-finished bedroom since I'd thrown in my job and I'd realised not only how much I loved it but also how much I wanted Jesse to love it too.

He didn't say anything.

'You hate it,' I said as a balloon of disappointment deflated in my chest with full farting sound effects to complete the feeling of failure.

'No!' He turned, his hand going to my forearm. 'No! I love it. Honestly, I wasn't sure if the lamp was going to work with it but it's brilliant. The whole thing ties in with the rest of the room perfectly too. This is definitely staying even if you don't.'

The cool, calm, possibly resting-bitch face that I'd cultivated over the years went out of the window, as it seemed to be doing far more often since I'd moved here. I beamed up at Jesse.

'You really love it?'

'I really do! Believe me, I'm not this good an actor.'

'Thank you.' My face was beginning to ache now but I couldn't seem to turn the smile wattage down. 'So you're not regretting your decision to bring me in as your interior designer on the property.'

'I wasn't regretting that anyway.'

'At least now you can be sure.'

'Like I said. I already was. Do you like it?'

'This?' I scurried over and plopped myself down in the pale-blue chair. 'I love it!'

'Good. There's Champagne in the fridge. Let's go and celebrate.'

'Why is there Champagne in the fridge?'

He gave me the head tilt again. 'Oh, Fliss. There should always be a bottle of Champagne in the fridge. You never know when you might need it.'

I was really beginning to like this man. If I was honest, perhaps a little too much. Even when I was arguing with him, I felt a connection to him that I hadn't felt with anyone for a long time. Not since Nanny. She'd been the only person in my life who'd made me feel as though just being me was enough. Now, decades later, I got that feeling once more with a man I hardly knew but wanted to know better. And that was kind of scary.

'You've got a strange look on your face. Everything all right?'

'Absolutely,' I replied, shaking the feeling off and stuffing it in a corner of my mind to be dealt with another time. 'Lead the way.'

14

Jesse and I watched as Dermot the surveyor walked towards us, clipboard in one hand, bright-yellow hard hat on his head.

'Oh God, I feel sick,' I whispered.

'Let's just see what he says first.' Jesse put an arm around my shoulder, gave a quick squeeze and then dropped his hands back to his sides. Which was probably for the best.

'Do you want the good news or the bad news?'

'The good. If there is any,' I replied.

'The good news is that the house doesn't need to be torn down.'

That wasn't even something I'd considered so I didn't especially see this as news. Obviously, it was good. Extremely good considering the bloody thing wasn't insured. Otherwise I might have been happy to take the money and run.

'And the bad news?'

'Although the house is technically safe, it's pretty obvious that it isn't liveable. When the tree came through the roof, it also took out the water tank in the attic so there's no chance of a heating system working for a bit, plus, from what I can see, the bedroom that took the biggest hit was the one room that appeared to be in the best state of repair before the storm. I assume you've been living elsewhere while the renovations are being done?'

'No. I've not long bought the place and I've been living here.' I looked up at the house. 'Briefly.'

'Oh. I see. Is there somewhere you can stay while the roof is being repaired at least?'

'Yes.' Jesse answered before I had a chance.

'Good. Good,' Dermot continued, tapping at his clipboard. 'There's a few things I need to go through.' He looked up at the sky, which, in contrast to yesterday's blue, today was a heavy pewter grey and was now beginning to deposit large, fat droplets of rain. 'Shall we meet up at Julie's and discuss it? Things are always better over a cuppa.'

The only way I could imagine making this better was to pour gin in the teapot, but that approach had been what landed me in this predicament in the first place. And there was, as Dermot had said, some good news. It was the bad news I was more concerned about.

Jesse and I headed back to the pick-up and drove past my pancaked car.

'Have you heard from the insurance company yet?'

'The money should supposedly be in my bank this week apparently. They can't say when exactly.'

'That's good though. Car shopping next on the list, then?'

I let out a heartfelt sigh. 'Yes. I suppose so.'

'The enthusiasm is rolling off you in waves.'

'Yes.' I gave a small laugh that was half air and little humour. 'Sorry. Yes, it's definitely next on the list. I'll start looking when we get back.'

He glanced over as he drove down the driveway to the house, even more rutted since the heavy crane had been brought in.

'I'm not rushing you. Just making conversation.'

'No. I know. Sorry.'

'Nothing to apologise for. You've got a lot on your plate. Talking of good news, I had a chat with the sheep farmer Joe had ordered those sheep from. He's agreed to cancel the deal in good faith, bearing in mind the circumstances.'

'He has?'

'If that's what you want.'

'Definitely. Chickens are my limit at the moment, I think!' I said with a relieved laugh. Pat and his wife had offered to see to the hens when they came up with Maisie to see Honey until I was back home so that was one worry off of my mind.

'That's fair enough. Baby steps. You can always reassess the sheep situation when you get more settled.'

'You say that like it's a certainty, which is interesting bearing in mind the state of things right now.'

'It'll all work out. You'll see.'

We rode the rest of the way in a comfortable silence until Jesse pulled into a space outside his sister's café behind the surveyor's car. Now that the heavens had well and truly opened, we made a mad dash to the door.

Inside was warm and cosy with the fuggy, comforting scent of baking floating on the air. Julie waved as she saw us come in then turned and continued prepping the order she was working on.

'Just an excuse to pop in here, I reckon,' Jesse said as we sat down at a table for four, opposite Dermot.

'How did you know?' he said with a smile. 'Spent hours doing that rain dance last night.' He grinned. He had a boyish-looking face but the smattering of grey at his temples suggested he was older than he first appeared. I knew from the fact that Jesse had chosen him he was experienced and someone to be trusted.

'Hello all!' Julie rushed up to us. 'How's things? Are you here to look at Fliss' house then, Dermot?'

'Hi, Jules. Yep, that's right. Bit of a state, eh?'

She placed a hand on my shoulder and gave a little squeeze as her brother had done earlier. 'Luckily, Fliss wasn't hurt though. That's the important thing.'

Yes, that's the important thing...

Jesse shot me a look as if reading my mind.

I offered up the expected smile and stayed silent.

'Now, what can I get you?'

We placed our order and Dermot proceeded to show us his full findings and lay out his thoughts. As he continued, my brain came off the rails and began a three-word chant, making it difficult to concentrate.

So much money!
So much money!
So much money!

Money, which was dwindling. Yes, I'd made a killing on the London flat, but it couldn't sustain me forever and as Dermot's list grew, including things that should have already been done before I'd bought the house and had clearly either been skimped on or missed entirely, the potential bill was rolling out in my head like a cartoon till roll. As my eyes glazed over, I felt the lightest touch of a hand, just above my knee. Hesitant but there. I looked across and met Jesse's questioning eyes. My smile was automatic and the weight of his hand increased.

I unballed the fists I hadn't even realised I'd made and laid them flat on the table. My hands were bereft of jewellery and I realised that they had been ever since that fateful meeting with Jesse in the DIY shop. I'd taken off the rings I'd bought myself over the years and headed out to buy wood, practically brained Jesse in the process and that was the last time they'd been on.

Once I'd noticed every little thing about my appearance, because those in the circles I'd mixed in would be noticing every little thing too. But here nobody seemed to care. Or at least I didn't feel as scrutinised amongst these relative strangers as I had amongst my friends and colleagues.

'So, that's the main rub of it,' Dermot concluded.

I nodded because that seemed like the right thing to do, but my head was swimming with numbers.

'Thanks for coming out so quickly, Dermot,' Jesse replied, his fingers tightening just enough on my leg to kick away the panic. 'We really appreciate it.'

'Not a problem,' he replied and drained the last of his cappuccino before wiping away the foamy moustache it had left him with. 'It was good to see you again, Jesse, and to meet you, Felicity. Although of course I wish it hadn't been under such dramatic circumstances, but with this man on the case, you don't have to worry.'

A faint blush touched Jesse's cheekbones as he dipped his head and fished in his pocket with his free hand for his wallet.

'I'm getting this,' I said.

He turned to argue, then, seeing my face, thought better of it. He was learning.

'Right, I'll leave you to it. I'll send over the full report later today. Tomorrow at the latest so you can get it in to the insurers.'

'That's great, thank you so much,' I said, brightly, standing and holding out my hand for Dermot to shake, which he took, puzzlement now creasing his face, the cogs whirring.

'It's not insured, is it?'

'Nope,' Jesse replied as he too shook the man's hand.

'Can I ask a question?'

'Yes.'

'How come you're smiling?'

'Well, it's either this or full hysteria, so right now, I'm going to keep trying to pull this off for as long as I can.'

'That makes sense. And I wish you all the best with it. I'm sure I'll see you again before too long but if there's anything I can do in the meantime, don't hesitate to shout.'

'Thanks, mate. Appreciated,' Jesse replied.

Dermot gave a final wave and dashed to his car in the still biblical rain.

* * *

'How are you feeling?' Jesse asked as we retook our seats for a moment.

'A little shell-shocked, I think, but I'll get over it.'

'You will.'

'Thanks. I mean... for...' I shrugged one shoulder.

Highly articulate, Felicity.

'You're welcome to stay at my place for as long as it takes.'

'Oh no!' I said, finding my voice again. 'I couldn't possibly do that.'

'Why not?'

'I... I just couldn't. Dermot has confirmed it's not going to fall down around my ears now so I can move back in now.'

'In where?' Jesse asked. 'The one room that was partly habitable is now the worst of them all!'

'Yes, thank you for pointing that out.'

He pinched the bridge of his nose. 'Sorry. It just doesn't seem like the best idea. You're going to be cold. There's no heating or running water at the moment, for a start.'

Bugger. I'd forgotten that.

'Look,' Jesse said, 'how about a compromise?'

'Go on.'

'As the tree took out your water tank and the boiler is nearly as old as the house, it could be a good opportunity to replace it with a combi. It doesn't need a tank so that's one less thing to think about replacing and it'll be more efficient. How about you stay until that's done at least?'

I fiddled with the salt cellar as I thought about it. Annoyingly, he did make some excellent points.

'If it's taking you that long to think of an excuse to say no, why don't we just agree on that for now?'

I looked up at him with a flash of irritation but all it did was make him laugh. 'That's settled, then,' he said as his sister walked over to the table, a piece of paper in her hand. 'You all right, Jules?'

'Umm, yeah. I think so. This just came.' She handed him the paper to read. As he did so, a wide smile broke on his face.

'Nominated for Best Small Business in the County award?' He stood and swept his sibling up in a huge hug. 'That's fantastic!' Jesse stood back, having now placed his sister back on the floor. 'How come you don't look more pleased? This,' he waved the paper, 'is great!'

'It is! I know. And I'm thrilled. Just a bit shocked, I guess.'

'And?'

'And what?'

'I know you, remember. There's something else.'

'What is it?' I asked, pulling out a chair at our table. She plopped down into it and looked at Jesse, who'd now retaken his own seat, then me.

'These awards. They're quite fancy.'

'Good excuse for a new dress.' I grinned.

'That's the thing. That's not really me. I don't do fancy. What would I do with a pricey dress? I'd probably only wear it that once. And then there's my hair—'

'Which is beautiful.' It was the truth. Thick and dark like her brother's but, unlike his short crop, Julie's tumbled down her back in soft waves, although most of the time, she kept it pulled back in a low ponytail.

'I'm not sure I can go. It's too much expense for one night. I might not even win anyway!'

'Of course you're going to win. And you have to go!' Jesse frowned.

'I don't have to do anything, thank you,' she snipped back.

'It would be a shame not to go, Jules,' I said, the familiar term coming naturally as I stepped in as mediator, 'and I think I've got a plan.'

The siblings both looked at me, expectant. Hope showed in Jesse's eyes, nerves in his sister's.

'As you were kind enough to lend me some clothes when the sky fell in, how about I return the favour? I've got plenty of outfits that would be perfect for that type of event and you'd absolutely rock them.'

'Oh no, I couldn't. If you wear Armani to clear out a shed, I dread to think how much your dresses cost!' She was half laughing but it was clear she meant the comment.

'The money is already spent, Jules, and right now they're just hanging there looking unloved. I'd love it if you'd take one to wear. There are shoes too if you'd like. You could come and choose something or I can bring a few over to you that I think would suit you so you can try them on without freezing your arse off as there's no heat at my place.'

'Are you sure you don't mind?' Jules asked, some of the earlier tension beginning to melt away.

'Not at all. I'd be thrilled at the opportunity to help.'

'I don't suppose you could give me any make-up tips while you were at it, could you?' Her hand went to her face. 'I only ever wear a tinted moisturiser, maybe mascara if I'm feeling fancy.'

I grinned. 'I can do better than that. You'll be red-carpet ready by the time we're done.'

Jules' hesitant smile began to widen as she looked at her brother.

'You shall go to the ball!' he said, laughing and taking one of our hands in each of his. 'And you're going to win that bloody award!' He leant over and kissed her on the cheek. 'Well done, sis.'

Julie gave me a huge hug, wiped her slightly teary eyes and hurried back to the counter.

We both watched her go before Jesse turned back to me. 'Thank you.'

I shook my head. 'Not at all. It really is my pleasure.'

We both stood, Jesse tucked the cash I'd got out for the coffees under the condiments set, motioned to his sister about it, then took my hand and we pulled open the door, ready to sprint through the rain to the car.

'Oh. My. God.' The tones were loud, educated and unmistakable. 'Felicity DeVere.'

'Get in the bloody door, Minty. It's pissing down out here.'

Jesse's hand momentarily tightened around mine then dropped away. Araminta Montagu-Greer stepped in, followed by the owner of the male voice, who pushed the door closed behind him. A few people looked up. Jules glanced over and a coolness I'd never seen veiled her face.

'Jesse.'

'Magnus.' The one word sounded like ice. Nothing at all like the usual warm tones I'd quickly been getting used to.

'And who's this?' Magnus turned to me with interest. 'I don't believe we've been introduced.'

Minty took charge. As always. 'Oh my God, Magnus, this is like, so bizarre. Felicity and I went to school together! And now we just happen to run into each other in some rando little coffee shop!'

Then she saw Jesse.

'But, oh my, it looks like you landed on your feet after all that mess. Hello. I'm Araminta.' She flashed a winning, and likely very expensive judging by its perfection, smile at Jesse and held out her hand. I curled my fingers into my palms, hiding the state of my own nails. The last manicure I'd had seemed so long ago and by the sounds of the work that needed to be done on the house, the next one wouldn't be any time soon.

Jesse quickly took her hand. 'Hello.' He let it go just as quickly and I saw a flash of disappointment and confusion on Minty's face. She had always been used to being the centre of attention at school and apparently not a lot had changed in the last twenty-five years.

'So, what are you doing here?' she asked, her eyes still soaking Jesse in despite his coolness. Araminta never had been one to give up on anything easily if she wanted it. If that something belonged to someone else, then so much the better.

'I live here.'

Magnus gave me a confused look, then looked back at Minty. 'You never told me someone you went to school with was here.'

'I didn't know, did I?' she snapped back. 'I thought you still lived in London,' she continued, turning back to me.

'I did. Until a short time ago.'

'Well, I can see what drew you away.'

Magnus rolled his eyes and Jesse looked at his phone. I held my back rigid and refused the bait.

'I'm just down visiting,' she continued. 'Magnus is my cousin. Another cousin of ours is getting married shortly so this is all just the preliminaries. You know how it is.' She pulled a face, showing us all how bored she was by it, but Araminta Montagu-Greer had never done anything she didn't want to and I highly doubted that she'd changed in that regard.

'So how long have you two been together?' Her eyes strayed once again to Jesse before returning to my face. 'I have to say well done. Revenge is so sweet, isn't it?'

'We're not together,' I replied. From the corner of my eye, I saw Magnus throw Jesse a glance. 'And I'm sorry, what revenge?'

'Oh!' She put her perfectly manicured and expertly tanned hand up to cover her plumped lips and gave a little giggle. 'I thought you two... I mean, Adrian might be married to that heiress now, but he always did hate to be outdone. And believe me, you've certainly gone up a few leagues here.'

Mortified was an understatement.

'Sorry about all that though. I hope you're OK.'

'Perfectly fine,' I replied automatically.

'Your family and marriage don't seem to have a lot of luck, do they?' She pulled a pouty face, which I guessed was supposed to be sympathetic but Araminta wouldn't know empathy if it got up and slapped her across the face with a wet lobster.

'We'd better go, Fliss. We're going to be late.' Jesse slid the phone back in his pocket and I met his eyes. There was nothing to be late for, but he knew. He knew what needed to happen.

'Oh, that's such a shame. We should meet up.' Minty checked her Apple watch as she spoke and scrolled through a couple of messages before looking back at me. 'I'm absolutely rammed this week but I'll be down for longer for the wedding so we'll have time then. Just give Magnus your details and I'll call you. Ciao!' She tilted her head at Jesse. 'See you soon. I hope.'

Jesse gave a nod so brief, a sneeze would have been longer but Minty didn't seem to take offence. She had him in her sights and not a lot else mattered when that was the case. The result was usually the same: Minty got her way.

Jesse held the door for me and we both hurried through the rain to the pick-up and dived in.

'Everything all right?' he asked as we pulled on our seatbelts.

'Yes, thanks.' I gave a dismissive wave and flashed a smile.

And it was. Yes, I was in the middle of a personal disaster but I was making friends and perhaps really starting a new life. Maybe that was what I'd needed all along. I'd just gone about it in a rather dramatic way. But it was all good. Until Araminta had walked back in and dragged the past with her.

'Sorry if you were embarrassed. I had no idea she had relations down here.'

'Takes a lot more than that to embarrass me.'

'Good to know,' I replied.

'Do you know him?' Jesse asked.

'Who?'

'Magnus Montagu-Peak.'

'No. Do you?'

'Yes. Unfortunately.'

'Not friends, then.'

'Definitely not friends.'

I waited for the explanation but Jesse didn't offer one.

'Does he live locally?'

'Seen the big place on the hill about half a mile before you get into the village?'

'Briefly, I think.'

'That's his. Well, his parents' really, but they couldn't be bothered running it any more so live in an apartment within it and Magnus runs the estate. Or rather gets people to run it for him. He couldn't manage a business if his life depended on it. Obviously, he takes all the credit, naturally.'

'Sounds like they share a lot of family traits,' I said.

'Yeah?'

'Definitely.'

'Is he married?'

Jesse looked round sharply and the look in his eyes pinned me to the seat.

'Believe me, I'm not interested! I was just making conversation.'

'It's up to you if you're interested. And no, he's not.'

I rested my hand on Jesse's forearm. His fingers had tightened on the steering wheel at my question. 'I'm definitely not interested.'

I saw his Adam's apple bob. 'Like I said, not my business.'

'But I'm saying it anyway.'

'OK.'

Silence drifted around us and not an entirely comfortable one.

'So he basically still lives at home with his mummy?'

Jesse's laugh broke through the awkwardness. 'Yes, I guess he does when you put it like that.'

'Always a bonus for a prospective partner.' I rolled my eyes and mimed waving a tiny banner. 'Red flag.'

He laughed again and I basked in the sound, happy that the silence and the strangeness had dissipated.

'I'm not sure it's the same in the higher echelons of society? Although... sorry. That was probably out of line.'

'No need to apologise. I'm far from there these days but I suppose, like most things, it depends on the person. Even if I'd not had either of my falls from grace, that wouldn't have appealed to me. I mean, I'm sure they're lovely but...'

Jesse shot me a look.

'I'm trying to be polite.'

'Let's just say good old Magnus is a real chip off the block.'

'Ahh.'

We pulled up on the drive and Jesse switched off the engine as the automatic gate closed behind us. The rain pattered on the roof and windows of the vehicle and the view quickly became distorted through the droplets running down the glass.

'Any particular reason you two don't like each other?'

'His friends killed my wife then hired expensive barristers to try and get away with it.'

15

Jesse exited the pick-up and the sound of the door swinging closed jolted me out of my shock. I snapped my jaw shut and went to open my door but Jesse was already there, holding out a hand to help me step down. He knew I didn't need assistance, which was what made it all the more special. And right now, I was grateful for it as my brain was still busy trying to process what he'd just said.

We hurried to the front door and Jesse grabbed a package from the parcel box beside the porch before following me in. I felt around for the stair and sat down to pull off my boots. I stood and Jesse looked down at me. 'Sorry. I shouldn't have just landed that on you like that.'

'I... I'm sorry. I don't know what to say.'

'It's fine. I shouldn't have said anything.'

I grabbed his arm. 'Jesse! Of course you should. I want to understand you. I...' I cleared my throat. 'I care about you. Something as important, as huge, as that? Then of course I want to know. To try and understand. But only if you want to tell me.'

I followed as Jesse turned and walked into the kitchen, placed the keys down in a dark-green glass bowl that stood on the dresser, put the parcel alongside then took a deep breath.

'Alice was driving back from the next village after meeting an old school friend for dinner. I'd offered to take her and bring her back so that she could have a drink but she insisted. She didn't want to drink as we were planning to head off early for a weekend away in the Cotswolds the following day anyway. So I said OK, kissed her goodbye and that was the last time I saw her alive.'

'Jesse...'

'You don't have to say anything.' His hand brushed mine for a moment before resting back on the worktop, the fingers splayed.

'Magnus' lot were coming down for a weekend party at his place. Huge great Range Rover with five of them in speeding along these tiny roads. A couple of people outside the pub saw them tearing by, music blaring, shouting and laughing, and the car was weaving across the road.'

He turned and rested against the sink, his gaze on a point on the horizon but I could only guess what his mind's eye was actually seeing. I doubted it was the bucolic scene outside the window in front of him.

'Alice never stood a chance in her little Fiat. I'd suggested she take the pick-up but she always said it was too big and she loved that car. She'd been so proud when we'd picked it up. Baby blue with a white interior. I swear she was happier the day we picked up that stupid car than she was on our wedding day.' He let out a laugh but it was one without even the thinnest layer of humour masking heartbreak. 'Not that it would have made much of a difference. At least, that's what the report said.' He swallowed hard. 'The Range Rover came up behind her and started beeping and flashing its lights for her to get out of the way, apparently. They denied all that, of course. But Jason was working in the field that backs onto the lane. He's got this ridiculously big tractor. We all took the piss out of him for it, but it turned out the joke was on us because it meant he saw the whole thing.' He dipped his head and rubbed Ned's head. The dog leant against his master's leg, apparently sensing something was wrong. 'Not that I would wish that on anyone,' he finished quietly before turning and sliding down the cabinet door to sit on the floor so that his dog could get closer. Jesse fussed him as he continued.

'It's a one-lane road so where the hell they thought Alice was supposed to go, God knows. And she never drove particularly slow so what speed they were doing... Jason reckoned a good eighty.' His teeth were gritted, his jaw tense and set. I wanted to tell him he didn't need to tell me, that I hated seeing him so upset, but I also wanted to know. I wanted to know everything about him.

'Anyway, when they got to a passing place, the moron driving went for it. Of course, it was never going to end well. Had it been any of the other places, she'd have probably just gone into a ditch. Not ideal, obviously, but, you know...'

I met his eyes as the stormy gaze briefly lifted. I knew.

'But the place he tried to pass her was more open. At least at the edge. As he went into the passing place to overtake, he quickly ran out of space and immediately came back onto the road again right alongside Alice. The force sent her car flying, literally. It landed on the driver's side and rolled three times before it hit a tree.' He cleared his throat. 'The coroner said she was most likely killed at the first impact when it landed, which is something, I guess. I can't imagine how terrified she was in those moments and the sooner that ended was for the best.'

'Oh, Jesse, I'm so sorry.'

It sounded so impotent. *Sorry*. The same word you use when you step on a toe, or accidentally nudge someone's elbow. Society can invent ridiculous words like 'chillax' and give the credit of 'word of the year' to a laughing emoji but when the worst thing in the world happens to someone you care about, the only words you have in your arsenal are 'I'm sorry'.

'I know.' He made the reply without looking up, which I was glad for. His focus was on the loyal dog so he didn't see my eyes washed with tears for a woman I'd never met and her broken-hearted husband.

'They actually tried to drive off, would you believe?'

'What?' Shock and disgust wrapped themselves around the word.

He looked up now. 'I know. Unbelievable. By this time, Jason had called the police and motored down there in his tractor and blocked the road so they weren't going anywhere. When Jason got out, he could smell the alcohol on the driver, well, all of them really, but they said they'd just taken a swig now because they were all in shock.' His teeth were gritted again now. 'Cowards. Lying bastard cowards.'

I got up from the chair and sat down on the floor near him. I wasn't sure if it was the right thing to do. He was talking about his wife, a wife he had loved very much. But when I did, he reached an arm around me and scooted me closer on the floor next to him.

'Are you sure you want to hear all this?'

'If you're sure you want to tell me.'

'Yeah. I do.'

I stroked Ned's head, now lying in Jesse's lap as his owner's hand rested on the dog's back.

'By the time the police turned up, Magnus' parents had arrived as well and, of course, Magnus and his father tried to get it all swept under the carpet. A few years prior, it probably would have worked too. It's amazing what money can do.' He flicked his gaze to me. 'Sorry. I don't mean to imply that you or your family would have...'

'Carry on.'

'It went to court. There was no way on God's green earth that I was letting that bastard walk. He killed Alice just as if he'd put his hands around her throat. The difficulty was proving it. Once they'd swigged the drink, it was harder to prove and the driver refused the breathalyser. They were all guilty as far as I was concerned but they played the victims.'

'The victims? How on earth could they do that?'

'Claimed that they were being victimised by the locals, that it had been Alice's fault, that Jason hadn't seen anything and had made it all up then threatened them. Although the last bit is true. He did threaten them but he'd just come back from what was left of Alice's car and saw them trying to drive away.'

'What did he say?'

'That if they tried, he'd drive over their car with his tractor with them in it. And at that moment in time, he probably would have. He and Alice went to school together and were good friends.'

'It must have been traumatic for him.'

'Yeah. Horrible. It took some work but a few of us talked him into going to therapy and that seemed to help, thank God.'

'They didn't get away with it?'

'No. Blood samples were taken at the police station and, despite the amount of money all their families, plus Magnus and his father, threw at the case, it ended up pretty clear cut. The driver was eventually found to have been three times over the limit plus high. It's likely they all were but the rest of them wriggled out of any charges. Basically threw the driver under the bus.'

'Nice. And the driver went to prison?'

'Yes. Fifteen years and a hefty fine. Not that the fine was

anything. Pocket change to people like that. I doubt he'll do the whole term. There were a couple of appeals but it was upheld. Which is probably just as well.'

He turned to look at me. 'I don't know what I would have done if he'd walked free but it wouldn't have been good.' His gaze flicked down to the dog. 'I'm not proud of that thought and Alice would be livid with me. She was very much the pacifist.'

'But if the situation had been reversed, there's no saying that she wouldn't have felt the same. Extreme circumstances cause people to think, and sometimes do, extreme things. But I'm glad you didn't.'

Jesse tilted his head back so that it rested on the cabinet door and his eyes focused on the ceiling.

'So am I.' He blew out a breath, slowly. 'So am I.'

We sat on the kitchen floor together for several more minutes. His hand still rested around my waist, each of us having one hand on the dog. My bum was numb and I had a cramp in my leg but I was prepared to sit there for as long as Jesse wanted.

Another minute passed and he patted my leg a couple of times. 'I have something for you.' Quickly, he got up and pulled me up with him. Ned gave himself a shake, executed a fabulous Downward Dog and waited to see what exciting thing would happen next.

I wiggled my toes on the heated floor, loving that this house was always warm. Even before the heating had been scuppered by the storm, 'warm' was still not really a concept my house had yet become well acquainted with.

'This is for you.' He pointed to the package he'd retrieved from the parcel box earlier.

'Me?'

He nodded.

'What is it?' I asked, excitement fizzing within me.

'Open it and you'll see,' he replied, the smile back in his voice now.

I did as he said and tore off the cardboard. Inside was a tissue-wrapped package, which I undid more carefully. Within that lay all the stationery I could ever want for starting my new business. Beautiful paper for printed invoices and quotes. I knew from before that some people still liked a printed copy, even in these days of email and digital everything. Pastel sticky notes – how did he know I had an aversion to the neon ones? Envelopes, the most beautiful planner, three emerald-green, suede-touch notebooks with the word 'Notes' embossed in gold script lettering.

'Jesse, this is wonderful! Thank you. But I have to pay you for it.'

'It's a gift.'

'Jesse.'

'Fliss.'

'You shouldn't have.'

'I wanted to. Don't you like them?' For a moment, something in his expression wavered.

My hand automatically went to his. 'I love them. They're perfect. They're exactly what I would have chosen myself. But—'

'There is no but. You needed stationery. Now you have it. There's something else though.'

'Something else?'

'Dermot sent me over the pictures of the survey.' He pulled up something on his phone. 'Is this your laptop?'

I looked at the photo on the screen as Jesse pinched it to enlarge the image. It was of my bedroom. And there, on the water-stained and beyond-hope bedside table was my equally beyond-hope computer.

'Oh, God. Yes. I forgot I'd taken it in there. Ironically, I'd been looking up house insurance before I went to sleep.'

Jesse let loose a giggle and then sucked his lips as if to try and pull it back in.

I gave him a whack. 'It's not funny!' It was another blow and right now, I wasn't sure how many more of them I could take.

'No. No. I know. Sorry.' And then he giggled again.

'Jesse!' I snapped at him but now I could hear the laughter in my own voice. 'Stop laughing!'

'I'm not laughing,' he said, his action making his statement an outright lie.

'You are!'

'So are you!'

'Oh God, I'm a disaster, aren't I?'

His hand reached out and took mine, pulling me close. His other brushed my cheek tenderly until it reached my chin, which he then tilted up so that my eyes met his. 'No. You're not a disaster. I know you'd prefer that none of this had happened and, believe me, I wish I could make all this better for you right now, but I'd be lying if I said I wished none of this had happened because then I wouldn't have got to meet you. To spend time with you. To...' He swallowed hard, his eyes dropping to our joined hands.

'Me too,' I replied, and his gaze returned immediately to mine. His hands dropped away and brushed down the side of my body until they reached my bum, whereupon Jesse lifted me and I automatically wrapped my legs around his tight waist as his lips met mine. The kiss was tentative to begin with, but soon all reservations were scattered as my hands gripped his collar then his hair and he rested me against the cool marble of the worksurface. It was cold against my skin but the heat from this man blotted out everything.

16

'You must be Maisie?' I called as I waved to the young girl wrapped up against the chill as she brushed down the pony that had now taken up residence in the top paddock. I'd been meaning to walk down and meet her ever since I'd told Pat to get the pony back here but what with the house renovation and more work enquiries coming my way, I'd never seemed to have the time. Not to mention that any spare moment I had, I wanted to spend with Jesse, which was a novel experience for me when it came to relationships, but thankfully, one that the man in question appeared to share. However, this weekend I'd made a point of finally coming over to say hello.

Maisie kept hold of the bridle as she turned a little to face me and gave a tentative wave back.

'Hi.'

'It's lovely to meet you. I'm Felicity. You can call me Fliss if you like.' I shook Maisie's hand in lieu of knowing what else to do. I'd not spent much time around kids and had been far too focused on building a career and financial security than to give much thought to having any of my own. Forty wasn't too far in the distance and I'd come to terms with that fact that I wasn't going to be a mother. Oddly, it hadn't been that hard. Some unasked-for advice from a psychologist one of my friends had been dating had diagnosed that this was likely due to a lack of love in my own childhood. I'd sent him a haughty stare and he'd got the message, but the fact was he'd probably hit the nail on the head. So here I was shaking hands with a ten-year-old and wondering what to say next.

'This must be Honey. She's absolutely beautiful.' I gave the pony a stroke and Maisie beamed.

'She's the best. Thanks ever so much for letting me keep her back here.' She turned away and resumed her brushing of the pony's coat.

'You're very welcome.' I racked my brain for something to say next.

'I thought I might have to sell her.'

'Really?' My eyes drifted to the tack box on the ground next to the little girl. 'Mind if I help?' I asked. 'It's been ages since I got to do this.'

'You had a pony too?' she asked, enthusiasm back in her voice now.

'I did.' I picked up another brush from the box and moved around the pony's head to her other side and began slowly grooming her. 'Her name was Poppy.'

'What colour was she?'

'Black, just like the centre of a poppy.'

'That's cool.'

'I loved her so much. I couldn't wait for the holidays so that I could spend all day with her.'

'You spent the whole day with her?'

'When I could, yes. I found her very calming to be around. And a very good listener.'

Maisie giggled.

'So why did you think you might have to sell Honey?'

'The man here before you wouldn't let us keep her here any more. Mum found a place but I know it was really expensive and Dad had to get up extra early to take me over there in the morning to check on her before he went to work. It was about half an hour away from our house and they said everything was OK but when he lost his job, I overheard them talking one night when I couldn't sleep...' She went quiet. I didn't rush to fill the gap in conversation. Birdsong and gently baaing sheep from the neighbouring farm took over until Maisie began again. 'I wasn't earwigging!' Her earnest face popped over the back of the pony.

'I'm sure you weren't.' I smiled back.

'I had a tummy ache so I'd gone down to Mum.'

I felt an unexpected stab in my chest at the simple statement and quickly pushed it away, intent on listening to Maisie.

'But I'd heard them when I was on the stairs. They were worried about money and I felt bad.'

'That just shows you're a very caring person. But you don't have to worry about any of that any more, OK? Honey can stay here as long as you want.' I was suddenly eager to make sure that Maisie never worried again about having to sell her beloved pony or felt guilty for the expense.

'Thanks.' There was a pause. 'Dad said you were nice.' She moved to the pony's nose and as she did, something over my shoulder caught her eye. 'Hi, Jesse! Hi, Ned!' Maisie bent down as Ned hared over and began wiggling his bum in delight at the attention, both his reaction and Maisie's giggles making me smile.

'Hi, Maisie. Honey settling in?' Jesse asked, giving the pony a quick pat.

'Yeah. Fliss and I were just giving her a groom.'

'So I see. Has Fliss mentioned anything about Honey's new home?'

'What?' Maisie looked between us, her face suddenly creased with concern, and I could have kicked him.

'No! It's good news!' I said, hurriedly, wrapping an arm around her shoulder. 'She's still going to be here, just in a better stable.'

'A better one?' the little girl asked, still slightly wary.

'Yes. Do you want to come and see?'

'Oh... OK.' She looked away for a moment and Jesse pulled a face and mouthed the word, 'Sorry'.

'Everything's ready,' Jesse said. 'We could take Honey up there now if you like.'

A few minutes later, Maisie was leading her pony up the paddock towards the one nearer the house. We left the old field through a new gate Jesse had fitted to replace the old rusted one that I'd fallen arse over tit from and up into the top paddock where the mini Victorian stable block stood. The uneven flooring had been fixed and I'd given the place a good sweep out myself this morning, giving everything one last check over to make sure Honey would be as comfortable as possible.

Maisie looked from one of us to the other, her face serious. 'Here?'

'Is it all right?' I asked, my stomach knotted with unexpected nerves.

'Yeah. I mean, yes, it's great.' She peered inside and around, all the while keeping hold of Maisie's reins. 'It's got running water and proper flooring and everything.'

I looked at Jesse, confused as to why she wasn't as pleased as I'd hoped she'd be. I'd been excited getting things ready up here for Honey but I was now wondering what I'd missed. Jesse gave a shrug, clearly just as baffled.

'Maisie?' he asked.

'How much is it?' She turned to me.

'Sorry? How much is what?'

'To keep Honey up here instead of down there.' She pointed to the field we'd just come from.

'Umm, nothing. I mean...' I looked at Jesse for help. Kids were apparently more confusing than I'd thought.

'Fliss agreed with your dad that Honey can stay here free for the next six months.'

'That was the other place.'

'It's the same deal, Maisie. I promise. I just thought...' I cleared my throat. 'I knew that Poppy would have preferred this shelter and thought Honey might too. It'll be easier for you to wash her down when it's muddy and stuff too.' I indicated the tap.

'The man that was here before you—'

'Fliss is nothing like him, Maisie,' Jesse said, dropping down to his haunches to be on a better level with the petite little girl. 'She's a good person. You know, when I showed Fliss where Honey had been staying, she was having none of it! Said it wasn't good enough for you or your pony. She wanted you to have a proper stable for Honey to make it better for both of you.'

I'd begun studying my wellies – now a bright pink pair in the correct size – feeling an unaccustomed swell of emotion at Jesse's eagerness to put Maisie's mind at rest as well as stand up for me. It felt like a long time since someone had done that. Not since Nanny...

I raised my head when he stopped talking. Maisie looked at me for a moment, shoved the reins into Jesse's hand and ran over to me, her arms wrapping tightly around my waist.

'Thank you, thank you, thank you!'

Automatically, I wrapped my own arms around her. 'You're very welcome, Maisie. I'm so glad you like it.'

'I love it!' she said, tilting her head back to look up at me.

My smile was so wide, it almost hurt. 'Mind if I come and say hi and maybe help you groom Honey occasionally?'

'That'd be awesome!'

Jesse and I left Honey and her owner making themselves comfortable in the pony's new home and began walking back towards the house.

'Somebody's happy.'

'I am! She was so thrilled.'

He chuckled. 'I was talking about Maisie.'

'Oh!' I replied, laughing. 'Yes. She did seem so, didn't she? I thought I'd messed up for a minute.'

'Nope. You just made that kid's year.'

'It was your idea.'

'But not one you had to act on. That was all you. As was the decision not to charge her family anything for keeping Honey here. And don't think I haven't noticed you've been back in there with the broom again this morning.'

'Least I could do,' I said, giving him a shake of my head as though that was obvious. 'I'm desperate for a coffee. Have you got time to have one with me?'

His smile was slow and sexy. 'Always.'

17

'Watch out. Incoming,' Jesse said with a grin as we took our seats at a table in Jules' café. It was the first time since that initial incredible night that we'd been into the café together.

'What?'

'Oh my God!' Jules plonked herself down at one of the spare seats and stared first at me, then at her brother, before her face broke into a huge beaming smile. 'I knew it! I knew it the moment I first saw you together.'

'Jules.' Jesse's one-word warning was enough.

'Sorry. Of course. You know people will find out soon enough though, right?'

'Find out what?' I asked.

Julie gave me a head tilt.

'I meant what is it they will conclude?'

'That you're together. I mean, you are together, aren't you? The look on both your faces says you are.'

'I... we...' I looked across at Jesse. The truth was, after that first night, we hadn't actually got as far as what *it* was. Apart from mind-blowing and the best ever. Well, for me at least, but I was pretty sure Jesse had had a good time too. At least twice. Life with him had slotted into place in a far more natural way than I'd ever experienced. I no longer slept in the guest bedroom. The night after that first one, I'd not wanted to presume but as we'd headed upstairs and I'd taken a step towards the other room, Jesse had caught my hand. He hadn't spoken. He didn't need to. Everything was there for me to read in his eyes. Further than that, we hadn't discussed. I knew it was complicated – at least on his side. If I was honest, maybe part of me didn't want to know what he called it in case it wasn't the same as me. For once in my life, I was enjoying the moment rather than plotting out a five, ten or fifteen year plan.

'We are,' Jesse replied, unflustered. 'But,' he added.

'But what?' Julie asked.

'But I don't want our love life being the talk of the village.'

'Would I?' A hand went to her hip.

'No. I'm just saying.'

'Well, you don't need to just say. And when you've stopped being a grouch about it all, am I allowed to say I'm so happy – for you both?'

'Slow down there, sis,' Jesse said, laughing, which saved me from having to say anything. He rolled his eyes as he looked back at me. 'I even look at a girl and she's picking out hats.'

Jules stood and clipped the back of his head with her hand. 'I am not. And excuse me for wanting you to be happy,' she added, her voice almost a whisper.

'I know. Thanks. Jules?'

'Yes.'

'Can we order now?'

* * *

Following lunch at the café again a few days later, I hoisted myself back up into the pick-up before Jesse could get to the door and slid down in the seat. I'd test-driven a four-wheel-drive Mini last week and put down a deposit. By the end of tomorrow, I would finally have my own transportation again. Jesse had already said I could borrow his car but, as kind as that offer was, it wasn't the same. My car was my independence. Plus I didn't fancy pranging his shiny sports car, which, bearing in mind the state of some of the back roads around here, was a distinct possibility. Earlier, we'd just managed to avoid one pothole so deep, I was pretty sure if you looked hard enough, you could see the Earth's core bubbling nicely away.

'You look like you're hiding.'

'I am.'

'Oh. Any particular reason?' Jesse asked, turning over the engine and checking over his shoulder before he pulled out of the space and onto the main road.

'Because I need to get home and take this sign off my back.'

He briefly squinted over at me. 'What sign?'

'The one that, judging by the looks and whispers I've seen today, clearly says I'm shagging Jesse Woods.'

'Ohhh, that one.'

'Is it always like this?'

He threw me a glance that was less amused than the first.

'I don't make a habit of sleeping with every woman that comes into the village so I can't answer that.'

'That's not what I meant.' I heaved out a sigh. 'I don't even know what I meant. Sorry. I'm just not used to this. I could walk through London stark naked and hardly anyone would bat an eyelid.'

His eyes stayed on the road but I could see the grin. 'I'd definitely bat one.'

'You know what I mean. Nobody cares what anyone does so long as it doesn't affect them. Here everyone knows everyone else and all their business. It's just a bit... unsettling.'

'I know.' He put the handbrake on as we waited at a red light and then reached over for my hand. 'They'll get bored soon and talk about something else. You're still relatively new to the place. Fresh meat.'

'And you haven't dated anyone in five years.'

He let go of my hand as the lights began to change.

'Who told you that?'

'A lady two behind me at the chemist. She also told me how pleased she was but that she'd never thought you'd be happy with a city girl, added in "no offence" there, and that perhaps it's for the best as that way you wouldn't be comparing me to your wife as much.'

Jesse dragged a hand down his face. 'Jesus. Sorry, Fliss. Maybe this wasn't such a good idea after all.' He looked across. 'I have to admit it wasn't my brain doing a lot of the thinking that first night.'

'I know. And no, maybe it's not the best idea, like you say. You've had enough gossip to last a lifetime, even if it was well-meaning back then.'

Suddenly, he pulled the truck over, flicked the hazards on and turned in his seat.

'I don't give a shit what people say about me, Fliss, whether they're well-meaning or not. What I do care about is you. I'm happy with you and despite what you might have thought, frankly I'd wanted to kiss you since I first saw you flailing about in the mud in that ridiculous paper suit.'

'Kinky,' I replied, squishing the tears, kicking and screaming, back down the way they'd come. I'd never cried in front of people

Reach for the Stars

and I wasn't about to do it in front of Jesse for a second time, even if we were seeing each other.

'There's other things higher up on that particular list, but we can certainly hold it in reserve for posterity.' The sexy smile flashed briefly before his expression returned serious. 'I care about you, Fliss. I know you've been through your own stuff.'

'Losing my allowance hardly equates to losing a spouse, Jesse.'

'It's not a competition. And you didn't just lose your allowance, did you? You lost your whole way of life and everything you'd known.'

'And I made it all up again.'

He paused for a beat. 'Did you though?'

'What's that supposed to mean?'

'You made the money, sure. But you don't have any contact with your family, do you?'

'No, and I don't want any. My father made his choice a long time ago.'

'And what about friends?'

'What about them?'

'Where are they?'

I sat up straighter. 'What do you mean?'

'It's just that I've never heard you refer to one friend, or have one person visit. You certainly didn't seem keen to keep up contact with that Minty woman, although I can't say I'm sorry about that, bearing in mind who she's related to.'

'She's not a friend. Anyway, it's not like there's a luxurious country house for them to stay in, is it? And what has that got to do with anything anyway?'

'You could have met up for the day somewhere though, couldn't you? If they did come down and didn't want to stay in the village, there's bigger hotels not that far.'

'What's your point, Jesse?' I was getting edgy now.

'My point is that I think this is where you're supposed to be, and I think you know that too otherwise you'd have already found a way to sell up and hotfoot it back to London. And I don't want some busybody's gossip spooking you.'

'It takes a lot more than people's words to spook this nag. Believe me, I've heard way worse.'

His hand cupped my face. 'You are not a nag. And for the record, if I hear anyone referring to you even the slightest bit detrimentally, I will not be happy.'

'Jesse Woods, are you going all alpha on me?'

His lips tilted up just a little. 'And what if I am?'

'Then...' I leant over, my voice low '...I suggest you get this truck back on the road as soon as possible.'

Believe me, I was as amazed as anyone that I would find this a turn-on. I never relied on anyone but myself. Maybe I'd given off that vibe – or maybe I'd just not met the right men – but every time Jesse did something for me, whether that was opening a door or switching me to the inside of the pavement or – well, let's just say sex with Jesse had been a revelation in more ways than one – I got a rush of warmth through me that wasn't just attraction but something deeper, closer. With the smallest gesture, Jesse made me feel as if I was the most important person in the world and that was both a huge turn-on and scared the crap out of me at the same time.

He gave me a long look. 'I've got a better idea.' He pulled the truck back onto the road then took a left almost immediately down a heavily wooded lane.

* * *

The next few weeks passed in a blur of activity. The house was moving along and I was gaining more work, not only from Jesse's properties, but quickly through word of mouth, and the fresh diary that Jesse had given me was rapidly filling. I was now staying at my house but that wasn't to say there weren't sleepovers at Jesse's.

'I need to go home and get changed. I hadn't planned on staying last night.' More than once, Jesse had suggested that I start keeping some clothes at his, but I was adamant about keeping my clothes in situ.

'Why won't you bring some over?' he asked, looking ridiculously hot as he lounged in the bed on a rare lie-in Sunday morning.

'I'm just happier with them where they are.'

'Why?'

The truth sounded silly so I fobbed him off. Or at least I tried to. 'It's easier.'

'Going back to your house to change your clothes, having had a shower here, is easier? Pull the other one, it's got bells on.'

Laughter bubbled out of me. 'I haven't heard that phrase for ages. Nanny used to say it to me when I was trying to get away with something. It never did work.' I smiled at the memory.

Jesse sat up a little, the pure white sheet contrasting against his skin and the line of dark hair that ran down his abdomen. I turned away to continue getting changed – otherwise things were going to take a lot longer and I had things to do today.

'She's the only person you ever speak about with any affection. Whom you ever speak about at all, really.'

I brushed my hair out and then tied it into a high ponytail. 'Nanny?'

'Yes.'

'I suppose that's because she's the only one I've ever felt much affection for – or from.' I bent to pick up a pot of moisturiser from my washbag on the bedside table and Jesse hooked his arm around my waist, pulling me onto the bed.

'Jesse,' I said, laughing. 'I have things to do.'

'I can think of some too,' he replied, his darkening gaze latching onto mine.

I batted him off, still laughing. 'I mean it.'

'OK, OK. I'll behave, I promise,' he said, not letting go. 'Just stay a little longer. Tell me about Nanny. She clearly meant a lot to you.'

I dropped my gaze to my bare hands. My jewellery, for the moment, was locked in Jesse's safe. I had amassed some expensive items over the years and my house wasn't exactly Fort Knox. But the most treasured possession in that small collection was the one piece that, monetarily, was worth the least. The ring that Nanny had given me.

'I'm sure you don't want to hear all this,' I said, making to push away, but Jesse held me gently in place.

'I'm sure I do. I want to know all about you, Fliss.'

'A grown woman talking about her nanny?' I pulled a face of disbelief.

'No. A woman I care about very much talking about someone who meant such a lot to her.'

I looked up and met his eyes. 'Tell me,' he said, softly.

'What do you want to know?'

He pulled me closer and placed a kiss on my forehead. 'All of it.'

Jesse leant back against the pile of pillows and I let myself follow, leaning against his solid chest as he gently pulled out the ponytail and let my hair drape back over my shoulders.

'I don't know where to start.'

'Was she there when you came back from school that day?'

'She was. Once my father tore himself away from trying to placate Estelle for five minutes, he dismissed Nanny. She'd been with our family since I was born and he just let her go like that,' I snapped my fingers, 'without a backward glance.' Tension returned to my body at the remembered moment, the shock and pain of having to say goodbye to the one person I knew loved me, and whom I loved just as fiercely.

Jesse's arms tightened momentarily around me, his thumb rubbing gently to and fro on my forearm, bringing me back.

'We vowed to keep in touch and we did. I couldn't imagine a future without that contact. If she hadn't wanted to, if she'd wanted to cut ties after such treatment, which I wouldn't have blamed her for, I honestly don't know what I'd have done. Of course, she'd long since stopped being my nanny at that point, but I'd never called her anything else and every weekend, I would take the train and then the bus out to the little flat she'd retired to.' I closed my eyes. 'I lived for those days and I'd cry every time I had to leave.'

Jesse's embrace tightened just that little bit more.

'But she'd wipe my eyes like she'd done when I was little and told me to dry those tears and that she'd see me again soon.'

'She sounds like a very special lady.'

'She was,' I said, my throat constricting as I replied, causing the last word to crack. I dropped my gaze to Jesse's arms and drew a finger back and forth on one as I talked. 'Mother was very loving, from what Nanny told me, but I don't remember her at all. I wish I did, but then at other times I wonder if it's best that I don't so that it doesn't hurt as much. I don't know if that makes sense.'

'I know what you mean. The "is it better to have loved and lost than to have never loved at all" question.'

'Yes.'

'There are arguments for either side as you say. So you carried on seeing Nanny?'

'Yes. Until the day she died. I don't think I've ever felt so alone as I did the day she passed. She knew she was going and asked me to come over. I almost didn't go. After all she had done for me, I thought about refusing to go. Isn't that awful?' I still felt shame from those moments of doubt.

'Why didn't you want to go?'

'Because I didn't want to face the fact she was… leaving. And in my twisted psyche, for a few moments I thought if I didn't go, I could delay the inevitable.'

'But you went.' It wasn't a question.

'Yes. She had lots of friends she'd made moving out there. That made me happy. That she'd had more of a life than she'd had living with us. In truth, she could have left a long time before my father's bankruptcy. I was long past needing a nanny but she stayed anyway. I'll never be able to thank her enough for that.'

'It sounds like you were incredibly special to her. She could have left and she didn't.'

'Probably because I begged her not to. Selfish, now when I think of it.'

'No, I don't think so. From the sounds of it you were a little girl without a mother and she was next best thing. It might have been different if your father had acted better but there's nothing to be ashamed of in wanting to be loved by someone, Fliss. And when it came to it, she wanted you there, at the end. That says just how much you meant to her.'

I nodded against him. 'There's a ring in your safe. A thin gold band with an amber setting. It's not worth anything much but to me it means everything. If anyone robbed the rest, I wouldn't care so long as they left that. I usually wear it all the time but at the moment, trying to get stuck into things on the house, I'm afraid I'll break or lose it.'

'She gave it to you?'

'Yes. She always wore it. Her mother had given it to her on her twenty-first birthday and she'd worn it ever since. She wanted me to have it. She held my hand, slipped it onto my finger and held on for a few more moments. Then she patted my hand, closed her eyes and...' The tears were flowing now as I relived that heart-wrenching day. The day my heart had truly broken. If I was honest, it had never quite fitted back together the same since then.

Jesse didn't speak, just held me close and kissed my hair until I was done. After a while, he shifted position and sat us both up, turning to kiss me on the lips this time.

'Thank you.'

I wiped my fingers under my eyes. 'I probably look a complete fright now.'

But he shook his head. 'As beautiful as ever. In fact, even more so.'

I smiled back. 'I've never told anyone about Nanny.'

'Your ex-fiancé must have known about someone that important to you, surely.'

I dropped my gaze. 'No. He didn't. No one did.'

Jesse's finger caught under my chin, lifting it enough for me to meet his eyes. 'Then thank you for trusting me enough.'

Trust. That most elusive of feelings. I'd only ever trusted one person in my life, and now I'd trusted someone else enough to tell them about her.

We sat together, not speaking, for a while longer. The truth was I didn't really want to move but I had things to do and so, reluctantly, I eventually pushed away to finish getting ready.

'So, getting back to why you don't leave clothes here...'

I looked back at him as I redid my ponytail. 'It's a good job you're handsome, because you can be terribly annoying at times – you do know that, don't you?'

'Noted. And thank you. But now the reason.'

'Ugh! Jesse!' I said, sitting heavily on the bed to pull on my jeans.

Two strong arms hooked themselves around my waist and lifted me back up the bed so that I landed across Jesse's lap.

'Are you moaning?'

I stayed silent and he read my eyes.

'I didn't mean that kind but...' His eyes flashed with mischief and one hand slid under my top.

'No-o-o-o! Come on,' I said. 'We've got lunch with your sister in an hour, you've got to give Ned a run and I've got some notes to make on that new project before that.'

'You're not working today.'

'I'll work when I bloody well like, thank you.'

'Fliss, you were up until 1 a.m. working.'

'I'm enjoying it.'

'I know, but it's not healthy. You need rest.'

'You can talk!'

'Fine. Yes, I know.' He shot me a look that perfectly illustrated another reason I was short of sleep. 'But come on, tell me why you won't move your clothes.'

'Because...'

'That's it? Because?'

'Fine. I don't want to jinx it. There. Happy now?' I made to wriggle off his lap but his arms tightened.

'Jinx what?'

'This. Whatever this is. You. Me. Here.'

'You won't jinx it.' He lifted one hand and hooked his finger beside my chin, turning my head gently towards him. 'I promise.'

'I'd just rather not take the chance.'

He studied me for a moment more. 'OK.'

'Thank you. Now get your arse out of that bed and get ready or you can explain to your sister why we're late.'

'I am never discussing my sex life with my sister.'

'Then I suggest you get moving.'

18

Pete and Jules were, appropriately, sitting in a cosy love seat by the fire in the pub we'd arranged to meet at. It was a few villages across and gave us all a chance to chat with less likelihood of everyone in the room scrutinising our every move.

'They look good together.' I nudged Jesse as he closed the heavy oak door behind us. Ned sat and rested against my leg. The two had been seeing each other a little longer than we had but still had that 'new relationship' glow.

He watched them for a moment before coming to a decision. A decision he didn't share with me.

'Don't you agree?'

'I do,' he replied, his hand snaking around my waist and resting on the waistband of my Levi's.

'How come you took such a long time to think about it?'

'I didn't. I was just thinking that I hope he doesn't mess up. I really like Pete but nobody hurts my sister.'

'Aww, you're a big softie really, aren't you?' I turned slightly so that I was resting against his chest, looking up at the defined jaw, now shaved clean, and those mesmerising grey eyes that now hooked onto mine.

'If you continue to make slanderous accusations like that, I'm not going to help you on your house any more.'

'Is that so?'

'It is,' he said, linking his hands behind me so that they rested at the top of my bum.

'Then that just means you're stuck with me using your place as an office for even longer.'

'Hmm. That is true. Well, in that case, go ahead and tell anyone you like.' His smile spread and mine mirrored it as he dipped his head and kissed me softly on the lips. 'Come on, we'd better go and join Jules and Pete.'

Hugs were exchanged before we were ushered through to the dining area of the pub and settled at a table. The waitress took our drinks order and left us some menus to peruse. Ned immediately scooted underneath and curled up to doze.

'What's the latest news on the house, then?' Pete asked.

'It's fixable. Coming along slowly. The roof's done, complete with the alterations that Fliss wanted, like the extra skylight in the main bedroom. Personally, I don't think it's particularly habitable but what do I know?'

'Dermot's report was quite clear. It is entirely habitable, it's just not ideal. Now the new boiler is in though, I've at least got heating and running water.'

'Not that the heating is much good until the last few windows are replaced,' Jesse countered.

I took a sip of my white wine that had now arrived, and rolled my eyes at my companions.

'There's a lot to do on it still. I just need to go through and make a plan.'

'*We* need to go through it and make a plan,' I repeated, adjusting Jesse's words.

'Of course. You know what I mean.'

I did, but something inside forced me to clarify things. As much as I appreciated Jesse's help, I wasn't about to let anyone take control of my life again. I'd worked hard to get to where I was and, although I might have made a misstep of gigantic proportions buying the house, it was important that I knew exactly what was going on.

'Someone came in to the café yesterday asking for you,' Jules said as we clinked our glasses to friends, health and happiness.

I looked up from my wine. 'Me?'

'Yeah. Marion was in. Told me that woman who came in before with Magnus Montagu-Peak was back asking where she could find you.'

'Araminta?'

'So why did Marion feel the need to tell you?' Jesse's brow creased and his expression darkened.

Jules ignored him and continued. 'So, are they friends of yours? Apparently she told her you're close?'

'You know better than to listen to gossip, Jules.' I could feel Jesse's tension. In fact, there had been a distinct shift in the atmosphere ever since his sister had brought up the subject of Araminta.

'What? No. Definitely not close. I mean, I knew Araminta before...' Jesse caught my eye, '...before I moved schools, but I hadn't seen her since. I had no idea she was related to anyone down here.'

Had I known, that would have been enough to put me off buying in the area. But then I wouldn't have met Jesse...

'Apparently her cousin, Magnus, is very interested in meeting you, seeing as you two are such good friends.'

'He's interested in anyone he thinks might amuse him for a while,' Jesse muttered.

'Excuse me?'

Jesse sat up straighter. 'Sorry. That... that didn't come out how I meant it.'

'How exactly did you mean it?' I asked before turning back to Jules. 'And as I already stated, contrary to whatever Araminta said, she and I are far from close. I haven't seen her since school and have absolutely no interest in rekindling any acquaintance with her or any member of her family.'

Across the table, Pete downed the rest of his pint. 'I'm just going to get us some more drinks. Jules, d'you want to give me a hand?'

Jules got up but I didn't miss the dark look her brother shot her as she left. This was certainly not how I'd envisioned lunch going. We were barely five minutes in and the other couple were already making excuses to vacate the table. The mention of Araminta and her cousin had unsettled me and the usual warmth in Jules' tone was distinctly absent.

'This is going well.'

Jesse took a sip from his beer. 'Yeah.'

'So, as we've now apparently been given space, what was that comment about?'

'Nothing.'

'Jesse. I don't have time for games.' My words came out sharper than I meant them to but at least it got his attention.

His brows drew close as he turned to look at me, his normally calm expression now like a stormy sea.

'You think all this is a game?'

'Of course not! But I'm suddenly getting the cold shoulder from Jules and I don't know what I've done and now you're making insinuations that I'm likely to go and dally with some bloke just because his cousin is someone I used to know!'

Arguing was exhausting and definitely not something I'd planned on, especially after such a perfect, and emotional, morning. But arguing in a whisper while pretending to all around that everything was fine was even more tiring.

Jesse didn't say anything. I glanced over at the bar and noticed Jules and Pete surreptitiously watching.

'OK.' I put my napkin on the table. 'I don't know what the hell is going on, but I thought we were coming here to have a nice meal. I'm not sure what the point of that toast to friendship and happiness was, but I guess it didn't include me because ever since Araminta's name came up, I seem to have become public enemy number one.'

'It's not her.'

'What?'

'Your friend. It's not her. It's him. Magnus.'

'So what the *fuck* has that got to do with me and, I'm sorry, but did you miss the bit when I poured my heart out to you and told you just how shitty everyone at that school was when they found out I wasn't rich any more?'

'No.'

'Then I'd appreciate it if everyone would stop calling Araminta my friend. As I just told you all, she most certainly isn't and I have no interest in changing that situation or beginning any sort of acquaintance with her cousin. Do you really think I'd have anything to do with someone who'd been party to causing you pain, not to mention I thought *we* were seeing each other, but maybe I've got that wrong too?'

I let out a breath, took in another slowly and then let it out again.

'I think it's best if I leave you to have your meal with your sister and friend in peace. Perhaps you could explain the situation to her too.' I heard my voice catch on the last word and wanted to kick myself.

'No.' Jesse caught my hand. 'Stay. Please. I'm sorry.' His fingers curled around mine. 'I'll speak to Jules too. Now. I'll tell her. She's just being protective.'

'Then she should have asked me directly rather than ambush me at what I thought was going to be a pleasant meal.'

'I know. I'm sorry. I didn't realise she was going to do that.'

'I thought we were friends.' I did my best to keep the crushing sadness out of my tone but I knew there was no fooling Jesse.

'So did she. But then she heard about that woman coming in, calling you a close friend…'

'So, what? Because we sound similar, it means we must be close? She'd rather take the word of a complete stranger over someone who's supposed to be an actual friend?'

'I know! Look, let's start again.'

'Is it worth it? To be honest, right now I just want to go home.'

He looked down at the table then back at me. 'I can understand that and, if that's what you want, I'll take you.'

'I don't mean your house. I mean home.'

His eyes narrowed just a little. 'Your house?'

'Yes.'

'I thought you were staying tonight.'

'I know. I've changed my mind.'

He took in a deep breath before speaking. 'You know what, maybe you're right. This has been a disaster and we've only been here ten minutes. Maybe it's safest just to cut our losses now.' I wasn't sure if Jesse was referring just to the meal or our fledgling relationship and my pride wasn't about to let me check.

'I agree.' I kept my voice even and my back straight, just as Nanny had taught me all those years ago.

Don't let them see they've hurt you, love. They don't deserve to know.

I felt Jesse's eyes on me but I refused to meet them.

'Can you give me a minute to talk to the others?'

'Of course.'

How had everything gone so wrong in such a short space of time? When we'd come in the door, Jesse and I had been almost as one and now we were conversing like over-polite strangers.

He stood from the table and headed for the bar and I took a sip of my wine more for something to do than because I wanted it. It tasted sour in my mouth now, along with what had once promised to be a wonderful day.

I kept my head turned away from the direction that Jesse had strode off in and pretended to take an interest in the polished brasses tacked to the beams above me.

'Fliss?' Jules' voice was soft and I turned as she sat beside me. I kept my expression neutral. 'Sorry. I didn't mean to come across so hostile.'

'It's fine.' I gave her a smile but even I knew it hadn't reached my eyes. 'It's perfectly understandable you'd be protective of your brother, just as he is of you.'

'Yes.' She rolled her eyes but no one could mistake the love in them for her sibling. 'He's already told Pete if he hurts me, he'll be in the foundations of the next house he builds. Good job he's joking. I think.'

I did the smile again and hers slid from her face.

'Oh God, I'm really sorry about being snippy. I just thought...' She looked down at her nails, painted a vivid peacock green that went wonderfully with her dark looks. 'I don't know what I thought, if I'm honest. But I do know I should have spoken to you first before I said anything. That's what friends do.'

I'd begun to let my attention drift but at her words, I met her eyes.

'I'm a shitty friend, aren't I?'

'Not at all.'

'Obviously, I am, because you're doing that "being terribly polite" thing that people do when what they actually want to say or do is frowned upon in public. But go ahead. I deserve it.'

I felt a chink in my defence and the palest hint of light shine through.

'No, Jules, you don't. You were looking out for your brother. That's all.'

'I know, but I judged you in a way that I wouldn't someone I'd known for longer, or that grew up around here. That wasn't fair and I'm really sorry.' She tentatively laid a hand over mine, which had been clasped together neatly on the table in front of me the whole time. 'Can we start again?'

'Funny, your brother suggested the same thing.'

'I'm assuming you said no to him, bearing in mind he came over with a face like thunder to tell us you were leaving and that he's spitting mad with me because of it.'

'What? No, he shouldn't be. The last thing I want is for you to fall out because of me!'

'He should be angry. If it had been the other way around, I'd have given him a hefty kick by now.'

I gave a weak smile, knowing that much at least was true.

'I told him I'd fix things. I'm really sorry, Fliss.'

I nodded before looking back up at her.

'I'm starving.' A smile edged onto her face and this time mine reached my eyes.

'Me too,' I replied, moving my menu across so that we could both share it, our tummies rumbling as we scanned the delicious selections.

19

A few minutes later, the men were back at the table with another round of drinks and the atmosphere, thank goodness, was entirely different.

'I'm sorry it felt like I wasn't including you when talking about the house. Of course I meant us,' Jesse said quietly, reaching for my hand as he slipped back into the chair beside me.

'I know. I think I was just overreacting because I felt like I was suddenly on my guard,' I replied.

'Understandable. It was an honest mistake, but I realise now that it would have sounded like I was trying to take control because it had been in our family, or something... I promise I'm not.' He dipped his head before meeting my eyes once more, his face close to mine. 'It's been a long time since I was a "we" – it's going to take some getting used to. I would never make a decision without involving you or even think of doing so. It's your house.'

'Which you're working on for free for a reason I'm yet to understand.'

'I can remind you why later.' The smile I loved slid back onto his face and he kissed my cheek before returning to the table conversation. He took one look at his sister and pointed a finger. 'Don't.'

'I can't help it!' she said, dabbing at her eyes with the heel of her hand before tilting her shoulder in a one-sided shrug. 'I can't remember the last time I saw you looking this happy. No wonder you were so angry over there.'

'Let's forget all that now,' I said. 'Come on, let's order. I'm bloody starving!'

Thankfully, the rest of the afternoon was a complete reversal of the first part. Relaxed conversation and easy laughter. Although I understood it, and even the reason behind it, it was hard to completely forget that, as an outsider, I'd immediately been subject to a treatment that a local wouldn't have by someone I had considered my friend. Jules and I chatted and laughed but I think both of us knew, deep down, that something had shifted. I felt that, yet again, I was having to prove myself worthy of fitting in somewhere. And frankly, I was getting tired of it.

* * *

'You and Jules OK now?' Jesse asked as I climbed into bed that night, having returned to my original plan of staying over at his place after all.

'Absolutely.' I kept my tone light and breezy.

'Oh, good.'

Excellent. He bought it.

I turned to plump up my pillow and found Jesse looking at me.

'What?'

'You know I can tell when you're lying, don't you?'

'I'm not lying.'

'Yep, you are. You do this cute wrinkle thing with your nose when you fib. And your voice drops a little lower.'

'All right, Poirot. First of all, nothing I do is "cute". I'm not the "cute" type.'

'Oh, you really are. I've got a list if you want to hear?'

I kind of did but, as a matter of principle, that would have to wait.

'And, secondly, my voice is perfectly normal.'

'Fibber.' He reached over and scooted me onto his lap. 'So what's going on? Is this going to be a problem?'

'Of course not. There's no problem. She apologised and it's forgotten.'

'It's not though, is it?' There was no accusation in his tone.

'Jesse, I'm fine.' I pushed myself off and finished faffing with my pillows. 'I'm just tired.'

He leaned over and kissed me, paused a beat then snuggled down in the bed. I lay there for a moment before wriggling over towards him. His arm automatically went around me and held me close as I nestled into the gap between his collar bone and his neck, resting my thigh on his hip. He didn't believe a word I'd said, for good reason, but he was still there for me and that was enough.

* * *

Spring was now bursting into bloom. Plants once buried beneath the overgrown mess were now emerging from the earth and fighting their way through the brambles to the light. The garden was definitely a work in slow progress but I'd discovered hacking away at brambles to be a very therapeutic form of exercise.

The integrated solar panels on the new roof of the house were finally getting the chance to begin earning their keep a little as the sun shone down on Paradise Farm. If I stood back and squinted – a lot – I could almost see how it got its name. There was still an awful lot to do but the weeks were flying by in a haze of work, both on my fledgling interior design business, which was growing feathers remarkably quickly, as well as on the house itself.

Once the roof had gone on and it was warm enough to spend any length of time at the property not huddled under four blankets and a duvet, I'd decided to take the opportunity to evaluate what I had. Or rather what I no longer had. So much had been damaged by the rain the night of the storm, the only solution was to hire a skip and get rid of everything that wasn't salvageable. Once I'd assessed what was left, I began to realise that many of the items I'd brought with me either didn't suit what I was creating with this new property or held negative memories. A table Adrian and I had bought in Sienna, the lamps I'd bought for the guest bedroom when we'd had his parents to stay after we announced our engagement. I still appreciated the design of the pieces but the first thing I thought of when I saw them was Adrian. And that most definitely wasn't the vibe I was going for.

'Are you throwing those out?' Jesse asked when he saw them standing outside the front door. 'Also, good morning. You left without having breakfast.'

'I'm not hungry and good morning.' I reached up and linked my fingers behind his neck, my work-booted feet on tiptoe to reach him as I kissed his lips.

'You need to eat.' He handed me an apple.

'Thanks.'

'Coffee?' He held up two insulated travel mugs.

'Lifesaver, thank you!' I bit into the apple and took the mug he held out to me before perching on a low dry stone wall that bookended one side of the front garden.

'So?' Jesse pointed at the lamps and table. 'They don't look damaged.'

'They're not. But I don't want them any more. I was going to sell them.'

'They look pricey.'

'They were. Do you think Ray at the salvage yard would be interested?'

'I expect so. Might be tricky getting what they're worth though.'

'Unless you barter for me?' I fluttered my lashes at him.

He gave a low chuckle as he put his own mug to his lips. 'Oh no, you're not using that one on me again.'

'Funny, you didn't seem to mind last night.'

'Last night was going to happen whether you blinked those baby blues at me or not.'

He sent me a grin that made my toes curl with anticipation inside the pink steel-toed boots he had bought for me. 'Besides, it's time you took on Ray yourself.'

'Me?' My voice pitched up an octave.

'Yeah.'

'Oh... I don't think that's a good idea.'

'Why not?'

'They were expensive and I need all the money I can get to help fund this money pit!'

'Which is exactly why you can do it. You've got the drive.'

'He doesn't like me. He likes you! Please?'

Jesse swallowed his mouthful of coffee and turned to me with a frown. 'Who said he doesn't like you?'

'Well, nobody. But I can tell. He never talks to me and I'm sure he thinks I'm just a hooray from London playing about down here.'

Jesse shot me a look.

'He wouldn't be the only one. Even you thought that the first time you met me.'

'The first time I met you, I had tweety birds circling my head after you gave me concussion so that doesn't count. Ray doesn't dislike you so get that out of your head. He's just a bit shy. I've got an appointment in a couple of hours but nothing on right now other than working on my girlfriend's money pit. Fancy a ride up there?'

Jesse put out his hands to help me up from the wall and then scooped one arm under my bum, lifting me against him. I wrapped my legs around him and had the novel experience of looking into his face on the same level while vertical.

'Hello.'

'Hello.'

I felt him smile through his kiss before he placed me gently back down on the ground and hefted the three items into the back of the pick-up. The marble side table had taken both Adrian and me to lift it. Jesse did it alone.

'What are you smiling at?' he asked as he swung himself into the driver's seat and pulled the door closed.

'Nothing.'

'Liar,' he replied with a grin, then started up the truck and pointed it in the direction of Ray's Salvage Yard.

* * *

'I did it!' I said, practically bouncing back into the cab of the truck, my voice unnaturally squeaky. 'I got what I wanted for the pieces. Actually a bit more!' I flung my arms around Jesse's neck and did a little dance in the seat. 'I can't believe it!'

'Why not? Fliss, there's nothing you can't do if you put your mind to it. Haven't you noticed that yet?'

'It's not the same. Here, I mean. I'm... I knew that world. The world I was trying to get back into. How to be, how to talk, what to say. Everything's different here. And I'm different.'

'Yep, you've got a posh accent, but the rest of it? That's all you. People, for the most part, will treat you how you deserve to be treated. Do unto others and all that.'

'I didn't know you were religious.'

'I'm not. Not especially. Alice loved to go to Midnight Mass on Christmas Eve and I'd go along to that but she went periodically on her own. I don't think that particular rule has to be linked with any religion. It's just a good ethos for life in general.'

'You're right. It is.'

'Went well then, did it?'

'Yes! Ray's super nice, actually. I think you were right when you said he's just shy. But once I got him talking, he was fine.'

'So you don't think he hates you now?'

I stuck out my tongue.

'Want to know a secret?'

'What's that?'

'You know the reason Ray never spoke to you?'

'Why?'

'He has a crush on you.'

'Oh, he does not!'

'True. Told me in the pub after one too many beers.'

'Oh!' I thought about it. 'I'm sure that was just the beer talking anyway.'

'Nope. He remembered. The next time I came up here, he was all flustered and trying to apologise.'

'Why?'

Jesse gave a shrug. 'Guess he thought I'd be angry for some reason, or jealous? I don't know.'

'What did you say?'

'Told him I needed not to fuck it up because you were probably better off with him anyway.'

I giggled. 'That was very sweet of you.'

Jesse pulled a face. 'I do not do sweet. It was honest is what it was. Ray's a good bloke.'

'Why didn't you tell me earlier? Before I went in.'

'Promise not to get stroppy?'

I folded my arms and raised a brow.

'I didn't want you to know in case, you know...' He scratched the side of his jaw and made a rolling motion with his hand.

'No. I don't know.'

Jesse did a head wobble and rolled his eyes. 'In case you used it to your advantage.'

'You think I'd do that?'

'No. I don't. You're right, I should have told you. Some people would though.'

'I am not some people.'

'Like I said, you'd be better off with Ray. He's less likely to do stupid things like that.'

And then he threw me that grin that would keep me from ever looking anywhere else.

* * *

It had taken a few weeks for Jules and me to get back to where we'd been but, thankfully, with both of us wanting and working at it, we had. When I fancied a change of scene from my desk, I'd take my laptop and notes into the café and have lunch there at the discounted family rate, despite me trying to insist I pay full price. It had also been an opportunity to meet more of the villagers. They'd chat about the house, how it was coming along, and as time went on, the conversations felt more natural and relaxed. The questions weren't just about that, but also me. How was I settling in and how was the new business coming along? One couple had even asked for a card to pass on to friends who were looking for an interior designer.

I'd caught sight of myself in the hall mirror at Jesse's one morning, a hard hat at my hip, work boots on and the once carefully cut layers of my hair now overlong and growing out. I'd looked so different and in a way, it had felt as if I were seeing myself for the first time. The real me. The one who wasn't pretending to be anything she wasn't. The one who was happy to say, 'This is me, take it or leave it.' And then I'd called Ned and we'd both run to the Mini and jumped in to head out to survey another job.

* * *

'At last!' Daphne said, taking my hands. 'Come in, come in!' Jesse's mum bustled me in the door. Despite several invitations, neither Jesse nor I had felt ready for the whole "meet the parents" scenario but eventually, we'd had to bite the bullet. 'We were so looking forward to meeting you before and then that awful storm came along and then one thing and another, well, the time just goes, doesn't it? Thank *goodness* you were all right though. Jesse said at the time it was a close thing.'

'Let the poor girl breathe, Daph.'

I looked up from where Jesse was helping me off with my coat to see an older, greyer version of him striding along the hallway towards us, a broad smile on his face.

'Hello, son. Jules and Pete are already here. And you must be Felicity. It's a pleasure to meet you at last. I'm Doug.'

I held out my hand. 'Call me Fliss, please. It's a pleasure to meet you. Both of you,' I said, taking Daphne in as I spoke. Doug looked down at my hand.

'None of that here, lass. The way my two have been chatting about you, we feel like we already know you, don't we, Daph?'

'We really do,' she agreed, laughing as she snuck a quick glance up at her handsome son. 'Come on, give us a hug!'

I hugged them both, feeling the knots I'd tied myself in over the meeting already melting away. Jesse hadn't told me much about his parents, apparently in contrast to the amount they'd been told about me, but it didn't matter. They both had the same warmth that had emanated from Jules the first time I'd met her.

'Yes, yes, hello, you!' Doug said, bending down to fuss Ned. 'I expect you're looking forward to a nice bit of roast chicken, aren't you?'

Ned's ears pricked up and he began doing what I could only describe as a happy dance on the spot.

'You said the magic word, Dad.' Jesse laughed, bending down to give his dog a pat. 'Go on, boy.' He motioned towards the kitchen and Ned took off.

'Come on through and Doug can get you a drink. What would you like? I do love your dress. Isn't it beautiful? Jules did say you had wonderful style. I can see what she means now. Here, take a seat. Doug, where's that drink?'

'She hasn't had a chance to tell me what she wants yet.' He spread his hands on a laugh. 'Although I reckon this might hit the spot.' He turned back towards the fridge and a moment later had extracted a bottle of Veuve Clicquot. 'What do you say?'

'I say yes, please!' I replied, hugging Jules and Pete before taking a seat at the well-worn, long kitchen table.

'Good girl. Should always keep a bottle of Champagne in the fridge, I reckon,' he said, busying himself with glasses and I realised where Jesse had picked up the habit from.

Jesse sat beside me, his hand resting on my knee. 'You OK?' he asked quietly.

I smiled and nodded. I'd been nervous but within moments, I'd been made to feel entirely at home – but better. I'd never felt this comfortable or valued within my own family and I felt a pang as Jules said something to her dad as she helped him with the drinks. He responded, taking her hand as he did so. The love in each of their eyes was clear and I couldn't help but wish I knew what that felt like.

Jesse's hand moved to mine and I snapped out of my daze, my gaze hooking onto his. He said nothing but the gentle squeeze of his hand said more than any words ever could have.

We didn't leave until gone nine o'clock that evening, having been persuaded to stay for tea, Daphne insisting that we all must as otherwise, she and Doug would be eating leftovers for days.

'So lovely to meet you, Fliss,' Daphne said as I hugged her back tightly.

'And you. Thank you so much for having me.'

'Our pleasure, love,' Doug added as I hugged him too. 'Look forward to seeing you again soon.'

'Me too.' And I meant it. This had been one of the best days of my life. A wonderful Sunday roast with all the trimmings, and family around the table, talking, laughing, all enjoying each other's company – and I'd been a part of it. I'd been made to feel a part of it and I knew I'd never forget it.

20

'Goodness! It's like a peacock parade out there.' Gertie, one of the villagers I'd come to know through the time spent at Jules' café, bustled in and plopped her shopping bags down at her usual table. 'Hello, dear. How are you? Another warm one out there.' Spring had now merged into summer and, although some of my newly discovered garden plants were struggling somewhat, the rooftop solar panels for the heating were coming into their own for hot water.

'I'm fine, thanks, Gertie. You?'

'Oh, not too bad, not too bad. Not part of all that wedding hoo-ha up at the big house, then?' She cocked her head at the door.

'No, nothing to do with me.'

'That's a shame. Jules said you had some lovely frocks, didn't you, love?'

'Talking about me behind my back?' I asked, grinning at my friend.

'Not at all. We were discussing your wardrobe. With envy, I

might add. Do you want to try one of my chocolate shortbreads? It's a new recipe.'

'Jules, are you trying to distract me with baked goods?'

'Is it working?'

'Absolutely. Hand it over.'

The plate arrived and was as delicious as I'd come to expect from everything I'd had in the little café since I'd moved here.

'Verdict?'

Mouth full, I made a circle shape with my finger and thumb. Jules grinned and went back to serving her customers.

* * *

'Felicity?'

I looked around from where I was loading my laptop and the fresh chicken I'd got for tonight's supper into the boot of the Mini.

'Felicity DeVere, it is you!'

'Caro?'

'Felicity, darling! What a wonderful surprise. Are you here for the wedding too?' She hurried towards me with long, elegant strides on her five-inch heels and enveloped me in a hug and a cloud of Chanel No 5.

'No, I'm not. I actually live around here now.'

'You do? How perfectly marvellous! I heard you'd left the London company.'

'Oh, I'm sure you did,' I replied with amusement. Wildfire would have had nothing on that particular piece of gossip.

She grinned and flashed her eyes. I'd always loved working with Caro. She had impeccable taste, a wicked sense of humour and absolutely pots of money, which she was more than happy to spend. Caro bent closer.

'Did you really tell them to shove their job as you were going off to commune with nature?'

'Something like that. I'm not sure I used the word commune. It sounds like the tale has been embellished somewhat.'

Caro gave a dismissive wave. 'Don't worry about it. You know what people are like. Tiny, narrow little lives. But look at you!' She took my hands and held them out. 'You look amazing and, stuff that London lot, you *are* out in the countryside after all.'

'I am, and you're too kind.'

'Not at all. You know me well enough to know that if you looked like a wild woman, I'd have told you.'

'That is true.'

'You're positively glowing! The country air obviously agrees with you. I never did like Adrian anyway.'

'Yes. You made that quite clear a couple of times.'

'He was no good for you,' she replied, unapologetic, before her attention was caught by something over my shoulder. I turned.

'Hi.' Jesse smiled and, reaching me, bent to kiss me hello.

'Now I see why you're glowing,' Caro said. 'Hello. Caro Whitely. And you are?'

Jesse took the offered hand and shook it, shooting me a brief, confused look as he did so. 'Jesse Woods.'

'Caro is one of my oldest—'

She cleared her throat.

'Most established,' I corrected myself, 'clients from London.'

'I took my business elsewhere after they fired you. I demanded they rehire you and when they wouldn't, I told them where to stick their business too.'

'You did?'

'Darling, you know I couldn't work as well with anyone else as

I did with you. I've tried a couple of other interior designers, but it's not gone well.' She pulled a face at us both.

'You know Fliss has started her own business here?' Jesse said.

Her hand went to her throat. 'You have? Oh, my darling! Why didn't you say? Thank goodness for this hunk of a man filling in the blanks. Do you have a card? I have to go to this ghastly wedding this weekend and there's all sorts of extra "fun events" they have planned.' She rolled her eyes dramatically. 'Oh God,' she said quietly, 'here comes that dreadful Araminta.

'Minty, darling!' She held out her arms as she had done to me, pulling a face over her shoulder. 'Do you know Felicity DeVere and Jesse Woods?'

'Oh God, yes! We go back ages, don't we, Felicity?' Araminta said with an enthusiastic sincerity that, from the stolen glances she aimed at Jesse, I assumed she was still hoping would lead to a better acquaintance.

'We went to school together for a while,' I replied, my expression cool but polite. She slanted her gaze towards me. It might have been a long time ago but I hadn't forgotten Minty's behaviour towards me back when she and her cronies had made me feel worthless. But she didn't have that power any more. Nobody did. And Minty knew it.

'So how are you, Caro?' she asked, turning her back to me.

'Wonderful, thank you. You're blocking Felicity, darling,' Caro said, manoeuvring Minty into a more polite position. A pink flush appeared on Araminta's enhanced cheekbones as she made a fake apology.

'That's OK. We need to get home anyway.' Jesse and I still weren't actually living together but if Minty took it to mean that, then all the better. And from the look on her face, it worked. 'Caro, here's my card. If you have anything you want to chat about, then just give me a call.'

'I absolutely do! I hope you've got space in your diary. Since you left, I've been itching to get on with things. Finally!' She raised her expensively beringed hands to the sky. 'I'll call you next week. Lovely to see you again!' She gave me a hug with an added squeeze.

'And *very* lovely to meet you too.' She held out her arms to Jesse, who also received a hug. Minty tossed her hair and pretended not to care but I knew her of old. She hated anyone to be one up on her, which, of course, Caro knew too and was likely why she'd made such a display. When she winked at me out of sightline of Araminta, I was sure.

Jesse walked around and opened the driver's door for me.

'And manners too!' Caro called, sending a chef's kiss our way, causing Jesse to laugh and shake his head before folding himself into the passenger side.

'She's a character,' he said as I pulled out onto the road and pointed the car back towards Jesse's house. I was currently mid kitchen, although what was in already was looking amazing and I couldn't wait for it to be finished. I might not know how to cook but learning how to was on my list.

'That's an understatement,' I replied, laughing.

'She seems different from Araminta.'

'Chalk and cheese. She plays along because that's how things are done. But she's loyal to the people she actually cares about.'

'Like you.'

'Yes! Apparently!' I looked across at him for a moment before returning my eyes to the road.

'You seem surprised.'

'I am. We always got on really well and seemed to be very in sync in understanding what was needed. I got what Caro wanted so it was always just easy and enjoyable working with her, which I can't say about everyone.'

'She obviously felt the same way. Sounds like she might be sending some more work your way.'

'I'm trying not to think about it too much in case it doesn't happen but if it did, it'd be amazing. Some of my biggest commissions were Caro's, as well as the most fun.'

'Fingers crossed, then.'

'Fingers crossed!'

* * *

Caro, true to her word, had rung the following Tuesday – 'once the hangover had subsided, darling' – and on Thursday, I was being thoroughly wined and dined up in London as she and I spent several hours going through all the plans she had for what she called her 'projects'. I felt myself fizzing with excitement. Working with Caro had always been so much fun and this time, these well-paying commissions would be helping pay off the huge loans I'd taken out in order to make my house the paradise its title promised it was.

Three weeks later found me on a plane, first class, to Milan to 'do a little shopping' then on to Venice, where it transpired that Caro had invested in a stunning palazzo in need of a revamp, which was Caro-language for a complete makeover. Then there was the Chelsea apartment we'd done several years and one ex-husband ago, and she wanted a whole new look for that too.

'I was thinking of a Moroccan feel in the dining room. Or maybe Indian. I haven't decided yet. We'll have to have a couple of trips to help me get inspired.'

'Or I could pull together some mood boards for them?'

Caro threw up her hands. 'And where is the fun in that? You can do that once we've been inspired.' When it came down to it,

Caro loved to travel, and she loved to travel with people whose company she enjoyed even more. 'I was thinking of a colonial look for the garden room. All dark wood and exotic plants. Is that what it's called? Are we allowed to call it that any more?' She threw up her hands. 'I can't keep up. Anyway. That. That's what I want in there.' With that, she gave a discreet wave to a member of the cabin crew and moments later, two more glasses of Champagne appeared.

'I really missed this!' Caro said, tinking her glass against mine. 'Cheers!'

* * *

'Hello, stranger.' Jesse greeted me at the door and lifted the case into the hall. 'How was the trip? You look shattered.'

'Thanks. You look gorgeous.'

'I never said you didn't look hot. Just that you look shattered. Hot goes without saying.'

'Nice backpedal.'

I laughed as I hooked my hands behind his neck and cuddled up to the strong, solid body I'd missed so much.

'Just bloody well kiss me.'

And I did just that.

* * *

'Remind me where this time?' Jesse asked three days later as I tried my best to zip the case quietly by the light of my phone.

He pressed a button beside the bed and the blackout blinds began to rise. Ned, curled in his bed by the window, opened one eye, deemed it far too early to be awake and snuggled back down.

'New York. Go back to sleep. I was trying not to wake you.'

'Don't you dare ever leave without kissing me goodbye.'

'OK,' I said and dropped a butterfly kiss on his forehead as I rubbed hand cream into my hands and popped the tube back on the bedside table.

'I mean it,' he said, catching my hand. His face was taut, his grey eyes turning darker with emotion as they always did.

I lifted my hand to his cheek, the slight roughness tickling my palm. 'I know. And I promise.'

'Thank you. Now give me a proper goodbye kiss.'

A few minutes later, I hurried down the stairs, Jesse following me carrying the case and my carry-on bag with my laptop and necessities in it. The limo was waiting patiently outside, the engine purring quietly in the dawn.

'I miss you.'

'I miss you too. But once Caro's had her fill of travel, I'll be back home more again.'

'I know. And I'm really happy for you. It's good to see you being valued in your work.'

'Thanks. I've got some great ideas for Paddock House too.' Jesse was currently in the process of building a stunning, modern house for a couple who'd bought ten acres of paddock land that had had a decrepit little shack on it. The new build was all glass and cedar wood and was going to be magnificent when it was done. The couple had given me a few ideas as to what they wanted but I mostly had free rein, subject to approval.

'You OK doing that? I don't want you burning out.'

'No, it's great. I'm loving working again. Especially having the freedom to choose the jobs I do and don't want to do rather than being told what to do. That way, I get to work with friends and hot men.'

'Hot men, eh?'

'Don't look at me like that or I'm going to miss my flight.'

'I'll make it worth it.'

And I knew for sure that he absolutely would have. I grabbed a fistful of cotton T-shirt, pulled him close for another hasty kiss and willed myself into the open door of the limo Caro had sent.

* * *

That night, thanks to jet lag that not even travelling first class could magic away, I lay awake, staring at the red dot of the smoke alarm on the hotel ceiling, thinking about home. It seemed strange that I now thought of the village and the once disaster zone of a house I'd bought as home. Thanks to Jesse and the many favours he'd pulled in from people I was now lucky enough to also call friends, the place was really coming together. Having gone from hating the sight of it, I was now falling in love with it. Just as I'd fallen in love with the village, the landscape and, without doubt, Jesse Woods. Yet here I was, once again, thousands of miles away from all of them.

Neither of us had said the L word yet. Was I holding back, waiting for him to say it, just in case he didn't feel the same and saying it first might freak him out and scare him off? Not that he was a man that scared easily. Although he'd had a pink fit when he'd come in from the garage a couple of weeks ago when I was home briefly between sojourns abroad and found me balancing on the very top of the ladder to reach the top corner of the wall I was painting.

'Jesus Christ!' Jesse had grabbed the ladder with one hand and me with the other and unceremoniously plonked me down on the floor.

'What are you doing?'

'Preventing you from breaking your neck! What the hell were you thinking?'

'It was perfectly safe!'

'Fliss, when a ladder is tilting at a forty-five-degree angle, it is not "safe", perfectly or otherwise.'

'Stop exaggerating.'

'OK. Thirty-five. I've just aged ten years!'

I had shrugged. 'You look good on it.'

'Ha ha. I'm serious.'

'You're overreacting.'

'Fliss, you were about to go crashing to the floor!'

Admittedly, it had felt a little wobbly, but ladders never felt that secure, did they?

'I wasn't quite tall enough.'

'Then call me. Do not risk injury or worse by overreaching. Promise me!' There was no humour in his eyes and his mouth was set in a line.

'I promise. Sorry. I didn't mean to freak you out.'

'I'm not freaked out. I'm just... OK, yes. You freaked me out. I don't want anything to happen to you.' His hand had cupped my face.

'I know. I promise I'll call you next time, or wait.' I had placed my hand over his and turned my head, kissing his palm.

'Thank you.' He had wrapped his hand around my waist and looked around. 'It's looking good. You know you didn't have to do all this though, right? You've got more than enough on your plate to then start painting the house.'

'I know. And if I'm honest, I don't think I'm going to have time to do the rest. But I've never painted my own house. I wanted to do at least one room myself.'

The room I'd chosen was the dining room, which was now a beautifully soft duck-egg blue with white trim and woodwork. I'd been itching to do it as soon as it was ready, but Jesse had explained we needed to give it a few weeks to let the plaster dry out enough. Thankfully, the good weather had helped and then, when it was ready, he'd had the decorators do a mist coat with watered-down white paint to help seal the new plaster. Now that I'd finished my second coat of blue, it looked perfect. New, efficient glazed doors in a period design opened out on the garden. I'd rediscovered some plants now that the brambles were all removed but that was as far as I'd got on that front. However, the vision board I had been pulling together for it, when the time came, was looking fantastic.

But the truth was, I was exhausted and I knew it wasn't just down to the jet lag. My business had been steadily increasing and then, once Caro had booked me too, I was really running beyond capacity. Her projects alone were more than enough for one person. But I couldn't say no. And it wasn't as if I didn't enjoy the work. I loved it and I was good at it. But the backlog of plans Caro had built up was beyond even my expectations. Jesse had told me I didn't always have to say yes, but that was what he didn't get. I *did* always have to say yes. Not just because I loved Caro, but because, right now, I was still too scared to say no.

What if the work just dried up for whatever reason? It could happen. I'd gone from feast to famine once before and had worked my arse off to get a seat back at the feast before chucking it all away again. Had it not been for the kindness and generosity of Jesse and the rest of the village, I could very easily have been in real trouble. So, as tired as I was, as much as I hated being away from home and the man I loved, I couldn't turn down work. I had to keep building up that financial security so that I would never, ever be in that position again.

I watched the light on the ceiling blink on, off, on, off for another minute or two until it started irritating me. I grabbed one of the spare pillows, stuck it over my face and tried to sleep.

* * *

'Oh, wow!' I'd left my luggage at Jesse's and, despite him suggesting I take a nap after my flight back from New York, I was too excited to see the rooms after he'd told me he'd arranged to have them all painted as a welcome home surprise.

'What do you think?'

'I love it! It looks even better than I'd imagined!' I spun slowly, taking in the evening light as it shimmered and danced off the walls of the main bedroom now painted the colour of fresh cream. The colour gave a clean, crisp look but with a warmth that suited the period character of the original building. Ostensibly it looked the same, only much, much better, from outside, but inside the house was now far more economical to run thanks to the updated heating and a rainwater collection system buried in the ground outside.

'Do you like it?' I asked, reaching for his hand.

'I do. Very much.'

I looked across to the full-length windows and balcony that now faced the bed, taking in the view of what would eventually be the garden, and then up at the man beside me.

'What?' he asked, brushing a strand of hair that had broken free of my chignon back from my face, a soft smile on his face. The smile he reserved for me.

'No one's ever built me a balcony before.'

'That's because you were never with the right man before.'

I wrapped my arms around his waist and looked up. 'I think you might be right.'

'No doubt in my mind.'

I looked back at the window and Jesse released me. 'Go on, I know you're dying to.'

I grinned, went on tiptoes to kiss him and then turned the key. Opening the door, I stepped through onto the balcony that overlooked what I knew would become a beautiful garden with the fields beyond. With a change around of layout, following Jesse's suggestion, the bedroom had now been extended and become double aspect, but I'd chosen to place the bed this side because I knew I was more likely to sit here in the morning with a cup of herbal tea than I would in the evening. The opposite side had two squashy bedroom chairs that we could sit in to appreciate the sunset, the full-length windows there being framed by a smaller Juliet balcony.

Once we'd posited the idea of replacing the current windows with full-length ones, I'd mentioned to Jesse that I wanted to put a small seating area here to enjoy the view and get some morning light and air. A few hours later, he'd come to me with a drawing for a balcony extension off the bedroom and it was perfect. I hadn't even known I'd wanted it – but he'd known. It was just one of the many reasons I loved him.

'I love it so much. I can't wait to sit out here with you.'

Jesse leant against the frame of the balcony door. 'When you arrived, did you think you'd ever be standing here saying how much you loved this house?'

'Not for one moment. I thought it was the worst decision I'd ever made in my entire life.'

'And now?'

'Now I know it was the best.'

His smile lit up his face as the evening sun danced through the leaves of the trees, the warm tones bathing his skin.

'Best. Decision. Ever.'

'Good. Now, come on, you need some food, a hot bath and

your own bed after all those hotel ones. Well, my bed but as good as.'

'Oh-h-h-h.' I tipped my head back for a moment. 'That sounds absolutely perfect.'

We headed back down the stairs. The carpets and flooring were being laid over the next few days and I couldn't wait to see the final result. Then came the really fun bit – styling! And this time, I'd be doing it with Jesse. We'd already decided that this was going to be our home. We'd choose things together, make it really *our home*. The connection it had to his family and the fact that we'd been designing and working on it together made it seem the logical, and the right, decision. Together, we had made this house special. It was built with care, and thought – and love.

Love.

'Jesse?'

'Yeah?' He turned, his hand on the latch of the front door.

Terror knotted my inside but I knew I had to say it.

'What is it?' he asked, his brow crumpling in concern as he took a few steps back towards where I was standing on the uncarpeted bottom stair.

'I love you.'

He stopped dead.

Oh, shit! Abort! Abort!

'I mean I love—'

But I didn't get to finish the sentence because Jesse was there, his lips on mine, pulling me close and whispering he loved me too.

When we came up for air, I pulled back.

'You do?'

'Of course I do!' He laughed.

'Then why didn't you bloody say something?' I whacked him on the arm. It was like a flea biffing a hippo.

'Because I was shit scared I'd frighten you off!'

He wrapped his arms back around me, pinning mine to my sides to avoid any more flailing. 'Believe me, I've been trying to work out how and when to say it for months.'

'Months?'

He looked down at me. 'Months.'

I stepped out of the house entirely happy and feeling so lucky, after everything, that we had found each other. I should have known it was too good to last.

21

A large, shiny four-by-four was hurtling up the driveway, still currently full of potholes, dips and rises. Until all the machinery and deliveries were done with coming to and fro, we'd opted to leave it alone. I didn't recognise the vehicle but clearly Jesse did.

'What the fuck is he doing here?' he growled.

I looked back at him. 'Who is it?'

Jesse stayed silent, the relaxed posture of moments ago gone, replaced by a tension so visceral, he was practically vibrating. His hands had clenched into fists and his jaw was rigid.

'Jesse?' I asked again.

The car had now stopped. The door opened and out stepped Magnus Montagu-Peak.

Now it made sense.

'Hello, Felicity.' He sent Jesse a glance and the barest nod of acknowledgement.

'Magnus? Can I help you?'

'Yes. I believe we could be a lot of help to each other, actually.'

'What do you want?' Jesse's voice was practically a growl.

Magnus gave him a look, briefly considered ignoring him and

perhaps, wisely, sensing it would not be a good plan to antagonise an obviously already angry Jesse, answered.

'I've got a business proposal for Felicity.'

'She's not interested.'

'Jesse.' I kept my voice low and my temper in check. I absolutely understood why he wanted nothing to do with this man and why he didn't want me to have anything to do with him either, but it was my place to tell this arsehole exactly what he could do with his proposal, not Jesse's.

Jesse shot me a look, his face furious and dark.

'Why is he still even here? You know what he did!'

'Could we talk about this in private?' I asked Jesse, my voice low.

Magnus made a show of looking at his watch. 'Look. I don't really have time for your lovers' tiff. Long story short. We're acquiring a small chain of boutique, extremely high-end luxury hotels in the Indian Ocean area and we'll obviously be giving them a complete makeover. Caro tells me you're the best interior designer so that's what I want.' He pulled a piece of paper from the dashboard through the open window and handed it to me. 'I know you may have... reservations.' He gave Jesse a cold look. 'But I think this would overcome those. First-class travel, five-star accommodation, all that sort of thing,' he gave a flick of his hand, 'would be provided on top of that.'

I looked down at the paper, more as an automatic reaction than for any actual interest. There was no way I'd have anything to do with Magnus, whatever the fee – which I now saw was well over double my usual. It didn't matter. Magnus could take his offer and ram it up his—

'Seriously?' Jesse turned to me, his arms crossed over his chest.

I looked up at him. I was exhausted, jet-lagged, hungry and a little bit spaced. All I wanted to do was get this idiot off my property and go back with Jesse to the food, bath and bed he'd mentioned earlier.

'Sorry?' I asked, a little dazed at the whole strange scenario.

'You're *actually* considering it?'

'What? No, of course not!'

'You took a long time to decide. Big number, is it?' He tilted his head up and stared at the sky for a moment. When he turned back, his expression was icy.

'Jesse, I'm not—'

'You know what, Felicity? You do what you want.'

And with that, he strode to his pick-up, got in and started the engine.

Shock mixed with absolute rage filled me. Who the hell did either of these men think they were?

Before he could swing around Magnus' car, I stamped across and stood square in front of the pick-up.

'Get out of the way, Felicity!' Jesse shouted.

I ignored him, instead turning out to face Magnus.

'And you! This is what I think of your offer.' I screwed the paper up into a ball and threw it directly back into his car through the open window. Years of playing Goal Shooter at netball had finally come in useful. 'I'm guessing you've been talking to your cousin about my family's financial history?' Magnus shifted his weight but didn't answer. 'That's what I thought. And because of that, she thinks I've got a price.'

'Everybody has a price, Felicity. Don't be so obtuse!'

'No, Magnus. Some people most certainly do *not* have a price and I am one of those people! How *dare* you come here and try to buy me off just to get back at Jesse?'

Behind me, the engine of the pick-up went silent.

'Now,' I said, still facing Magnus, 'I'd appreciate it if you would get the fuck off my property and don't even think of *ever* coming back.'

Magnus' high colour was reaching peak purpleness.

'You stupid bitch!' he sneered. 'You think you're so much better than everyone! Even that idiot knows you thought about taking the money.' He jutted his chin at Jesse and the door slammed behind me, followed by heavy, quick footsteps. I didn't turn but I could feel Jesse beside me, the anger palpable.

'I suggest you go, Magnus. I'm extremely tired and the last thing I want to have to do right now is help him dispose of your body.'

Magnus tipped his nose up, as if the threat didn't bother him, but there was no disguising the fear in his eyes. Jesse was a big guy and right now, he was one very pissed-off big guy. I wasn't big but what I lacked in size, I could make up in pure rage. Wisely, he decided not to test either of our patience any further. Yanking open the door, he slid in, started the car and spun it round in the drive, scattering bits of gravel and building detritus as he did so before tearing off the way he'd come. As he hit one particularly large pothole, his wheel made a loud noise of protest and the car slowed to a fast limp until it was out of sight.

* * *

Now it was time to deal with Jesse. I turned round.

'Fliss?' A frown crumpled his forehead, brows drawing together as he took a step towards me.

'Don't you "Fliss" me! Who the hell do you think you are?'

'What?' Confusion covered his face.

'You! Telling that idiot that I wasn't interested in his offer!'

His expression darkened again. 'So you were?'

'Of course not! Good God, Jesse! Don't you know me at all? I would never have taken that job no matter how much he offered. Even if I'd been down to my last penny, I wouldn't have taken it!' I took a step closer to him. 'Do you have any idea what that means?'

'Fliss, I didn't mean—'

'I told you what happened when I was at school and ever since that day, I swore I would never, ever let that happen again. That I would never let a man, or anyone, have control over me again. Why do you think I've been taking all the jobs? Every single trip and project Caro offers, knocking myself out, forcing myself to be apart from you? It's because I am *terrified* of being in that position again.'

'I would never let that happen.' He reached for me but I stepped back. He swallowed before continuing. 'I'm sorry I butted in. You're right. Of course you're right. I should have kept my mouth shut. I just... When I see him, I see red. I can't help it.'

'I understand that. And that I could have forgiven. What I can't forgive is that you didn't trust *me*. You didn't trust me to not take the money.'

His arms were crossed once more as he shifted his weight. 'You looked like you were considering it! What was I supposed to think?' Jesse's voice sounded loud against the peaceful surroundings.

'You were supposed to think...' I bit back a sob. 'You were supposed to think, "I love this woman and I trust her." *That's* what you were supposed to think!' The words tore themselves out of my chest.

'Fliss...'

'Yes, Jesse, I looked at the offer. People hand you something, you look at it. It's automatic. Plus I haven't slept for...' I checked my watch, 'over seventeen hours, so excuse me if I wasn't as alert and on point as I usually am. And yes, to answer your question, it was a big number. It was a friggin' enormous number, if you must know. But it didn't matter what was written there. It could have been two, three, four times that and I *still* wouldn't have taken it. Do you understand what it means for me to say I'd rather be broke than take money from a person who hurt you so badly?'

Jesse looked down at me. The stormy grey eyes were washed with tears and it was only when he gently brushed a thumb across my cheek that I realised my own tears were already streaming down my face.

'I do.'

'Good. Then you know how much you just hurt me and why you now need to leave.'

'What? Fliss, don't.'

'No, Jesse.' I stepped back. 'That's it. We're done. My father lost my trust entirely the moment he picked his trophy wife over his own daughter, and it's taken a bloody long time for me to even think about trusting anyone other than Nanny again, let alone a man. But I trusted you. I trusted you with everything I had. But trust has to work both ways, Jesse.'

'Fliss, I do trust you!'

'Then you have a funny way of showing it. Now, I think it's best if you leave. I'll collect my things tomorrow.'

With that, I turned and walked back to the house, unlocked the door and went in. My legs felt weak and it was all I could do to close the door and lean against it, sliding slowly down, feeling a sort of shock settle around me. It was only when I finally heard the pick-up start and drive away that I gave in to the pain that was tearing at my insides and sobbed, my arms wrapped around my middle, until I fell asleep, exhausted, without having moved away from the door.

22

The next morning, I woke up stiff, sore and cold. Pushing myself up, I made my way upstairs to the en-suite bathroom, where the full extent of my crying showed in the blotchy face and dark circles under my eyes, enhanced by smeared make-up that I hadn't got around to removing.

I washed my face, brushed my teeth and got in the shower. Once that was done and I felt a little more human, I got dressed, reapplied some light make-up to hide the worst of the damage then headed into the village to get some basics. Having not expected to be waking up in my own house, I hadn't got any supplies in. The last thing I wanted to do right now was see anyone, but I'd put my armour on and I'd have to tackle the situation sooner or later. There was an emptiness inside me that I knew no food would fill. I wasn't even hungry. But I did need coffee.

* * *

'Hi! How was New York?' Jules called as I walked in the door. 'Are you OK?' She frowned at me. Obviously, she hadn't spoken to her brother yet. In a way, that was a relief.

'Yes, I'm fine, just a bit tired. I missed you though,' I said, giving her a hug as she came around the counter. It was true. I had missed her, and the village and the man I loved. Had loved... No. Still loved. And would for a long time to come.

'I missed you too! Please say you're home to stay for a while. Jesse's been missing you madly!' She looked past me. 'Is he with you?'

'Oh, err, no. I did see him last night though.' It wasn't a lie.

'Good. Hopefully, he'll stop being such a grump now. Honestly, I can't tell you how happy I am that you two got together. I really never thought I'd see him smile again. You know, from here.' She laid a hand on her heart. 'Are you sure you're all right?'

I squelched the tears back down. 'Yes. Sorry. Jet lag and overwhelm, I think.' Again, not a lie.

'You sit down. Have you eaten?'

'I'm not hungry but a coffee would be great.'

'I'll bring you a coffee and a croissant.'

'But I'm not—' I stopped when I saw her face. 'Thanks, that would be great.'

Jules smiled and kissed me on the cheek.

I still wasn't hungry despite the enticing smells that always wafted through the café, but she was probably right. I hadn't eaten since the plane and, with the time difference, my body clock was completely out of whack.

I sipped on the dark roast and savoured the taste, picking at the fresh, soft croissant, my mind drifting back to the night before and how things had gone from perfect to perfectly awful so fast. The café filled up around me and every time the tiny bell above the door tinkled, I half expected, and if I was honest, half wanted, Jesse to walk in, his frame filling the doorway as it always did, the smile he gave whenever he saw me and the feeling of peace and security that radiated through me when he did. But that was then.

When the door did next open, it was with a force that made everyone look up. Araminta strode in, her eyes laser focused on me.

'Who the *hell* do you think you are?'

The café fell silent. I looked up at her. I wasn't the insecure young girl she'd befriended then dropped the moment I was 'poor' any more.

'I assume you're talking to me.' I remained seated and took another sip of my coffee.

'Of course I'm bloody talking to you. Who the hell are you to reject an offer from Magnus Montagu-Peak?'

Now she definitely had everyone's attention. Jules caught my eye, mouthing, 'What offer?' but I looked away, back at Araminta.

'I have no wish to work with your cousin.'

'You do realise that price was well above what anyone else would ever pay you? Not to mention putting you up in the best hotels and flying you first class. Personally, I thought it was over the top but Magnus insisted.'

'And why would he do that? Why are you even interested in what I do and who I work with? You weren't interested in being there for me when my family lost all their money. When I needed a friend.'

The heads swivelled back.

'Your family didn't *lose* their money. Your father *spent* all the money, mostly on that trollop of a stepmother.'

Back to me.

'But you were behind Magnus coming to me with an offer.'

She stuck out a hip and put a hand on it. 'Yes. I thought it would help.'

'Help what, exactly, Minty?'

'You!'

'And why did you assume I needed help now when I'm finally settled and happy?'

'Happy? Here?' Her nose wrinkled at the thought. She appeared to be attempting to frown too but her Botox was having none of it.

Some of the customers exchanged dark looks.

'Yes.'

'Because what? You think this is your world? You think these people accept you? Don't be so bloody ridiculous, Felicity. Money is the only thing that matters to you. That's how you were brought up. It's in your blood and who you'll always be. Don't forget I know you of old. If it wasn't, why would you have done your utmost to claw your way back to that world? But suddenly you don't have a price?'

I drained my coffee slowly then pushed out my chair.

'No, Araminta, money is not the everything I once thought it was, and I'm unbelievably glad. I've realised that I am who I am today through my own choices. You're right. I did think I was supposed to be a part of the world I'd been brought up in. But I'm not. Because all of it, like you, was fake. People are either useful to you or they're not. That's your sole reason for being what you call friends with someone. But that's not friendship. I've not heard a single word from any of my so-called friends in London. It wasn't until I moved here I realised what true friendship is and you would never, ever understand. Let's face it, the real reason you're here is that you couldn't bear it, could you?'

'What?'

'That I was happy.'

'I don't care enough about you to bother whether you're happy or not.'

'And yet you still tried to ruin everything. How could I, poor little Felicity, who'd once been a part of your world, when I was so rudely kicked out, have the audacity to, as you put it, claw my way back in? Not content with that, when my life imploded, not only did I not roll over and beg someone to help me, but I went out and dared to find a good man and a good life. So, just like you always did at school, you found a way to try and ruin it.'

'You were the same. Don't go painting yourself as some angel.'

'I agree. I was a bitch. And although it seemed like the worst thing in the world at the time, what happened back then was the best thing for me. I thought I wanted to be back in that world. That I needed to prove to everyone, and myself, that I deserved to be there. But I was never happy. I'd seen the other side then. I'd seen you and the others for what you are. Thank God for Adrian being so spineless and dumping me to marry someone with a more "reliable" lineage, because if he hadn't, I'd have been trapped in that world.'

'Oh, and you think *this* is your world now?' She dropped her voice to a stage whisper. 'Newsflash. It isn't.' Her voice rose again. 'Your so-called friends here know, just as you do, that, when it comes down to it, it's all about the money for you.'

'So you thought you'd test me. See if I had a price?'

'Everyone has a price, Felicity.'

'No, Araminta. They don't. You do, as does your cousin. But good, decent people don't.'

'You just wait. You'll go begging to Magnus for that job. But guess what?' She sneered. 'You're too late.'

'So are you.'

'What?' Her face contorted, in the very small way that it could, into confusion.

'I'm not that girl any more. You don't intimidate me and you can't buy me. Your family acted disgustingly towards the man I love and I would never take a single penny from them for that reason alone. But even if that wasn't the case, I'd still have had no interest. I get to choose now and I choose not to associate myself with people like you and your cousin.'

'Then you're even more stupid than I thought you were. Enjoy your "life",' she made air quotes, 'here. Of course, you do realise that the moment you leave, they'll all be talking about you behind your back.' She glanced around coldly. 'Your so-called friends.'

'I think you've said quite enough.' Jules stepped forward. 'You can leave now.'

'I'll leave when I bloody well choose to, not when some country bumpkin tells me to.'

There was a collective gasp and, from the kitchen, Jesse stepped through into the café.

'My sister said leave. I suggest you do so.'

Araminta looked at him, then at me, and a small smile crept onto her over-plumped lips.

She might be a cow, but she'd never been slow. 'Oh-h-h-h. So the perfect man didn't work out for you after all, then?'

Julie's head snapped towards me, then Jesse, but neither of us reacted.

'That's what you wanted, isn't it?' I said. 'To break something that made someone else happy. Congratulations. But in the end, I win. I know I'm nothing like the person I was at school, a person I'm now thoroughly ashamed of. You, on the other hand,' I walked to the door and opened it, 'are entirely the same. Now, my friend asked you to leave.'

She glared at me for a moment, then turned and left.

I closed the door after her and felt all eyes on my back. When I turned around, Jesse had gone.

I returned to my chair, Jules watching me open-mouthed as I did so, hooked my bag onto my shoulder and left.

* * *

I'd been home nearly an hour when I glanced out to see Jules' car hurtling down the drive. Jesse had been about to call a friend to get a quote for finally having a proper one laid, but that task was something I'd need to add to my own to-do list now.

I opened the front door as she skidded the car to a halt and got out, knowing why she was there.

'What happened?'

'It didn't work out.'

'But... but why? Was it because of all that stuff that woman said?'

'Partly.'

'But can't you talk it out? You're so good together. Jesse adores you! You can't just walk out on him!'

'Jules, please don't. Don't put this all on me.'

'He said you told him it was over.'

'Did he tell you why?'

'Something about the offer.'

'Then please, as my friend, don't judge me until you know the whole story.'

'Then tell me the whole story!' she said, grabbing my arm, tears filling her eyes. 'He was happy! *You* were happy!'

'And now it's over. I'm sorry.'

I turned away. I understood that Jules had her alliances but it still hurt.

'You know he's leaving.'

I spun back. 'What?'

'Jesse's leaving.'

'Where?'

She shrugged, wiping away tears with the back of her hand.

'Where is he now?'

'Gone home to collect his things. He came to the café to say goodbye.'

It was for the best. At least I wouldn't have to risk running into him in the village. There was no chance of ever being 'just friends'. Our relationship was all or nothing.

'Did he say where he was going?'

'No. Just away. He'd talked about going away when Alice died but this is his home and, in the end, he decided to stay, but I don't think he's going to change his mind this time.'

'He'll be back, Jules. He has a home here, a business. Not to mention you and the rest of your family.'

'But he doesn't have you. And that outweighs everything. Because that's all he wanted.'

'And he's all I ever wanted!' I cried back at her. 'You know that! I never thought I'd ever be able to love, or be loved by, someone like him. I didn't even know love like that existed until I met your brother, so don't you dare make out that this is easy for me!'

'I know it's not!' She reached out and took my hands. The heat of the last few days had been building into thick and humid air. In the distance, a rumble sounded as a breeze began to rifle the thick, green canopy of the late summer trees. 'I know,' she said, more softly. 'But you need to know he won't come back. I know my brother.'

'Of course he will. He's not going to walk away from everything he has here.'

'I know him,' she repeated. 'He's done. Losing Alice here was bad enough and he never expected to be happy again. He'd accepted that. And then you came along and literally knocked him off his feet.' She laughed through her tears. 'He's never been the same since.' Jules sniffed. 'And I know he'll never be the same again. Please, Fliss. Talk to him at least! He made a mistake and I know how much that must have hurt you. But if you think he doesn't trust you, you're wrong. So, so wrong! Don't you see? He cocked up on this, yes. He's never been able to see straight when it comes to Magnus and, honestly, probably never will, but he trusts you! I can guarantee it. And you know how I know?' she asked, her voice louder now as the thunder got closer, big, fat droplets of rain bouncing on the ground around us. 'Because he gave you his heart. He trusted you with something he swore he'd never give away again.'

The rain poured down, mixing with the tears on both our faces, but neither of us moved. Jules' hands gripped mine and I wasn't sure when but I'd curled mine back around hers. Jesse had trusted me with his heart and I'd given him mine. And the truth was, I didn't want it back. I knew that now. All I wanted was Jesse.

'Where is he?'

A smile broke through my friend's tears. She held out her hand. 'Give me the keys. I'll drive.'

23

I handed the keys over to Jules and my Mini took off like a rally car towards her brother's house. She skidded to a halt on the drive.

Jesse was loading a large holdall into the back of the truck. Ned was already sitting in the front seat, his warm breath steaming up the window as he added nose prints to the glass. Jesse looked up at our arrival.

'Good luck.' She gripped my hand and waited for me to get out then, to my surprise, drove off. In my car.

I watched it leave for a moment, then turned back. My car being stolen wasn't my biggest priority right now. My broken heart was.

'What are you doing?' I asked.

He didn't even look at me, just turned and began walking back to the door. 'What I should have done a long time ago. Getting away.'

'From me?'

'From everything. And now you can take your all-expenses-paid trip out to the Indian Ocean and get as rich as Croesus guilt-free.'

'Don't you dare!'

He stopped.

'I swear to God if I had that piece of wood I knocked you on your arse with before, I'd smack you with it again! Maybe it might knock some sense into you.'

Stepping up to him, I halted him in his tracks.

'I told you last night and I will tell you again now for the last time. I would never, ever, take a commission from him. Not now, not ever. I don't know how much of the conversation in the café you heard...'

'Enough.'

'Good. Then I don't have to go over it again. I've done the best I can, Jesse. I didn't know who I was until I came here. I didn't have what you have. No support network. No family. So I did what I thought I was supposed to. But then I came here and I found everything I was missing. I found you. But I can't erase my past. I can't erase that fear of being broke and alone, but I'm trying the best I can. And I thought you knew me. I thought you loved me! But thinking I would ever take that job shows you don't know me at all and that...' I swallowed. 'It breaks my heart, and I don't know what to do with that as I've never had my heart broken before because I never dared give it to anyone. Until I met you. So if you still want to leave, then leave. But don't do it thinking I never cared about you or that I would ever put anything, or anyone, above you or your happiness.'

It seemed like an age until Jesse spoke and then his voice was deep and thick with emotion.

'I do know you, Fliss. And I do love you. More than I could ever put into words. I should have known you wouldn't have taken it. I did know, in truth. But we'd been apart so much, you living the high life, always jetting here and there first class, that I thought maybe you'd begun to regret things. I thought that you looking at it meant you were considering it, maybe thought even for a moment that the life you have here isn't enough. I don't think straight when that bastard is around and now I hate him even more because if this...' he indicated himself and then me '... this doesn't happen, then he's helped to destroy the two best things I've ever had in my life. I'm so sorry I doubted you. I *never* should have doubted you and if you take me back, I promise, I *absolutely promise*, I will never, ever do so again.'

He took a tentative step towards me. When I didn't move, he took another, then another, until he was close enough to take my hand. Lifting it to his lips, he kissed my palm, his eyes not leaving mine.

'I would hope that we would never be broke, although I can't guarantee it. But I can guarantee you this. That you will never, ever be alone again. Not as long as I live.' He reached for my other hand. 'Fliss. I never thought I would, or could, love anyone again. I wasn't even interested. And then you walked into my life and literally floored me. And I will be grateful every single day that you did if you'll just give us another chance.'

I looked into the eyes of the first, and last, man I would ever love.

I opened my mouth to speak but no words would come out. I nodded instead, my vision blurry with happy tears.

And then Jesse was kissing me, soft at first and then his hands were at my face, in my hair and pulling me close as though I could never be close enough and I knew how he felt because I felt the same. When we finally pulled apart, both our faces wet with tears, we were breathless and laughing with relief and joy and a tonne of other emotions we didn't have the energy to name.

'Can I just say something?' he asked, pulling back from me for a moment.

'Yes?'

'You were absolutely magnificent in that café. If I hadn't already been madly in love with you, I'd have fallen completely watching you stand up for yourself, and your friends.'

'My friends.' I repeated the word, loving the sound and the fact he had said it.

'Yes. Your friends. And don't you ever doubt it.'

'I won't. I promise.'

'Good.'

'Do you think one of those friends might give me a lift back to my house?' I asked, laughing and sniffing as I wiped my face with the back of my hand. 'Your sister appears to have stolen my car.'

'Will I do?'

I took the fabric of his shirt in my fingers and pulled him in for a kiss. 'Always,' I whispered.

EPILOGUE
NINE MONTHS LATER

'Oh, darling! *What* a beautiful wedding! And no, I'm not just saying that.' Caro was sitting in the warm spring sunshine, a glass of Champagne in one hand – her wedding present to us, all fifty crates – as she popped a canapé in her mouth with the other. 'Just perfect!' she said through the food.

'Thanks so much for coming, and for the Champagne.' I bent and hugged her again.

'My pleasure. And here's the man of the hour. Hello, handsome.'

'Caro.' Jesse grinned, bending down to kiss her on the cheek.

'I don't suppose you have an older brother or father free, do you? I've never been too fussy about age.'

'Parents still happily married. No brothers. One sister was enough.' Jesse chuckled.

'A sister who recently won the award from Best Small Business in the County and is being put forward for a national award,' I added, bursting with pride for my new family and feeling tears prickle as the word settled in my mind. *Family.* 'I have an extremely talented sister-in-law. Those canapés are all her work, you know.'

Caro picked another off a tray as the waiter circled by. 'Really? Absolutely delicious. Always on the lookout for a good caterer. You must give me her card.'

'I'll put you in touch.'

'Do! Do! And keep a lookout for a good man as well, won't you? It seems there's definitely something about the country air here.' She gave Jesse a wink and squeezed my arm.

A movement to our right caught my eye. 'Ray!' I flung my arms out to greet my friend. Now that I'd got over my nerves, and Ray had got over his crush, we were firm friends and he always kept an eye out for pieces that he thought I might like. Inevitably, he was always spot on too. Quite a few of the pieces we'd sourced for Caro's places had come via Ray.

'You look beautiful. As always.' He flushed a little as he said it and I gave him another squeeze.

'Thank you.'

'Jesse.' He held out his meaty hand and Jesse shook it. 'You look all right too.'

'Thanks,' my new husband replied, laughing.

'And who is this?' Caro said, rising from her chair like the queen that she was from a throne.

'Caro, this is Ray, one of my very best friends. He owns the salvage yard I've told you about.'

'Ray.' She held out her hand and Ray shook it carefully, as though afraid he might break it. Caro was petite and looked delicate, but she was tough as hell. I was so glad that something good – her friendship, not to mention work I enjoyed – had come out of my time in London. 'Felicity told me about the salvage yard, but she omitted to mention such a dashing, big bear of a man ran it.'

I tilted my head up to meet Ray's eyes. He looked both slightly bewildered and enormously happy.

'Could I get you some more Champagne?' he asked.

'You certainly may. In fact, I'll come with you.'

He offered his arm and Caro, delighted with his manners, placed her hand on it.

I caught her arm just before they moved off. 'If you hurt him, you're dead to me.'

Caro glanced up at him then back at me and kissed me on the cheek, her smile genuine and relaxed. 'Understood.'

We watched them walk back towards the marquee. Maisie was swishing her bridesmaid dress and playing with our ring-bearer, Ned, still looking wonderfully dapper in his silk bow tie. She waved when she saw me watching. I waved back and blew her a big kiss.

'Well, who'd have thought?' Jesse said, his attention still on Caro and Ray.

'It's not an obvious pairing but I think they'd be good for each other.'

He nodded. 'Yeah. Me too.' Then he wrapped his arms around my waist and pulled me closer. 'He was right about you looking beautiful. You're breathtaking. You know I nearly lost it when you walked in earlier.'

'Well, I'm glad you didn't. Do you know how long this make-up took this morning?'

Jesse stood back, his hands holding mine. 'How did I get so lucky?'

I let go of one of his hands and touched the tiny scar I'd given him that very first day.

'Maybe we were both just at the right place at the right time to meet the right person.'

'I guess we were.'

Then he kissed me again and I knew it was true.

ACKNOWLEDGEMENTS

Thank you so much for choosing to read Fliss and Jesse's story. I really hope you enjoyed it.

This book has come during quite an exciting year. In May, I was awarded the Romantic Novelists' Association award for RomCom of the Year for a previous book, *Just Do It*. Thankfully, I had absolutely no expectations of winning and therefore also no expectations of having to get up in front of a room full of people and speak. Had I even considered that, I'd have probably gone and hidden in the loo! Following on from that, my publisher recently advised that I'd passed the half a million sales with Boldwood Books.

It is fair to say that if I could tell Past Me this would all come to pass, things might have been a lot less stressful. Past Me probably also wouldn't have believed it which is fine because Current Me still finds it all quite a lot to take in – in a good way, of course!

Neither of these things would have occurred without the backing of the incredible team at Boldwood Books. Five years ago, I sent a manuscript to them and they believed in it, and me, enough to allow me to become one of their inaugural launch writers. They haven't let me down. Publishing is hard work and you need good people who will support and work hard for you and with you. I have been so lucky to find this at Boldwood Books and can only once again thank the amazing team for helping get yet another book out into the world. Special thanks, of course, go to Sarah Ritherdon, my editor, who has been there for the wobbles and the questions and the difficult times with unwavering support. The same goes for Marketing Queen, Nia Beynon who is also the sole reason I applied to Boldwood in the first place. And, of course, Leader of us all, the wonderful Amanda Ridout. I was lucky enough to be seated next to her at the awards dinner and had an absolute blast! Thank you for being the wonder that you are.

In addition, huge thanks go to Claire, Niamh, Issy, Ben, and all the rest of the Boldwood crew who keep the ship running smoothly. You are hugely appreciated. I'd also like to give special mention to my copy editor, Sue Smith. After a second bout of Covid, I developed further long Covid symptoms and that have given me extra challenges while writing this book. Sue's hard work, diligence and patience has been incredibly important in helping make this story the best it can be. Thank you, Sue. Also thanks to my proof reader, Emily Reader. And, once again, a fantastic cover from Leah Jacobs-Gordon has made the package complete.

Other thanks must go to my mum in law, Jose, also known as Mummy Number 2, for all the pony and netball information, neither of which I have any idea about but she has tonnes. Also thank you for being such a giggler too. Obviously, there's tonnes more to thank you for but all that won't fit in a few lines. We both love you so, so much.

Thank you also to all the readers who've been kind enough to buy and share lovely reviews of my books. It's so hard to get noticed amongst all the many, many books out there so every share, every lovely five star review, every pre order, really does help enormously and all are incredibly appreciated.

Finally, thank you to James. For everything.

ABOUT THE AUTHOR

Maxine Morrey is a bestselling romantic comedy author with over a dozen books to her name. When not word wrangling, Maxine can be found reading, sewing and listening to podcasts. As she's also partial to tea and cake, something vaguely physical is generally added to the mix.

Sign up to Maxine Morrey's mailing list for news, competitions and updates on future books.

You can contact Maxine here: hello@scribblermaxi.co.uk

Follow Maxine on social media:

- facebook.com/MaxineMorreyAuthor
- instagram.com/scribbler_maxi
- pinterest.com/ScribblerMaxi

ALSO BY MAXINE MORREY

#No Filter

My Year of Saying No

Winter at Wishington Bay

Things Are Looking Up

Living Your Best Life

You Only Live Once

Just Say Yes

You've Got This

Just Do It

Be Your Best Self

Reach for the Stars

LOVE NOTES

LOVE IN EVERY CHAPTER

WHERE ALL YOUR ROMANCE
DREAMS COME TRUE!

THE HOME OF BESTSELLING
ROMANCE AND WOMEN'S
FICTION

WARNING:
MAY CONTAIN SPICE

SIGN UP TO OUR
NEWSLETTER

https://bit.ly/Lovenotesnews

Boldwood

Boldwood Books is an award-winning fiction publishing company seeking out the best stories from around the world.

Find out more at www.boldwoodbooks.com

Join our reader community for brilliant books, competitions and offers!

Follow us
@BoldwoodBooks
@TheBoldBookClub

Sign up to our weekly deals newsletter

https://bit.ly/BoldwoodBNewsletter

Printed in Great Britain
by Amazon